WINGSPAN

Acclaim for the fiction of Karis Walsh

Harmony

"For those unsure of their decisions, those seeking a new life, and those who are stuck in a rut, this book will hit home. It is highly recommended for any romance or self-searching reader who enjoys lesbian sex scenes."—*GLBT Reviews from the Gay, Lesbian, Bisexual, and Transgender Round Table of the American Library Association*

Sea Glass Inn

"While I am not a lesbian, I found that the emotions in this book spoke for themselves and Karis Walsh gives us two very convincing women searching for love. The reason that I mentioned that I am not a lesbian is because this novel that happens to be about two women could actually be about anyone. So many who are burnt by love are ready to call it quits and we see here that love comes when least expected or even wanted."—*Reviews by Amos Lassen*

"Author Karis Walsh has again given her fans a lovely story of two women who overcome rejection to find their inner strength."—*RLynne,* Book reviewer

Mounting Danger

"The author is a professional riding instructor, and her knowledge and experience give the story an additional level of realism and significant detail that add to the plot conflict. *Mounting Danger*'s richly-detailed setting sets this romance apart, and adds to the fun of watching rakish Cal fall for rulebound Rachel. The mystery element adds an additional spice of intrigue to an already entertaining novel."—*Heroes and Heartbreakers.com*

Improvisation

"Walsh tells this story in achingly beautiful words, phrases and paragraphs, building a tension that is bittersweet....Improvisation is a true romantic tale, Walsh's fourth book, and she's evolving into a master romantic storyteller."—*Lambda Literary*

Visit us at www.boldstrokesbooks.com

By the Author

Harmony

Worth the Risk

Sea Glass Inn

Improvisation

Mounting Danger

Wingspan

WINGSPAN

by

Karis Walsh

WINGSPAN
© 2014 By Karis Walsh. All Rights Reserved.

ISBN 13: 978-1-60282-983-1

This Trade Paperback Original Is Published By
Bold Strokes Books, Inc.
P.O. Box 249
Valley Falls, NY 12185

First Edition: February 2014

CREDITS
Editor: Ruth Sternglantz
Production Design: Susan Ramundo
Cover Design By Sheri (graphicartist2020@hotmail.com)

Dedication

To the staff and volunteers at Wolf Haven, International

Their selfless and tireless work for the wolves of Washington brings the true meaning of the word "sanctuary" to life. They inspire me to be a better person.

CHAPTER ONE

Kendall Pearson paced back and forth in the small waiting room at Port Townsend's ferry dock. She could cross the small space in eight shortened steps or in five of her regular long strides. Every few circuits she paused and read the posters on the bulletin boards, catching words here and there, but not really processing the entire message. A quilt show would be held at the local grange sometime in the future, and several companies offered gray-whale-watching tours. Other signs cautioned not to disturb harbor seal pups if she found one on a beach and warned about the proximity restrictions on orcas in Puget Sound. An alarming number of notices alerted her about the likelihood of ferry cancellations due to bad weather.

A lone kayaker glided past the terminal's picture window. Ken focused on the broad stroke of the kayak's paddle instead of on the slow and steady approach of the large green-and-white ferry from Coupeville, on Whidbey Island. She wasn't sure why she was so nervous. She stepped outside of the ferry terminal and looked around. A steep bluff overlooked the dock, the hillside covered with yellow blooming weeds and topped with huge folk Victorian homes, their elaborately pretty facades most likely masking rather plain and simple interior structures. A steep staircase—four flights of concrete dotted with human beings—scaled the cliff. The spring sun was warm and seemed determined to break through the sparse but heavy clouds. Gulls and other seabirds swooped over the water or bobbed on the gentle swells. Virginia just might fall in love with this place, with its old brick buildings and quaint vintage shops. And the slow-paced Olympic Peninsula was close to the lights and energy of Seattle, giving them the best of both worlds.

Ken turned away from the bluff and sighed as the ferry bumped to a halt against the dock. Virginia *might* fall in love with this place, or she might not. Either way, Ken had her future and her savings tied up in an acre of land not far from here. This was her home now, no mights or maybes about it.

Cars began to disembark, driving off the metal ramp with loud and rhythmic clangs, obediently following the directions of the orange-vested ferry workers. Ginny Liang's maroon BMW was easy to spot, and Ken waved and gestured toward a public parking lot a few yards away. She cut through a tiny park next to the ferry landing and met Ginny as she was climbing out of her car. She quickly crossed the space between them and caught Ginny in a tight hug, as relieved to be getting on with the uncertain afternoon meeting as she was to see her lover.

"God, what's that smell?" Ginny asked, wrinkling her nose and stepping back when Ken released her.

"Just the paper mill," Ken said. She pointed at a thick plume of steam that rose from an industrial area beyond the dock. She had registered the odor, of course, but it had been merely background to the visual beauty around her. Part of the texture and character of the old waterfront town.

Ginny smoothed her unwrinkled gray pencil skirt. "I was hoping for some fresh air after an hour sitting in the bowels of two ferries and breathing nothing but diesel fumes. How can people complain about city air when this is the alternative? I think I'm seasick."

"Why didn't you get out of your car and ride on the upper decks?" Even as Ken asked the question, she knew the answer. Ginny rolled her eyes and tucked a strand of professionally straightened, glossy hair behind her ear. The lure of salt air and whirling seabirds wouldn't have been enough to make her endure the windy observation deck. Ken pushed back her irritation as quickly as it rose in her. She had first been attracted to Ginny because she was well-groomed and beautiful in an understated way. She couldn't complain about the efforts required to maintain such a suitable appearance when she herself knew the cost of fitting in.

"So, you got me out here, baby," Ginny said, looping her forearm around Ken's neck and kissing her on the cheek. Her mood seemed to be improving now that she was on land again. "What's the big surprise?"

"I thought we could spend the afternoon in Sequim," Ken said. Ginny appeared more relaxed as they talked, but Ken's agitation increased. "It's about an hour drive, but I'll buy you lunch at a marina once we're there. The best seafood on the Peninsula."

She started to walk toward her car, but Ginny called her back.

"Let's take mine," she said, handing Ken the keys.

Ken opened the passenger door for Ginny and then slid behind the wheel. She fished through the chaotic jumble of keys and pink feathery flamingo and stuffed leopard-print dice before she found the right one. Ginny's car was a pleasure to drive—smoothly quiet and as understatedly elegant as its owner—but Ken preferred the cramped interior and deep purr of her own '56 Corvette. Her past girlfriends had plenty in common, including an inexplicable dislike of her Vette. Ken adored it. She had gone shopping for a Lexus after carefully researching the appropriate vehicle for her age and income, but a brief detour at a tempting classic car lot had been her downfall.

Ken started the BMW's engine. None of the pedestrians nearby turned to look the way people did when Ken's Corvette leaped to life. Ken had truly meant to find a car like this one, one that didn't bring unnecessary attention to itself or to her, but she had been drawn to the silhouette of her little car. A vision of it fully restored and beautiful had superimposed itself over the chipped and faded fiberglass body in front of her, and she hadn't been able to resist the pull of either the fantasy or the neglected reality. She had bought the car and rented garage space for it outside the city, much to her then-girlfriend Lisa's disgust—or had it been Gretchen? They tended to blur in Ken's mind. Lisa— or Gretchen—had left her during the time-consuming restoration project, but Ken had barely noticed.

But now the restoration was complete, and Ken had once again managed to control her impulses. Her friends were now accustomed to seeing the two-toned cherry-red-and-white car as a sign of mild eccentricity, not as proof that she was too different, and she was able to drive under the radar again. She had found another girlfriend who was exactly what she wanted—someone stable and self-sufficient and popular in a mainstream way. Hopefully, in Ginny she had found not only her general type, but the specific woman who would be her partner and ally.

Hopefully. Ken asked questions about Ginny's job as she drove them out of town. She listened to Ginny's discussion about the new summer trends in clothing and accessories, but most of her mind was preoccupied with the shapes and colors alongside the road. Uneven stacks of plastic Adirondack-style chairs in a rainbow of colors lined the edge of a hardware store's parking area. Used boat lots were as prevalent as used car lots in inland cities. Shops selling bikes and ice cream and kites shared the streets with run-down grocery stores and garish Jiffy Lubes, revealing the identity of the town as both a tourist destination and an unpretentious permanent residence.

Ken wanted to point out the way the different styles of architecture spoke either of the comfort and security of home or of the transience and idealism of vacation, but she didn't bother. She knew from experience that Ginny wouldn't be interested in the gravity-defying stack of garden pots on the side of the road, any more than Ken was interested in the debate over the popularity of boot-cut jeans. She was satisfied to keep her observations internalized, where she was safe to express any thought or idea, no matter how unusual. Her external life, whether with a girlfriend or work associates, was unconnected to her inner life, just as it should be.

Once they were out of town and winding along the twists and elevation changes of Highway 20, Ken started to point out things of interest. The low-flying planes turning base as they approached Jefferson County's airport, the cedars and ferns encroaching on the highway, the glimpses of Discovery Bay through the forest as the road curved around it. She didn't need Ginny to love Port Townsend specifically, but she *did* need her to love the rugged and distinctly non-urban peninsula if she hoped to convince her to move here.

Although Ginny made the appropriate noises of appreciation at the beauty around her and asked polite questions about the area, Ken's earlier nervousness was replaced by a growing sense of resignation. They both fell silent as she merged onto Highway 101 and sped over the remaining miles to the town of Sequim. They passed sprawling horse farms and neatly ordered rows of lavender fields, and Ken knew Ginny might enjoy seeing them during a weekend vacation, but she was less likely to want to trade her skyscrapers and upscale restaurants for them on a permanent basis. Ken had been able to imagine Ginny living here with her, but now, actually seeing Ginny in this place and seeing the area through Ginny's eyes, Ken's vision of their life together started to blur. She bypassed her planned tour of Sequim and instead cut off the highway and took the shortest route to the marina.

Ken parked in the first of several lots along the waterfront. She had wanted to take Ginny directly to her property, but the marina was a more civilized and familiar version of her rugged, oceanfront acre. Here, the view of Sequim Bay was spectacular and soothing at the same time, with its border of forested hills and its calm waters. An eclectic variety of boats, from fancy yachts to decrepit old fishing trawlers, pulled gently against the ropes tethering them to the pier. Black cormorants, with their wings spread in the sun, perched like ancient sentries on rotting wooden pylons. She'd move Ginny from the city to her wild acre in gradual stages.

Ken felt more than heard Ginny sigh. "Very pretty, babe, but we could have had a similar view at the Fisherman's in Seattle. Why the sudden urge to get back to nature?"

"Come on," Ken said, instead of answering. She got out of the BMW and hurried around to the passenger side. She opened the door and reached out for Ginny's hand, keeping it tucked in hers as she shut the door and walked them across the parking lot.

Ken walked slowly along the concrete path that bordered the beach. She would have preferred to walk on the sand, but Ginny's high heels weren't as suited to the terrain as her own tennis shoes. She stopped at the top of a high bank and stared out at the water in silence for a moment, hoping the majesty of the setting would whisper to Ginny as it had to her the first time she had stood on her property, only a few short miles from here. *Home.* Yet another impulse Ken hadn't been able to resist. Ginny stood at an angle against the wind, pulling her long black hair over one shoulder and holding it as if her hand was a barrette.

"The firm is closing," Ken said. She had seen the signs for some time now. The housing market was down and buyers' tastes were changing, but the company she worked for hadn't adapted in response. They had continued to build on spec, the same beige houses in the same types of developments. Feeling like an outsider in the company—all she did was show up and design repetitive variations of the same unremarkable home—she had dispassionately watched the firm circle the drain. But what had she done with her prescient knowledge? Had she saved as much as possible? Explored the job market? Updated her monotonous portfolio? No. She'd gone out and bought a ridiculously expensive piece of land. She could barely afford the payments as it was, let alone the price of building her dream home and rent for an apartment until she could move there.

"You predicted that a few months ago," Ginny said. She moved so Ken was blocking most of the wind. "I thought you'd been looking for another job."

"Sort of," Ken said, hedging the truth. She had been explaining her regular trips to the Peninsula by making vague comments about checking out building sites and researching house plans. All true, in their own way, but not explicitly so. She had known she was being misleading, and that Ginny was being led to believe Ken was hunting for a new firm, but she had been afraid of Ginny's reaction to the property. Besides, Ken hadn't needed to look for a new job. One had found her—complete with a startling salary increase. Ken hadn't wanted to accept and had turned down the initial offer because she preferred to stay in her predictable and inconspicuous position, but now she had no choice. "I've been offered a place at Impetus Architecture in Bellevue."

Ginny's expression, usually unruffled by whatever emotions were seething below the surface, reflected her surprise. Her mouth dropped open as if she were about to say something but had forgotten what, and her hand dropped to her side, leaving her hair to fly wildly in the breeze.

"*Impetus?*" she repeated. "The firm that designs mansions for the rich and famous?"

Ken reached out and captured Ginny's intractable hair, sliding her fingers through the windblown tangles and trying to tame it into smooth submission. It felt as warm and silky and alive as Ginny's skin under her hands. "Yes. I didn't want to take it, but I'll be unemployed soon…"

"Wow. I didn't know you were *that* good," Ginny said. She wrinkled her nose and smiled with an apologetic look. "Sorry. That didn't come out right. I just—"

Ken held up her hand to stop the explanation. She wasn't convinced she was right for the job, so why should anyone else be? She had been happy designing her mass-produced box houses, and she wasn't comfortable with the gasps and awe elicited by the Impetus name.

"An old school friend of mine works there and he recommended me," she said. Dougie. One of the main reasons she hadn't wanted the job. Being around him would bring too many painful memories too close to the surface when they belonged deep down. Out of sight. "I'm not sure if I'll fit in there, but I'm out of options. I have to try."

"Well, congratulations," Ginny said with a genuine smile. She pulled Ken into a tight hug, her breasts pressed against Ken's ribs and her arms wrapped firmly around Ken's neck. In spite of the turmoil she had been in for the past few months, Ken felt her body respond to Ginny's touch. The area of contact between them felt hot in contrast to the cool wind buffeting Ken's back, and she wished she had gone against her own logic and had taken Ginny to her private and isolated property. Sex in that place could be wild, untamed. Fed by the throbbing beat of the waves.

"So, you'll be working in Bellevue? I'm so relieved," Ginny whispered against Ken's neck. The warmth of her breath would normally fuel Ken's passion, but Ginny's words doused it completely. "You've been so mysterious about today, I thought you might actually be thinking of moving out here." Ginny pulled back. "So, are we going to see the site of the first house you're building for Impetus? Who's it for? A Microsoft exec, or one of the Weyerhaeusers?"

"Gin, I *do* want to move here. I already bought a place and I want to build a house there and I want you to live in it with me. Please, don't say no yet. Come out and see what I have planned, and try to picture how great our life would be if we were here together."

"Ken—"

"Wait," Ken said, hearing a note of pleading in her voice. She wasn't sure who the object of her entreaty was. Ginny? Some god? The spirits of this place? The latter seemed omnipotent and not especially benevolent, because they had made her not only go against her plans and buy this land but had also ensured that she had to take the offer from Impetus. Pleas and prayers would have no effect on them.

"Remember the house I designed last year for the Pine Meadows development? We could build one like it, but with modifications so it'd be perfect for us." Ken started walking again, her hands in her pockets. She had been out to her acre earlier, jabbing stakes into the ground and joining them with string to demarcate the outline of a two-story home, based on one of her most popular floor plans. Ken had seen the house completed in several developments, and it wasn't exactly what she would have designed for her space, but she knew Ginny loved it. Ken rambled on, attempting to use words to create a vision of wood and skylights, stone paths and granite countertops, in Ginny's imagination. There'd be a weight room and gourmet kitchen for Ken. An airy sewing room for Ginny, and a huge deck where she could entertain by the light of tiki lamps. It should be perfect. Maybe, if Ken could make the fantasy seem solid and real, she'd be able to convince Ginny to stay.

"It sounds great, Ken," Ginny said when Ken ran out of words to say. Ginny gestured around them. "But why out here? If you want to live outside the city, there are plenty of developments in Auburn or Renton. We could build our dream home and still be close enough to enjoy Seattle and see our friends."

Ken held the door to the marina's restaurant open for Ginny and led her past the *Please seat yourself* sign and onto the slatted wood patio. She knew all the suburban developments around Seattle. She had designed homes for many of them—although, driving down streets lined with beige and pastel houses, even she had a hard time distinguishing her own work from any other architect's. The imaginary home Ken had been describing seemed more substantial to her than anything she had seen or touched.

"Do you want to at least visit the property before you decide?" Ken asked after they had scanned the menus in silence and placed their orders. She had read online reviews and menus from most of Sequim's restaurants, researching thoroughly before she invited Ginny to lunch and to see her property. The marina had seemed perfect, with its bright white-and-blue paint creating sharp lines and clear distinctions. Nothing blurred or iffy. The menu of seasonal and fresh seafood and produce was suited to Ken's taste, and expensive enough to prove it was on par with some of Seattle's top restaurants. But Ken could read Ginny's expression well enough to understand that outlining the house and choosing the restaurant had been fruitless endeavors.

"Maybe another day. This is a lot of news to process, and I need some time."

Time. Ken realized Ginny had already made up her mind. Ken had needed a nanosecond to feel a connection to this place. Ginny had needed the same amount to decide she wouldn't be staying here. She managed to smile and thank the waiter when he brought her drink, as if her world wasn't spinning horribly off its axis. Property she couldn't afford, a job she didn't want, and a relationship about to slip out of her grasp. Gravity had gone haywire, flinging the wrong things into her life and pulling the right ones away.

Ken toyed with the delicate stem of her wineglass between sips of the chilled Willamette Valley Pinot Grigio. "*Two* ferries," Ginny repeated. She picked the blue plastic skewer out of her martini glass and ate one of the olives. "And that just gets me to Mukilteo. From there, I'd still have a long commute into the city."

Ken closed her eyes and tilted her head toward the sun. Even as her mind raced, her body melted in the soft heat. The hint of salt in the air and the rhythmic splash of water against the wooden dock filled her ears and nose. Her outward senses were languid and relaxed, but inside—so deep no one would be able to detect it—she was frayed and edgy. Were they really going to break up over ferry rides? Granted, she had gotten accustomed to rolling out of bed twenty minutes before she had to be at work, taking a hasty shower, and speed walking the three blocks between her apartment and her firm's downtown Seattle office, but a place of her own was worth the extra time on the sea and the road. Besides, Ken loved the ferry rides. The sounds of calling gulls and splashing wake, the smells of diesel and fish, the taste of the ocean wind. There had been times over the past month when long ferry lines and delayed passages had left her feeling as exasperated as Ginny sounded. But then she had stood on her chunk of land, staring across the Strait of Juan de Fuca toward the San Juan Islands and Canada, as the natural beauty of the area settled her mind and soul. At those times, she knew she was willing to make whatever sacrifice necessary to be able to live on the Olympic Peninsula. Even if Ginny, and Ken's dream of a settled partnership with a suitable woman, were part of the price.

Ken opened her eyes and sat up when the waiter brought their food. The mussels in the small cast-iron skillet he placed in front of her were still steaming in their thyme- and garlic-infused broth. Ken inhaled and caught a hint of floral notes. Lavender. Interesting. She scooped a mussel out of its shell and ate it while Ginny cut her rib eye into precise, tiny bits, as if she were performing intricate surgery.

"I thought your plan was to buy a condo in my building," Ginny said, not looking up from her plate.

"I thought so, too," Ken said. She and Ginny had agreed that living close to each other was good, but living in the same apartment would be challenging. Ginny's building had seemed like an appropriate choice, fitting in perfectly with the type of places their friends had. But, like the Corvette, the acre of land brushed by ocean winds had made Ken forget her carefully formulated plans. "But I fell in love with the property."

Ginny took a bite of her steak and chewed it thoroughly before speaking again. "Why don't we build a little cottage there? It can be a vacation home. You can move in with me."

Ken knew the offer had been a difficult one for Ginny to make. Allowing Ken into her private space on a permanent basis, accepting that their finances would be tied up in a property and house she really didn't want—these hadn't been part of Ginny's life plan any more than buying the land had been part of Ken's. She chewed another tender mussel and swallowed, feeling the salty sweetness of the fresh shellfish ground her in this place. She belonged here and Ginny didn't. Simple as that.

"I want to live here full-time," she said, reaching out to cover Ginny's hand with her own. "This new job is going to be stressful, and I'll need a place to get away. And until I'm certain I'll be at Impetus longer than my two-month probationary period, I'll need to save as much money as I can. My lease is up in Seattle, and I'll be moving into an apartment here in Sequim. It'll be a hell of a lot cheaper than living in the city."

"So, that's it? I thought we wanted the same things."

Ken had, as well. She knew she wanted a woman like Ginny. She had already dated a string of them, confident in the general type but never finding the specific person she needed. And she wanted the life they had been building together. Her job, the condo she'd chosen, her friends—although, in truth, all their friends had originally been Ginny's. Ken had been working toward a settled and acceptable and inconspicuous life. Why did she insist on messing up every opportunity? *She* had been the one to buy the property, setting in motion the events that simultaneously drove Ginny away while pushing Ken into the Impetus firm. She couldn't blame fates or spirits when she had been the one to sign her name on the papers.

"I thought so, too," she repeated, but most of her thoughts were centered on the strange lack of feeling she had. She had just broken up with a sexy, intelligent, fun woman, but she felt more emotional about the exceptional plate of food in front of her than about the loss of her relationship. She wouldn't miss Ginny herself as much as she'd mourn the loss of security and legitimacy their relationship gave her. She was safe with someone like Ginny. Safe and accepted and part of society—not on the dangerous fringe.

Was she somehow incapable of feeling anything real for another woman? What was wrong with her? She continued to find the seemingly perfect woman, but constantly failed in her attempt to fall in love. To be fair, Ginny, calmly eating the rest of her steak and potatoes, seemed as little affected by the breakup as Ken was. Maybe there hadn't been enough emotion in the mix to cause either one of them much distress. She should be happy to have accomplished the split with minimal fuss and despair, and not paradoxically feel at a loss because she didn't feel a sense of loss.

The waiter brought their desserts. Ken cracked open the hard shell of her crème brûlée and ate a spoonful, letting the creamy sweetness coat her tongue. She and Ginny talked easily once decisions had been made and choices were clear. They would be civil through the rest of lunch, and then Ken would drive Ginny back to the ferry landing—not because Ginny wanted Ken to take care of her, but simply because Ken needed a ride back to her car. Ken had been attracted to Ginny because she didn't expect chivalry or protection, so she should be relieved now as they calmly parted ways. Ken would go on, putting her search for the ideal woman on hold until she could afford to get out of Impetus and back to a stable and less showy firm. In the meantime, she'd keep company with the sea, staying safe by remaining alone.

❖

Ken maneuvered as carefully as she could down the road leading to her property, avoiding the deeper potholes by driving instead through the thick grass lining the private lane. "I'm sure they'll eventually pave the road," she promised her car with a little pat on its dashboard, although she knew *eventually* was a long way in the future, if ever. "There are only a few houses out here now, but maybe once the rest of the lots are sold…"

Ken's voice trailed off. She parked on the side of the road, next to a for sale sign with a bright red *Sold* sticker cutting across it like a bloody gash. She got out of her car and let the now-familiar sense of peace steal over her. The land had caused her nothing but trouble, and still she couldn't help but love it.

Most of the one-acre property was a grassy meadow, dotted with dandelions and stiff lupine. Angular fir trees bordered the property, with salal and Oregon grape clustered around the base of their trunks. Ken saw the blemishes Ginny would no doubt have noticed—the unsightly and trash-littered scar where the previous owner's double-wide had rested until Ken had it removed, the invasive scotch broom sneaking onto the eastern edge of the lawn—but she also saw the grandeur of the spot. The energy of wind and wave as the Pacific Ocean pushed eagerly through the Strait of Juan de Fuca, calming only as it passed her house and entered Puget Sound. The hazy lumps of land that, on a clearer day, would be recognizable as Vancouver Island and the San Juans. Migrating whales and shipping traffic heading toward Seattle would parade by this place, and only a short hike down the bluff would land her on the rocky beach.

Ken walked along the path she had cut through the thick grass. Last weekend she had rented a truck and a lawn mower and had neatly trimmed the site she had picked for Ginny's house. Today she had measured and outlined the home she had wanted to build. She stepped over the yellow twine and stood inside what would have been the spacious living room. The image of the beige two-story was already beginning to fade from her mind. Ken turned in a circle, trying to picture the walls she had been able to see this morning, but all she saw now were the trees and grass around her. Ginny's presence was fading from this place as well.

Because she had envisioned Ginny inside the house the whole time. Ken had been able to imagine living in this place, walking along the bluff or the shore below, sitting on the lawn or under the stubby trees. But every time she had fantasized about living here with Ginny, she had been unable to visualize her outside the comfortable but boring two-story house.

Ken walked over the piece of twine marking the back wall of the house and headed toward the ocean. She came to the edge of the clearing, waded through the uncut grass, and nearly stepped on a large bird before it exploded in a flurry of feathers. She staggered back a step and saw a flash of white and brown as the bird struggled to fly away from her with one wing. The other dragged uselessly behind as it hopped through the thick grass. Ken backed away quietly. She had spent enough time hiking and exploring trails to know she should leave any wildlife alone and untouched if she came across a bird or animal, but this one looked seriously injured. She couldn't leave it there alone, where it would be easy prey for any passing dog or coyote.

She turned and jogged to her car. Was it an eagle? It didn't look big enough, but maybe it was young. She rummaged through her trunk and pulled out a clean towel she carried to wipe down her car. She dumped sketch pads and pencils out of a cardboard box, and slowly walked back to the home site. She had no idea how she was going to get the bird into the box without either damaging it or getting her eyeballs clawed out. She set the box down and approached the flapping bird with the towel in her outstretched hands like a matador. Didn't parrots think it was bedtime if someone draped a blanket over their cage? She wasn't convinced the frightened bird would meekly fall asleep in her arms because she threw a towel over its head, but she had to try.

And try again. By the time she finally managed to drape the towel over the bird, she was sweating and cursing and ready to lie down and catch her breath. But she quickly picked up the heaving ball of feathers before it could break out of its terry cloth prison, cradling its good wing against her body. The bird was heavier than she had expected, and she tried to hold it with one arm and support its wounded wing with her other as she carried it across the field and deposited it in the box as gently as she could. With a muttered sorry, she pushed its head down an inch and closed the box.

She opened the passenger-side door and put the box on the floor, setting a flat rock on top to keep the bird from pushing out. She stared at the box. Now what? She had been so intent on capturing the bird, but she hadn't given any thought to where she would take it. To the local small animal vet? Her apartment? She pulled out her phone and typed in *Olympic Peninsula, wild bird rescue.*

CHAPTER TWO

B ailey Chase changed outfits for the second time that
morning while she mentally reviewed her lengthy to-
do list. She pulled a soft, ancient football jersey over her head
as she counted the injured wings and talons and beaks she had
treated so far today. Once she was satisfied she hadn't forgotten
any of her patients, she walked back to her kitchen to prepare
lunch for herself and her charges. A large redtail watched Bailey
warily as she passed her cage in the living room. Bailey had
removed several BBs from her wing and body, but the bird was
healing nicely. She was stoic and resigned to sharing Bailey's
home, although she managed to take a sharp bite every time
Bailey let her attention slip for even a moment. The hawk would
be able to go into the flight cage soon, opening up much-needed
space in the interim cage.

Stacks of paperwork covered the kitchen table, reminding
Bailey of the less-urgent but just as demanding chores on her
list. She had been about to lose the land she leased for her
sanctuary last year, but an injured eagle—and the woman who
had found him on her property—had come into her life and
rescued *her* for a change. Vonda Selbert had been so moved by
the eagle's recovery and eventual release that she had bought
the sanctuary land and had arranged for Bailey's rehab center to

become a field study location for Washington State University's veterinary school. To be fair, the release of the eagle had been impressive as hell. He had been around four years old when he was injured and had arrived in transition, still sporting a mottled brown-and-white head, several brown tail feathers, and a grayish bill. By the time Bailey released him near the Selbert's waterfront home, he was in full adult plumage. The sight of the massive bird, with his bright yellow bill and sharply delineated white head and tail, launching off the ground had made even Bailey cry. Of course, she always cried at a release. But the eagle's had been truly spectacular. Vonda wasn't about to forget the experience. The arrangement had seemed like a dream come true to Bailey until the reality came crashing down onto her kitchen table. Massive amounts of paperwork, not to mention the interns and students who would be invading her privacy. Bailey's enthusiasm for the project had waned, but she had no choice but to push forward. She could afford to move to a smaller piece of land, but she would have to downsize. With the university's support, she'd be able to rescue far more birds than she could alone. End of story.

But she didn't have to face the extra work today, when she had been up for over twenty-four hours. Bailey turned her back on the table and took a bag of crickets and a box of sesame chicken out of her freezer. She put the plastic tray of chicken in the microwave and shut the door, opening it once again to make sure she had put *her* lunch in the oven and not her birds'. She wasn't about to make that mistake again. While she was setting the timer, the buzzer for her front gate sounded.

Bailey hurried into the living room, past the ruffled and annoyed-looking hawk, and pressed the button to open the gate. She stepped onto the front porch and waved in relief as Sue Adams, one of her closest friends and a fellow rehabber, parked her large white Buick and jumped out.

"Come here, honey. You look like you need a hug," Sue said as she bounded up the steps. She looked as exhausted as Bailey felt, but she always seemed to have energy in reserve.

"It's good to see you," Bailey said. She didn't particularly need a hug. She needed a bath, she needed some food, and she needed a hefty dose of caffeine, but she stepped forward and let Sue squeeze her tightly. She didn't move away until Sue did, guessing that Sue was actually the one who needed human contact. Bailey could easily go days with only the brush of feathers against her skin. "You look…tired."

Sue laughed. "That's a nice way of saying I look like hell, isn't it? Jim told me not to sit and rest anywhere near a cemetery because the caretakers might think I'd escaped and try to put me back in the ground."

Bailey smiled, but Sue's husband's playful warning wasn't far from the truth. Sue's face was unnaturally pale, and dark circles framed her eyes like smoky makeup. Her hair, cut in a simple wash-and-wear bob, was sticking up in front as if she'd been running her hands through it in weary exasperation. Bailey reached out and smoothed Sue's bangs. "Come in and rest for a while," she said. "I'll make you a cup of coffee strong enough to rouse the dead."

"Just what I need," Sue said, linking her arm with Bailey's as they walked into the house. "Hey, gorgeous." Sue acknowledged the redtail as they passed her cage on the way to the kitchen. "So, Bailey, what do you have for me?"

"An evening grosbeak," Bailey said. She gathered the papers she had strewn across the kitchen table and stacked them to one side, putting a bag of mealworms on top of the pile. "He had some deep cuts, probably from a cat. I cleaned them and stitched the worst of them. I don't know if he'll make it."

Bailey stopped tidying up and rubbed her stinging eyes. She had been up all night watching the small songbird, so fragile and delicate compared to her usual raptor patients. She had sat across the room and stared at the still form of the bird, willing him to survive until morning.

"First things first," Sue said. "Let's take a look at him, and then we'll have that cup of coffee."

"He's here in the pantry." Bailey opened the door next to her fridge. "I was worried he'd think he was going to be lunch if I kept him anywhere near my other patients."

Sue knelt and took the lid off the box, expertly catching the bright yellow bird. She splayed his black-striped wing and peered at Bailey's work.

"Beautiful job on these stitches," she said with a nod. She put the bird back and covered the box in one quick motion. "He'll heal just fine, don't you worry. Long way from the heart."

"But he's so quiet," Bailey protested. "I thought he was dead when I checked on him this morning."

"You're used to those vultures and raptors of yours. Ready to vomit on you or claw your eyes out every time you come near them. The songbirds are different." Sue sat at the kitchen table with a tired-sounding sigh. "This little guy is just lonely, but I have a crossbill that's all alone in my small flight cage. I'm sure they'll be besties before long."

Sue's confidence was exactly what Bailey had needed. She pulled a bag of locally roasted coffee beans out of her freezer and ground enough for two double espressos. She and Sue referred people to each other, directing raptors and songbirds to the appropriate rehab facility or—as was the case with the grosbeak—taking care of emergency care for the other when needed. The grosbeak had been left in a shoebox by her gate, and Sue had been unable to get here until this afternoon. Bailey had, of course, worked on small birds before, but their delicacy always made her nervous.

She poured some milk into a stainless steel pitcher, bypassing the skim and going straight for the whole milk, and heated it until it grew frothy and thick. Sue seemed matter-of-fact and unaffected by the plight of the little grosbeak, but Bailey knew the truth. She wouldn't be doing this job if she didn't care. Bailey brought the cappuccinos and a box of Oreos to the table and sat down, her sigh echoing the one Sue had made earlier.

"What a treat," Sue said, pushing the mealworms aside so she could reach the sugar bowl. She put a heaping spoonful in her coffee and passed the bowl to Bailey, who did the same. "Plus, Jim's parents have the kids for the weekend, so I'm really in heaven."

"I don't know how you do it," Bailey said, dunking a cookie in her coffee and watching the dark chocolate specks flake onto the white foam. Sue had three kids under eight years old, plus a husband and an endless flock of resident birds. Bailey could barely care for herself and her patients, let alone a family.

"Truthfully? I don't either. But they all help, out of necessity." Sue laughed and picked up a second Oreo. "You should see us at night. All sitting in front of the television with a bird or two on our laps, worms and seeds spilling everywhere. Crazy. But somebody's got to do it."

Crazy? It sounded perfect to Bailey. She would have loved to grow up in a household like Sue's. Chaotic and messy and more avian than human. A family gathered together with little bits of feather and heartbeat on their laps. She drank her strong coffee and wiped a mustache of foam off her upper lip.

"Do you have a minute to read something?" she asked, changing the subject from family life to her professional one. She pulled the stack of papers toward her. "I have to teach a two-week seminar every term as part of my deal with WSU, starting with the summer session. I wrote some notes for the first class, and I'd like your opinion."

"You're so lucky," Sue said. "All those vet students helping you clean cages and feed. Getting to teach classes and shape the young minds of future rehabbers—"

"Really?" Bailey asked in disbelief. "I'm dreading it."

"All that lovely money," Sue continued, undeterred by Bailey's interruption. "The new surgical room and bigger flight cages…"

"Well, I *do* like those parts of it," Bailey said. The cost of them was too great, though. But she'd sacrifice her precious time and solitude for her birds.

Sue shook her head. "Okay, I'll put my jealousy aside and help you, but only if you send an occasional intern over to my house to clean bird shit. Preferably a handsome male intern."

"You can have all of them," Bailey said. Male or female, she didn't care. She wasn't looking for dates, and she didn't want some inept students mucking about with her birds. "I decided to do my first seminar on removing foreign objects from birds."

"Charming," Sue said with a grimace.

"It's a big part of what we do. Plastic, fishing wire, BBs. That sort of thing."

"You're right. Why don't you give me the lecture instead of having me read your notes?"

Bailey took a gulp of her coffee and cleared her throat. She was nervous enough reading to Sue. She didn't know how she'd handle having a room full of students staring at her while she spoke. She loved talking about birds—anything to do with birds—but she knew from experience that her audiences never were as interested as she was. A few people were, like Sue and some of the women Bailey met at wildlife rehab conferences, but not many. Bailey had figured out how to curb her zealous enthusiasm for all things avian somewhere during fourth grade, but she had already established a reputation as an oddball since the same students had followed her through junior high and high school in the small town of Bremerton. She hadn't really minded, being content to keep her all-consuming hobby to herself unless she found a kindred spirit like Sue, but now she was being forced to do exactly what she had learned the hard way *not* to do. Talk birds.

Once she started, however, she lost herself in the subject. What did she think these kids were going to do, anyway? Steal her lunch money or pull her hair? She was thirty-two and they were students. She'd be fine as long as she kept talking. Her speech sounded a little too fast to her ears, probably fueled by the caffeine. But her attentiveness was still dulled by lack of sleep, and she was describing in intricate detail how to remove plastic pop-bottle rings from a bird's neck when she realized Sue was waving her hand and trying to interrupt.

"What? Did I say something wrong?"

Sue rubbed a hand over her mouth, as if she was stalling while she searched for the right words. "No. Your knowledge of the subject is very…thorough. But you might want to work on your delivery. Add some pauses now and then for questions, and make eye contact. You're reciting information in a monotone, and your students might lose interest. You want to entertain them."

"*Entertain* them? But it's a lecture. I'm supposed to teach them what I know."

"Of course, but just break it up a bit. Maybe add a joke or two."

"A *joke*?"

"A humorous story intended to make people laugh," Sue said, shaking her head. "Don't look so horrified. I'm sure once you get in front of the students, you'll relax and have fun with it."

Bailey was sure of the exact opposite reaction. The students would laugh *at* her, not with her. She'd make a fool of herself. Maybe she could back out now, while she still had some pride and dignity left. "I don't think I know any jokes."

"Okay, not jokes then. But tell some humorous anecdotes. I'm sure you have a million of them."

Bailey rubbed her forehead. This was more complicated than she had expected. It had taken her weeks to find the energy and time to sit down and write lecture notes. Now she had to add inflection and comedic timing to the task? The whole WSU mess was turning into a joke on her, but the punch line felt more like a punch in the stomach. She dimly heard a car pull up outside the house, but she didn't feel like moving. Someone had come through the gate she'd left open when Sue had arrived. Yet another person or bird here to make demands on her.

Sue got up and moved the kitchen curtain aside. "Oh, yum," she said. She dropped the curtain back in place and went to the pantry door. "Thanks for the coffee, Bailey dear, but I think I'll take this little guy home now and leave you alone to take care of your visitor."

Bailey peered out the window at the fancy little sports car and the equally impressive woman who was climbing out of it. Long legs, sharp clothes, and refined features. Bailey's mind echoed Sue's *yum* even as she noticed the vivid contrast between her rundown property and the obviously well-off newcomer.

"She must be lost," Bailey said to Sue. "Stay here and finish your coffee. I'll give her directions and send her on her way."

CHAPTER THREE

K en drove slowly up the gravel driveway. The road was filled with potholes and nearly overgrown by brush. She winced as a branch from a shrub scraped against the side of her car. The damned bird had better appreciate what she was sacrificing to bring him to this place. She parked in front of the huge old house and sat in the car for a moment. She hoped she was actually doing the bird a favor by taking him here. The setting would be perfect for a Halloween haunted house, ramshackle and rambling, with chipped paint and a broken shutter hanging askew on one of the front windows. She considered taking her passenger somewhere else, but she could see two enormous mesh cages in the yard beside the house. The grass in this area had been neatly trimmed, and the cages appeared roomy and clean. There was no sign anywhere identifying this as the Chase Raptor Rehabilitation Center, but she could see several large birds perched on limbs inside the mesh walls. As she watched, one of them soared smoothly to a higher perch from which it regarded her warily.

Ken had seen birds of prey in the sky and a few in zoos, but something about the birds in these cages stirred her. They were wild—she could almost feel their yearning to get out and be free—biding time here until they were healed enough to be released. A transition place, between two worlds, and whoever was taking care of them seemed to have made their welfare a priority. Yard and house be damned, all attention and effort seemed to have been lavished on the birds.

"I guess this is your best chance, birdie," she said. Her passenger didn't answer. It had been frighteningly silent during the entire drive, and Ken had a sinking feeling she'd open the box and it would be dead. Had she aggravated its injury when she stuffed it in the box? Stressed it out during the long drive? She sighed and stepped out of her car. Might as well find out. And then let a professional deal with the wounded creature while she got back to her own life. She preferred wood and stone to fragile flesh-and-feathers creatures.

Ken carefully shut her car door and walked to the passenger side. She paused with her hand on the door when two women came out of the house. The first one, wearing Birkenstocks, capri-length gray sweatpants, and a faded Seattle Seahawks jersey, caught and held Ken's attention. She looked like a teenager, but once she was close Ken saw she was in her early thirties. Auburn hair was pulled into a slightly off-center ponytail, and pale skin accentuated the dark circles under her eyes. Tired, uneasy eyes, almost the same glossy red-brown of her hair. The woman didn't have on even a hint of makeup—in fact, it looked as if there had been few intermediary steps between bed and being in public. Unpolished and slightly eccentric, but with a natural elegance and beauty that her old, baggy clothes couldn't hide.

"I'm Ken," she said, forcing herself to acknowledge both women, although her focus remained on the one closest to her. The other woman answered first.

"I'm Sue, but I'm leaving." Sue put a box, much like the one Ken had brought, in the front seat of her Buick. Another bird in transport? Convenient. One out, and Ken's could move in. She waved as Sue drove past her car and continued down the driveway.

"Bailey Chase." Bailey looked at the hand Ken offered for a moment before she moved closer and shook it. She glanced at the dust cloud made by Sue's car, as if she wanted to follow it down the road.

"Nice to meet you, Dr. Chase." Ken struggled to keep her expression neutral when Bailey came near, bringing a powerful acidic scent with her. The odor quickly shifted her from eccentric to weird.

Bailey moved away again. "You can call me Bailey. And I'm sorry about the smell," she said. Apparently Ken hadn't been as successful at hiding her reaction as she'd hoped. "A vulture threw up on me this morning. I haven't had a chance to shower yet."

"A vulture. Threw up on you," Ken repeated. She had to laugh at what was probably the most absurd statement anyone had ever said to her. She tried to imagine how Ginny would have reacted if the vulture had chosen her as its target instead of the apparently unperturbed Bailey. Ginny would have required hospitalization and a handful of valium.

"Occupational hazard," Bailey said, a protective tone creeping into her voice. "It's a defense mechanism. He was injured and frightened."

All right, crazy bird lady. "Will he be okay?" Ken asked, to be polite. She wasn't sure why someone would go out of her way to rescue a defensive and stinky vulture, but the bird seemed to matter to Bailey.

"He was tangled on some fishing line and it took me a few hours to catch him, so he was very stressed. He has some lacerations on his feet, and I had to amputate one of his talons, but he should heal well. He's young and strong."

"Oh. Well, that's good news." Ken was about to reach out and touch Bailey's shoulder, but she stopped herself in time so her hand only flinched. She had a feeling Bailey had been as stressed by the chase as the vulture, and she had the unexpected—and unwelcome—urge to offer some comfort. Bailey was too fragile for Ken's tastes. Not weak, since Bailey appeared strong and healthy, and she obviously was walking her own path with her nontraditional career. But sensitive. Too sensitive. Ken had learned long ago that she couldn't afford to care too much in return. She wasn't strong enough to protect such a fragile soul from the harsh realities of life.

Bailey stared at Ken, trying to decide whether she was being sincere or sarcastic. Ken looked like she understood a thing or two about defenses. Dressed in stark black and white, with her straight hair simply styled and just brushing her shoulders, she was stunning but wasn't trying to call attention to her looks. Her turquoise eyes were expressionless, and even without crossing her arms or closing herself off, she managed to convey distance with her body language. She seemed stiff and controlled, as if she was ready to block any unwanted touch. Bailey had long ago developed the habit of scanning people's faces and bodies for any clues about their emotional states, and if she hadn't been paying such close attention, she would have missed the brief responses Ken revealed before carefully bringing them under control. Her small wince at the residual vulture odor. Her amusement at Bailey's explanation.

Now, there was no sign of emotion, so Bailey changed the subject. "Why are you here?" she asked.

"I brought you another bird," Ken said, seeming undeterred by Bailey's abrupt question. She nodded toward her car. "Hopefully this one won't vomit on you."

She leaned into her sports car and lifted the large box easily. "Where do you want it?" she asked.

"Wait," Bailey said, irked by Ken's assumption that she would automatically take the bird. Well, she would, of course, but she wanted to be the one making the decisions. Bailey was getting tired of bossy people disrupting her chaotic but comfortable life. Vonda, WSU's dean, and now the composed and assertive Ken. She blocked Ken's path as she started walking toward the flight cages. "What kind is it?"

Ken shrugged. "A big one. I saw white, so maybe it's an eagle?"

Bailey sighed. The last "eagle" someone had brought had actually been a large band-tailed pigeon. She gestured toward the house. "The surgery is inside. Follow me."

Ken shifted the box in her hands, careful not to jar its occupant or dislodge the rock that still held it closed. She walked behind Bailey, noticing how even such baggy and unbecoming clothes managed to show off her slender figure. Who would have thought ratty old sweatpants could make an ass look so good? Too bad the woman inside the sweats was so odd. Definitely not Ken's type. Bailey was different, while Ken was accustomed to cookie-cutter women—the type she herself aspired to be. Ken felt a momentary pang of compassion as she thought how difficult life must have been in school for oddball Bailey. Ken had been there herself, but she had learned how to fit in. And part of fitting in meant she had to avoid being connected with people on the fringe.

Ken sidled past Bailey as she held the screen door open. She'd drop off the bird and get out of here. She had rescued it from the edge of her field, possibly pulling it back from the brink of death, but she had reached the limit of her usefulness. She might even have done more harm than good by following her misguided instincts and clumsily putting the bird in a box rather than leaving it alone. Either way, she couldn't do any more for it, or for Bailey. Bailey only served as a reminder of how far Ken had come since junior high. And how close her new job brought her to being shoved back to the outskirts of society, where she had verged with her friends Dougie and Steve.

The dangerous zone.

Ken had managed to get accepted into the mainstream, and she had to be on guard so she didn't get pegged as an outsider ever again. Once her house was built and she could get a job somewhere besides Impetus, she'd be fine. She'd find another socially acceptable girlfriend like Ginny—but maybe one who stirred her soul a little more deeply—and she'd be all set. Or maybe she'd just live by herself once she built her new home.

Ken followed Bailey through her living room. At first glance, it seemed like a normal, comfortable room, complete with cushy sofas and hand-knitted quilts. Normal, except for the regal hawk that watched their every move. Ken returned its unblinking stare as she walked across the room, but she was first to break the intense eye contact.

"Set it on the examination table," Bailey said when they entered what must have been a bedroom before it was turned into a makeshift examination room. The closet door had been removed and now held shelves of latex gloves and bandages and syringes. The hardwood floors and large window would have made it an elegant and airy room, but a clear plastic lining covered the floor, and the window was darkened by a heavy shutter. A bright lamp and metal table were the only light spots— clinical and functional as they were—in the room.

Ken put the box where directed and inched toward the door Bailey had closed behind them. She had done her part and now it was time to leave, but she was mesmerized by Bailey's sudden transformation. Instead of the awkward woman Ken had first met, she now had a fluidity and grace about her as she put on a pair of heavy gloves and opened the box. For a brief moment, the bird spread its wings as if about to fly away—its wingspan easily as long as Bailey's five-and-a-half foot height—before she expertly bundled it in a cloth and covered its face and lethally sharp beak with a leather hood. The hint of elegance Ken had noticed earlier was clearly evident now as she handled the large raptor with practiced ease. Even if Ken hadn't spent a sweaty half hour trying to wrestle with the ungainly bird, she would have recognized skill and finesse when she saw it.

"Put your hands here…and here," Bailey instructed, breaking Ken out of her reverie.

"I really can't stay." She groped behind her back for the door handle. "I just expected to drop off the bird and go. I don't have any experience with—"

"Put your hands here…and here," Bailey repeated, not looking at Ken.

Ken walked over to the examination table. So she spent a few more minutes in the company of sexy bird lady Bailey. What could it hurt? Well, it might hurt the poor bird. She replaced Bailey's expert hands with her own less-adept ones. She felt the steady rhythm of the bird's heart beneath her touch. The twitch of muscles, the latent power. Even as part of her wanted to leave, she couldn't stop her instinctive response to the powerful living creature she held.

"It's an osprey." Bailey spoke quietly as she gathered supplies from her shelves. "Probably a male, judging by his size. They're a bit smaller than the females."

Ken felt the bunched muscles of the bird pushing against her restricting hands. This one seemed plenty huge, and she was relieved she hadn't found a female instead. She'd never have gotten her in the box. Suddenly her bundle lurched and a foot broke out of its wrapper and scrabbled against the metal table. Ken caught a glimpse of a white leg with two gray toes facing forward and two backward before Bailey came over and eased the leg back into the cloth. She covered Ken's hand with her own and changed her position slightly. Even through the heavy glove, Ken felt the assured skill of Bailey's touch. Confident and gentle. Ken focused on the bird again, concentrating on containing it rather than on the effect of Bailey's pressure against her skin.

Bailey filled a syringe and swiftly injected the bird. She seemed to have a sense of the osprey's anatomy, even when it was covered with cloth, and Ken soon felt the taut muscles beneath her hands loosen and relax. Within minutes, she was carefully cradling a dozing bird, its slow heartbeat thrumming against her wrist.

"Put this on," Bailey said, handing Ken a heavy apron. "I'll need to take an X-ray."

Ken took the garment and draped it over her torso while Bailey set up a decrepit portable X-ray machine. Ken had somehow been drafted into the position of surgical assistant, but she gave up any pretense of wanting to leave as she watched Bailey manipulate the osprey's injured wing. Bailey seemed unaware of her presence most of the time as she spoke soothingly to the anesthetized bird, but occasionally she raised her voice enough to give Ken instructions about how to hold the wing, or to ask for an instrument.

Ken didn't know much about ospreys, but she realized what a privilege it was to have such close contact with a wild animal. The raptor was dark brown with a white head and belly, its glossy feathers at once pliable and stiff. While Bailey examined the X-rays, Ken trailed her fingertip over the leading edge of the bird's wing and along the wing tips, tracing the delicate structure.

"Looks like a clean break," she said, looking at the backlit X-ray with a feeling of relief. Bailey *had* to be able to fix the injury. Ken didn't think she could bear to hear that the osprey would never fly again.

"Well, yes, it is." Bailey's voice sounded more cautious than Ken liked. "A break in the humerus. It isn't close to the joint, so it has a good chance of healing."

"But?" Ken prompted.

Bailey turned away from the X-ray and came over to the table. She spread the feathers on the osprey's belly. "But…do you see these small cuts? And these here, near the broken bone? He most likely was hit by a car. The scrapes are minor, and the break isn't the worst I've seen, but he might have internal damage that I can't fix. I'll wrap the wing and suture a couple of the larger cuts, but we won't know the extent of his injuries for a few days."

Bailey's voice was matter-of-fact, as if she were reading the information out of a textbook, but her hands told a different story. Her gentle touch on the bird's wing, the light brush of a fingertip over the osprey's white head. Ken had no doubt Bailey would be devastated if the bird didn't survive. She had a feeling Bailey had seen plenty of heartbreaking cases in this room and that her detached manner of stating possible outcomes was a way to protect herself from the pain of losing a patient. She let her fingers briefly rest on Bailey's arm.

"I know you'll do your best," she said. "Tell me how I can help."

Bailey pulled her arm away and muttered something about needing to get some supplies. She left the room and leaned against the wall, just out of sight of Ken. She had been fighting back the emotions that always arose when she saw a hurt bird. She would feel its pain, as if she herself were injured, and every time it was necessary for her to push those sympathetic feelings down and do her job with what detachment she could muster. Ken's touch had almost made her lose control, had almost made her focus on the ache of injury rather than the logistics of healing.

Bailey went into the room next door and searched for something she could bring back into the room to support her excuse for leaving so abruptly. She was comforted by the brush of feathers, but the touch of human skin was sometimes too abrasive, too intrusive. Ken's hand had been anything but. Her touch had spoken to Bailey, given her an assurance of help and protection and understanding. Promises Bailey couldn't trust because they had been broken too many times in the past. Ken was here for the moment, only reluctantly staying to help hold the osprey. She looked as out of place here as Bailey would be— with her vulture smell and casual, ripped clothes—in the world she imagined Ken inhabited. Bailey wished she could take back her insistent order for Ken to help. She'd be better off handling the bird alone rather than being distracted and vulnerable because of Ken's nearness. And aroused, damn it.

Bailey picked up a towel and went back to the surgery. Her first priority was to take care of the osprey. She didn't have a reasonable excuse to make Ken leave now, but she could handle the situation by keeping her distance. No more touching, and she would think of Ken as an impersonal assistant. Better yet, she could use Ken as a guinea pig and try to incorporate some of Sue's suggestions for teaching as she instructed Ken in her nurse duties. Bailey hurried back to the surgery, more comfortable now that she had a plan in place.

Unfortunately, her plan didn't keep her from noticing the way Ken smelled of spicy soap, exotic and mysterious as a pirate at sea. Bailey tossed the towel on the table next to her and arranged the instruments she'd need for the osprey. She'd have to pretend she was instructing an intern. How to start? Tell a joke, Sue had said. *A hawk walked into a bar. "Drinks for everyone! Put them on my bill!"* Bailey coughed to cover her laughter.

"Are you okay?" Ken asked. She was still holding the osprey as if he'd suddenly wake up and take flight.

"Allergies," Bailey said. Only the seriously exhausted would laugh at her lame joke, so she kept it to herself. So, no jokes. Maybe an anecdote.

"You aren't the only person to mistake an osprey for an eagle," she said. "The dark carpals and flight feathers contrasting with the lighter-colored axillaries and belly can appear similar to a juvenile bald eagle. At least from a distance." Bailey paused. Sue had said *personal* anecdote, not mini-lecture. She wasn't sure how to make the information personal. "I have a book that shows pictures of them side by side, and I can show you later. Hand me a packet of gauze from the cupboard, please."

Ken found the gauze, and then the cotton and antibiotics as Bailey asked for them. Bailey had seemed nervous when she came back with the towel, but as she concentrated on the osprey she became less chatty, and her aura of calm returned. Ken hadn't wanted to stay, but she found herself helping as much as she could. A different kind of help than she'd been called on to offer before. Instead of pretending to be strong and fighting to protect someone weak, she was working together with Bailey. She felt a new sense of connection as she fetched items, snipped gauze, and held the massive wing steady while Bailey joined the ends of the broken bone and wrapped it tightly. She watched Bailey's hands at work the entire time, even as she listened to the quiet instructions and marveled at the fragile yet strong creature on the operating table.

Ken had seen plenty of beautiful hands. Slender wrists, tapered fingers, neatly manicured nails. And skilled hands—whether they were designing or drafting or making love. But Bailey's hands were different. They somehow had personality beyond their delicate shape and obvious proficiency. They managed to convey compassion and tenderness and single-minded focus.

"That's it," Bailey said, breaking Ken out of her trance. "I'll put him in the recovery room."

Ken followed as Bailey carried the large bird into yet another converted bedroom. There were several cages of varying size in the otherwise empty room. Bailey nudged open the door of one of them—one short enough so the bird couldn't attempt to fly—and she gently put the osprey onto a nest of blankets before shutting the door and draping a heavy blanket over the cage.

"Now what?" Ken asked. She had been determined to drop off the bird and leave, but now she felt a strange reluctance to go. She wouldn't mind a tour of the facilities, an up-close look at some of the recuperating patients. Perhaps another hour or two assisting Bailey with rehab work. Ken was sure she'd come away from the afternoon with new ideas and images to file away for later use in her own designs. She had gotten out of the habit of flexing her mental muscles and examining the shape of the world around her, but she'd need those skills in her new job. In her previous work, her creative output had been as limited as the fuel she had been giving it over the past years. Bailey—no, not Bailey, but the raptors she tended—had given Ken a sudden surge of energy, a sudden desire to look more closely at something and see what connections she might find.

"Now you fill out an admittance form, and then you're free to go." Bailey deflated Ken's plans, her manner abrupt again now that her hands had stopped working. "Ospreys are migratory, so I have to file federal and state paperwork."

Ken took a last look at the covered cage before she walked out the door Bailey held open for her. "What about my bird?" she asked as they went down the short hall, past the staring hawk, and into the kitchen. "How do I find out what happens to him?"

"*Your* bird?" Bailey repeated with a shake of her head. She pulled a form out of the pile of papers on her kitchen table. "He's wild. He doesn't belong to you or me."

Ken crossed her arms over her chest and refused to take the pen Bailey held out to her. The osprey had been on her property. And she had just spent an hour up-close and personal with him.

She didn't own him, but she damned sure deserved to know his fate.

"Fine," Bailey said after a long pause. "You can call in a week and I'll let you know how he's doing." She tapped the pen against the form before holding it out again. This time Ken took it and sat down at the table.

Obviously Dr. Chase had excellent bird skills but completely lacked people skills. Ken filled out her name and phone number, the date, and a description of the osprey and its injuries. She hesitated when she came to the blank asking where she had found the bird. She glanced at Bailey where she stood at the counter, mixing what looked like moistened dog food with some sort of meat. Unappetizing. Well, the food was. Bailey herself was definitely tempting, but she had a quirky streak that made Ken uncomfortable. Ken guessed she was the type of person who would be unwavering in her beliefs. Unyielding in her fight for what she perceived as justice. All very good if one was an injured raptor in need of her help. But what would Bailey think of Ken's plan to develop her waterfront property? If she put the actual address where she had found the osprey, would she go visit the site one day and find Bailey chained to one of her trees?

Ken filled in the address of her new firm. What difference did it make where she had actually found the bird? She put down her pen and leaned back in her chair, looking around the spacious kitchen. Like every other room Ken had seen in Bailey's house, this one appeared to be dedicated to the raptor center. A stack of empty dog crates lined one wall, and an upright freezer—filled with God-knew-what—took up most of the dining area. The kitchen table, covered with feeding charts and local maps and ornithology books, was crammed in between the counter and the stove. A bag of something that looked disturbingly like a mass of fat worms sat uncomfortably close to Ken's elbow. The room was certainly not user-friendly for the gourmet cook, not that Bailey seemed to use the kitchen for anything beyond making bird dinners. The only visible appliance designed for purely human use was a gleaming professional-quality espresso machine with a coffee grinder sitting next to it. Ken would have paid a lot of money for just five minutes alone with that machine. She was certain she could make magic with it.

"You found the osprey in Bellevue?"

Bailey swiped the form off the table while Ken was staring at her espresso machine. She thought she read guilt in one of Ken's unguarded moments before her expression closed again.

"I've seen birds in the city," Ken said.

"Yes, but did you see *this* bird in the city?"

"Does it matter where I found him?"

Bailey paused, fighting the temptation to answer Ken's question with another question. This could go on all afternoon. "Yes, it does," she said instead. Appeal to reason. "The data is used to track migration patterns. And if I'm eventually able to release the bird, I'll want to let him go as close as I can to where he was found."

"Fine," Ken said, snatching the form out of Bailey's hands. She crossed out the Bellevue address and filled in one from Sequim.

"Do you live there?" Bailey asked, curious about why Ken had lied in the first place.

"I will. It's just a vacant lot now, but I'm having a house built."

Bailey was familiar with the area. Private and quiet. Probably close to the water. And judging by the quality of Ken's clothes and her fancy-looking sports car, the house was bound to be something special. Classier than a rundown old house filled with raptor cages. Bailey wouldn't trade her center for a mansion by the ocean, but she occasionally felt like a prisoner in her home. So many beaks to feed, and whenever one patient recovered and moved on, there were always several more injured and ready to move in.

"Will you really release the osprey at my place?" Ken asked. Bailey had seen too many people who wanted birds *out* of their yards, but Ken seemed pleased by the idea.

"Maybe not right in your backyard," Bailey said. "It'll depend on the neighborhood and how busy it is. But close-by, at least."

"I'd like to be there when you do."

"Maybe," Bailey said. She wouldn't commit to anything just yet. She had been in the rehab business too long to make promises of any sort. She had no idea whether the osprey would even make it through the night, let alone survive long enough to be released. She didn't encourage people who brought injured birds to the center to keep in touch because she hated them to have to share her disappointment if she was unable to save them. Ken had only given her glimpses of emotions, but Bailey couldn't bear to have one of them be sadness, no matter how fleeting. She wasn't sure why she felt protective when Ken seemed perfectly capable of putting up her own defenses. Maybe because the emotions Ken *did* show were so pure and clear. Bailey had learned how to hide her feelings as well, and she didn't want to be responsible for building more walls around other people.

Besides, the last time Bailey had let an outsider get involved in the release of a bird, she had gotten trapped in the university's grip. Vonda Selbert had been determined to stay involved when she brought the young eagle to her after he had flown into her picture window and fractured his bill. Bailey had wired his beak together and overwintered him while his growth plate regrew. In the spring, Bailey had returned to Vonda's home—where Vonda had filled every window with decals and hanging streamers— and together they had released the now-mature eagle. Vonda had been so moved she had wanted to help as many birds as possible. Bailey appreciated the thought, but she resented the new impositions in her life. Who knew what damage Ken would do to Bailey's life if she were allowed to stick around during the osprey's recovery? Bailey didn't want to find out. Vonda had succeeded in wearing down Bailey's energy. Ken seemed capable of breaking hearts.

Bailey walked Ken to the door, promising again to give her an update when she called. She watched the small red-and-white car ease its way up the rutted driveway before she returned to the kitchen and got the meal she had prepared for a barred owlet that was living in her downstairs bathroom. She sat cross-legged on the floor and fed the hungry bird while she thought about the osprey. Most likely, she'd never hear from Ken again. Most people were relieved to pass on the burden of caring for a wounded bird. They cared enough to contact her, to find help for the bird they had found, but then they returned to their normal routines and forgot about both Bailey and the winged creature that had touched their lives momentarily. Bailey was usually happy to see them go, to be left alone with her charges again. She fed the owl another morsel of food and wondered why this time felt different.

She would never admit it to WSU's dean, who called her daily offering the assistance of interns, but she had been happy to have help while she treated the osprey. Usually she was juggling bird, syringes, and bandages on her own. Ken's competent and confident assistance had made the procedure much smoother and quicker, both important things when dealing with an anesthetized raptor. Ken had been respectful and gentle with the fragile osprey, watching the whole procedure as if fascinated while still following Bailey's instructions to the letter. Bailey worried that her interns would be less likely to listen to her and follow her methods without question. They might think they knew enough to make decisions on their own. To change or ignore her routines…

The owlet squawked when Bailey paused with the tweezers held just above his head. She hurriedly dropped the food into his open mouth. Ken had proved to be the ideal assistant today, but Bailey had been intrigued by her for other reasons as well. On the surface, Ken looked like a typical successful young professional. Well dressed and well groomed, but in subtle ways. She could be dropped into any office, any profession and look like she belonged. But when she had been intently watching Bailey wrap the osprey's wing and she'd leaned over for a closer look, Bailey had been distracted by the tantalizing edge of tattoos just visible in the slightly gaping V of her conservative button-down shirt. An ornate dragon with a ruby eye peeked over the plain white bra above her left breast, and the wing of some creature was barely discernible in the shadowed area above Ken's navel. The unique and hidden tattoos—like the brief flashes of emotion that crossed Ken's face—told Bailey there was more to her, just below the surface, than her conventional exterior suggested. And they told Bailey there was more to her awareness of Ken than was safe. She had nearly stabbed herself with the suturing needle while she was distracted by the delicate web of ink on Ken's skin.

But it didn't matter, because even if Ken actually did contact her about the osprey, Bailey would never have a chance to learn more about her hidden, protected self. Bailey watched the sated owlet burrow under his blanket before she went into the recovery room and peeked under the drapes at the osprey. He was stirring, but still sedated. Bailey willed him to wake up soon, to heal and grow strong enough to be released. For his sake, and for Ken's. She dropped the dark cloth again and quietly left the room.

CHAPTER FOUR

Ken held herself stiffly in the Eames chair, resisting its siren call. She refused to succumb to the comfort of its well-designed aluminum frame and its too-damned-cushy white leather-covered pads. She didn't belong here, refused to get too comfortable here, and she wanted to leave no doubt about it. She had dressed carefully in the most conservative outfit she could find in her closet, although she knew the dress code at Impetus was casual. She had opted to have all her tattoos—and all her individuality—carefully covered by a pressed cream-colored shirt and a navy blazer and slacks. All of her inner turmoil reduced to simple neutrals—as bland as the beige houses she designed.

She watched Joe Bently, CEO of Impetus, flip through the designs and blueprints in her large black leather portfolio. His expression never changed, but Ken could read his opinion of her work in the rhythm of his page turning. If he was truly impressed by anything he saw, he'd hurry through early planning stages to arrive at the finished design, or he'd pause and examine whatever caught his eye in more detail. Instead, the movement of his hand was as steady as a metronome. Boring, mass-produced houses built with the intention of fitting seamlessly and unobtrusively into boring, mass-produced developments. Every sketch had the same straight lines and predictable proportions, but even worse were the glossy photos of the finished houses. Once the skeletons she had drawn were hidden behind the palest of pastel siding—colors strictly controlled and approved by the homeowners' associations—there was nothing to identify the houses as her own.

Ken tilted her chin slightly, even though Joe seemed unaware of her presence in the room as he continued to flip through uninspiring pages. She had no reason to be ashamed of her work. Her designs were popular and her homes were easy to inhabit. She was good at what she did, creating livable homes that appealed to a wide market. She wanted to defend herself, to point out details in the designs that often weren't noticed until the walls were up and someone reached for a light switch or door handle. She had a knack for imagining 3-D versions of her designs in her head. She would look at simple lines on grid paper and be able to put herself in the room she had just drawn. Adjust a door frame or move a closet a few inches to the left. Minor touches, but they made a big difference in daily life.

But she kept her mouth shut. As her emotions grew more conflicted internally, she felt her expression and posture become conversely more still. No smile, no frown. No fidgeting. She wanted Joe to change his mind, tell her she wasn't Impetus material and let her go. She could find another developer—one who would appreciate her unexceptional and reliable work and, hopefully, one who wouldn't go bust before she got a modest home built on her property. Everything she had done so far that day, from her portfolio to the impression her style of clothing gave, was designed to help her out of this mess.

Well, almost everything. Joe's hand paused in midair when he came to the last pages in her portfolio, and Ken snapped her head sharply as she looked away from him. She studied the photos on his office wall while he slowly went through the final designs, but she noticed in her peripheral vision as he took his time moving forward and back through her final sketches. She felt a growing sense of panic as she struggled against the desire to rip her portfolio out of his hands until her attention was caught by a series of photographs of an eagle, taking off in flight.

She had barely registered the details at first, but she forgot about Joe and her drawings as she slowed down and studied each frame. The first showed a large wooden box and a woman leaning over it. Her back was to the camera as she seemed to be unsnapping a metal latch. The sunlight brought out deep red tones in her braided auburn hair—contrasting beautifully with the vivid green grass and blue-gray water behind her. Her faded and torn jeans fit her distractingly well. Ken quickly shifted her attention to the next picture. In this one, the eagle stood, poised and calm, on a wooden platform. A brief moment of calm before the third photo, and the bird's powerful launch into the air. The photos were exquisite, and Ken could feel the energies of confinement, suspension, and freedom pulse out of the still shots and into her.

"That's Bailey, isn't it?" She added inflection as if asking a question, but she would have recognized Bailey—any part of her—without hesitation. "I mean, Dr. Chase."

"The wild bird rehabilitator, yes," Joe said. "Do you know her?"

"Not really," Ken said with what she hoped was an indifferent shrug. "I have a small piece of property near Sequim and I found a wounded osprey there last weekend. I took him to Dr. Chase's sanctuary."

"Incredible," he said, looking at her with the same intense focus he had shown while looking through her final sketches.

Ken gestured toward the photos, waving his attention off her. "It was a beautiful bird, but nowhere near the impressive size of that eagle."

"It's magnificent, isn't it?" Joe left her portfolio lying open on his desk as he got up and walked over to the wall. He tapped his finger on a photograph of a huge glass-fronted A-frame. "I designed this house in Poulsbo for some friends of mine, the Selberts. Gave them a lovely view of Puget Sound, but unfortunately an eagle flew smack into the center of an upper story window. Nearly killed him, but Dr. Chase fixed him up. Vonda took these pictures of his release and sent them to me. I think she blamed me for the damned bird getting hurt."

Ken wasn't sure how to respond, so she stayed silent and looked through the pictures once more. Bailey. She had been on Ken's mind since they had met, and she was partly to blame for Ken's discomfort right now. Ken had been thinking how much one of her old architectural drawings would have suited Bailey, and she had dug the series of sketches out of a box in her closet. And then she had stuck them in her portfolio on a whim. Yes, this was Bailey's fault.

Joe came around to the front of his desk and propped himself on its edge. "You should see the house now. She has stickers and dangly crap covering every window, so no birds will fly into the glass. Looks like shit, but it makes her happy. That's architecture, isn't it? We design a house, but the owner turns it into a home. What they choose to hang in the windows is out of our hands."

Ken struggled to come up with a suitable response. Fortunately, Joe seemed to have his own agenda and didn't expect her to make conversation.

"I have questions about you, Ken," Joe said, before she had time to formulate a comment about the Selberts and their house. "Maybe you can answer this one. Were you underutilized at your last job?"

Ken frowned. She didn't want to raise questions in anyone's mind. She wanted to be clear about what she wanted and who she was and where she was going, but she didn't seem to be doing a good job of providing forceful explanations for any of those—to Joe or to herself.

"I was one of the senior architects at the firm. I designed the three top-selling floor plans, and I made modifications for every new development—"

Joe held up a hand. "I didn't mean underutilized in terms of time, but in talent. I've seen how many new housing communities have been built in the last decade, and I know there's been no shortage of work for someone with your skill. You create well-thought-out plans, and I can imagine people living happily in the houses you've designed."

He reached back and slid two sheets of paper out of their protective covers, setting them side by side on the desk in front of her. One was a plain and boxy two-story she had designed a year ago. The other was one of the series she had added to her portfolio this morning. Nine whimsical sketches she had made in junior high, when she had first begun to study architectural drawing in earnest. One house for each of the classical muses. The one he had chosen was for Urania, muse of astronomy. Ken still didn't fully understand why she had added them. She had been stubbornly set on defying the climate and identity of Impetus by showing only her monochromatic work, but instead she had slipped the nine drawings and detailed plans into the back of her book. Was it pride? A need to prove she really could design more than a box? Her self-control seemed to fail every time she had a strong urge to assert her individuality—the very times she needed to remain strong and silent, her actions shouted out how different she really was.

Ken stared at the two drawings without speaking. If she hadn't been the one holding the drafting pencil, she wouldn't believe they were the work of the same hand. Urania's house was her favorite of the group, and she felt perversely glad that Joe had picked it out of the series. Where most houses seemed to be rooted in the ground, her structure pushed heavenward. Three overlapping isosceles triangles in harmonious accord, reaching toward the sky. She was relieved he hadn't chosen Euterpe's house instead, with its large indoor atrium. Ken had originally designed it with Sappho in mind, but now she could only see Bailey living there. She wouldn't have been able to remain so composed if Joe had been holding that one in front of her.

"These nine sketches are brilliant," Joe said. "They're striking and unique to look at, but anyone with artistic talent could draw a pretty building. The trick is making something unusual from the outside, yet structurally sound and functional for the person living *inside*. You've done that, with a level of skill I've rarely encountered. But I can see you were a novice when you made these. They were dreams—well-executed dreams, but not ready to be made in reality. My question stands. Were you underutilized at this place?" Joe picked up her two-story and waved it before tossing it back on the desk with a flick of his wrist. It slid across his computer keyboard and onto the floor. He picked up Urania's house and held it by the two upper corners. "Or were these early drawings just flukes? Beginner's luck? Which is the real you?"

Ken reached out and gently took the paper from him. Had she deserted her muses, or had they deserted her? She understood the question, but she didn't have an answer. She knew what had happened in her life between the fantastical sketches and the mundane, but she wasn't certain what had been her choice and what had been forced on her by necessity.

"I don't know," she said. She felt defeated by her own drawings. Why had she given Joe any reason to expect something special from her?

"I don't, either," he said. He took the drawing back, just as gently as she had taken it from him. "But I'm willing to give us both time to find out. When you're ready."

"Okay," Ken said. *Thank you* might have been more appropriate, but she wasn't feeling grateful. She was angry because she had opened herself up to the vulnerability her Muse houses represented and confused because she had just passively fought for a job she didn't even want. No, not grateful at all. She pushed out of the enfolding arms of the white chair and picked up her fallen floor plan. She put it back in the portfolio—not bothering to slide it in its plastic sleeve—and reached out her hand for the other drawing.

"Can I keep this for a few days?" he asked. "My daughter Lydia is an astronomy buff and she'd love to see it. She'll be after me to build a triangular extension onto her room so she can have a telescope viewing area like the one on the south face of this house."

"Go ahead and keep it," Ken said. She folded the leather cover over her portfolio and snapped it in place. "I don't have any use for it."

"You might, someday, so I'll take good care of it and bring it back to you."

"Thanks," Ken said, her shoulder rising and falling in a reflexive shrug even though she felt relieved with the assurance that she'd get her drawing back.

"Don't mention it. If Lydia manages to talk me into building her an observatory, I'll have you design it." He returned to his desk chair and sat down, pulling a stack of papers in front of him and looking as distant now as he had seemed fatherly and caring only moments before. "We have a new project starting next week, and it'll be managed by your old school friend, Douglas. It'll be a good fit for you, and an easy way for you to learn the Impetus methods. In the meantime, Jessica has agreed to let you tag along with her this week. She's working on the finishing touches for a major renovation we're doing for one of our top clients. She's my senior architect, has been with me for years, and you can learn a lot from her. Take advantage of the opportunity."

"Yes…sir," Ken said, hesitating over what to call her new boss.

"Joe," he said, without looking up.

Ken shut the door behind her and leaned against it. She felt too many different emotions to be able to clearly identify or manage any of them. He thought he was easing her transition into the company by putting her to work with Dougie—on whose recommendation she'd been given this job in the first place—but he was one of the main reasons Ken didn't want to be here. Being with him would bring up too many painful memories, but Ken had already started the journey back in time by bringing her Muse drawings today. Ken wanted to go back to her safe life, back to Ginny and the Seattle apartment and her comfortable old job, but if she was being honest, a tiny rebellious part of her was excited about being at Impetus. She longed to have a pencil in hand and feel the ideas flowing from mere suggestions and hints until they solidified into three-dimensional homes and buildings in her mind. She pushed away from the doorframe and went in search of Jessica.

CHAPTER FIVE

Bailey adjusted her hold on the bulky wooden crate she carried, wrapping one arm protectively around it while reaching for a drooping cedar bough with the other. The fallen tree in front of her—at least three feet in diameter—blocked the barely defined deer track she was following through the dense woods. She stepped her left foot onto the decaying trunk, using the cedar limb for balance as she hoisted herself and her precious cargo onto the log. She felt her sneaker slip on the thick coating of moss, and her grip tightened on both the crate and the bough as she teetered on the arced surface. The branch she held was too slender to give solid support, but luckily it didn't snap off in her hand. She hovered on top of the trunk for a moment, leaning back beyond her balance point, before she was able to right herself. Instead of risking another close call on the way down, she bent her knees until she was sitting on the damp moss that covered the trunk. The springy cushion underneath her triggered memories of mossy trunks and rocks she had sat on as a kid. They had been her thrones and her reading chairs, more comfortable than anything she found in her own home.

Bailey dropped off the log and shifted the crate again, clenching her fingers around the handle on its lid. She pushed through a stand of Indian plum, weaving among the thin, spaced limbs of the shrub. The long, soft leaves brushed against her face and hands with a gentle touch, as if welcoming her back to the woods. She was miles away from the forests around Bremerton that had been her sanctuary in childhood, but the smells and cool forest air were as familiar as her old haunts. The air was draped with fog, the trees with moss and lacy lichen. Ethereal and otherworldly. When she was a young girl, Bailey had been a fairy queen in the forest, shutting out the loneliness and pain of the human world as she fit seamlessly into the forest realm. Now, as an adult, Bailey knew her respite from the troubling and intrusive civilized world was only temporary, but she appreciated it just as much.

The deer path widened slightly, and Bailey paused for a moment. She set the crate on a cushioned bed of sword ferns and pulled off her dark red sweatshirt so she was wearing only a white sports bra. The creatures of the woods wouldn't care how inappropriately she was dressed. A picture of Ken, so well dressed and buttoned-up, came into her mind. What would it take to get Ken out of that pressed shirt and let Bailey get a look at what was underneath? Bailey wasn't interested in Ken's skin, just the tattoos etched across her chest. Well...she wouldn't mind seeing the skin, either. She used the sleeve of her shirt to wipe a mist of perspiration off her forehead before tying it around her waist. The early morning air was cool, but the long uphill hike had warmed her body. The thought of Ken, stripped to her waist, wasn't helping her rising body temperature. She picked a twig out of her bangs and refastened the white plastic barrette that held her long hair off her face before picking up the crate and resuming her hike. She pushed her thoughts off Ken and back to childhood hikes, when she used to wear a mask made of feathers she found on the forest floor. She would weave twigs and wildflowers and leaves in her hair and her clothing, as if by covering herself with these things she would be able to fully merge with the forest.

The woods behind her childhood home hadn't been nearly as big or as wild as the ones Bailey was in today, but they had seemed as limitless and hopeful as her childish imagination had been. Escaping the routine fights between her mother and father, Bailey had first sought refuge in the woods and had later learned everything she could about its flora and fauna. She had been particularly focused on the birds flitting through the branches or calling from just out of sight. She had convinced herself that she had been born in a nest and had accidentally fallen to the forest floor, where her human parents had discovered her. Instead of the raptor parents who would fight to protect their child, the human ones fought over and because of her. As an adult looking back, Bailey was able to separate the arguments in her mind into three phases. First, her mom and dad had simply fought with each other. Once they decided to divorce, they had used her as a pawn. After the divorce, when they each had started to date again, they argued against their hard-won custody rights. But young Bailey had only heard the yelling and breaking glass as her parents fought because of her—while ignoring her.

As she neared the top of the hill, the heavy forest vegetation began to thin. She walked with a longer stride, anxious to get her small charge out of his confining quarters. With every step, she left her worries a little farther behind her. She had grown out of her childhood belief that she could eventually leave the world of humans completely and live in the forest with birds and animals as her only companions. Now she knew the necessity of coexisting with people, but she still had done her best to remain isolated. Her big rambling house was set in the exact center of the ten-acre piece of property, and her roommates were wild and temporary—injured birds of prey that resided with her until they were able to return to freedom. She had a few friends in Sequim and the surrounding areas on the Olympic Peninsula, and she occasionally had visitors when people dropped off wounded birds, but she could go for days without talking to another human.

Quiet solitude. Not a perfect life—lonely sometimes, and always consuming her time and energy—but it was the one she had chosen. But now the cage she had willingly built around herself was about to be breached. It had been over a year since Vonda and her eagle had landed on her doorstep, nothing unusual at the Chase Raptor Center, but so very different this time. The chain of events had been set in motion then, and now the university was about to barge in and expand and send interns and students to mess up Bailey's ordered life.

She pulled in a lungful of mountain air, tasting bark and fresh greens and the hint of salt from the nearby Strait of Juan de Fuca. She had left her house early this morning, partly because she wanted to arrive at her destination not long after sunrise, but mostly because she wanted to be away when the vet med's dean made his routine morning call to ask if she had reviewed the internship applications or if she had created lesson plans and reading lists for the seminars she would be teaching. Bailey hadn't done much of the work he was asking her to do, and she knew her passive resistance was fueled by the desperate hope that he would eventually give up and go away.

Bailey came to a stream, running swift and deeper than she had expected due to the late spring thaw in the Olympic Mountains. Out of habit, she looked for Ratty and Mole before she turned her attention to crossing the rivulet. There were several widely spaced boulders that were flat enough for her to stand on and close enough for her to make a big leap from stone to stone as she crossed the water. But, while the risk of a fall into the icy water was okay with her, it wasn't acceptable for the small raptor she carried. Instead, she waded into the stream, feeling for each foothold on the slimy rocks as she held the crate over her head. She might fall during the crossing, but she wasn't about to get her bird wet.

At the deepest point, the water barely reached her knees. Bailey balanced her cautious progress with the need to get across before she lost all feeling in her feet and could no longer tell where she was stepping. She exhaled with a loud puff when she reached the pebbled bank. She hadn't realized she had been holding her breath until she let it go. She paused and leaned against an oak tree to regain her composure, resting against the supportive trunk. She had climbed a tree like this one once, long ago, when she had found a Cooper's hawk nestling on the ground. She had carefully scaled the tree with the tiny nestling cradled inside her sweater and against her beating heart. She had pushed aside her fear of heights in her desperate need to return the baby to its parents, climbing until she was level with the nest. The branch hadn't looked strong enough to support her weight, so she had reached as far as she could and plopped the nestling back in its home.

Unfortunately, the long reach had put her off balance, and Bailey had fallen through the branches and onto the ground with a thud and a crack. A neighbor had heard her screams and had found her lying in a heap with her broken tibia jutting out of her shin. Bailey leaned over and rubbed her leg where the scar was now hidden by her jeans. She hadn't been allowed back into the woods after the accident, and her mom had moved them out of the Bremerton house soon after. She had never had a chance to return to the tree and find out if her baby bird had survived.

Bailey shivered as the memory washed over her. The loud and unnatural crack of bone followed by the deafening silence of pain. She had screamed as much to lessen that silence as to get help. She shook her head as she straightened and noticed a cluster of chanterelles at the foot of the oak tree. She'd stop and gather some on her way back. They'd make a nice addition to the ramen noodles she had for dinner most nights. Feeding and preparing food for her bird patients rarely left her with the time or energy to make an elaborate meal for herself, but the mushrooms would add some nice flavor and a touch of elegance to her simple dinner. She thought of candlelight and soft music, someone like Ken sitting across from her as they ate. The fantasy was ridiculous, but it chased away the residual pain of Bailey's childhood fall and the events following it. She moved away from the tree with a more purposeful stride.

Another easy quarter mile or so, and Bailey waded through a yielding thicket of snowberry bushes—their pink-purple unopened buds looking like minuscule clumps of grapes—and stepped into a small meadow that covered the top of the hill. Tightly budded lupine stood at attention amidst the thick grass. She could see a valley below her, with horse pastures and gray-green lavender fields showing only a hint of the purple blossoms that would explode in a week or two. The whole region seemed to be holding its breath, waiting to exhale with a rush into spring. Except for a seagull circling one of the pastures, Bailey didn't see any sign of the strait that lay just beyond the next hill.

Bailey felt a curious conflict within herself as she set the crate on the ground. She felt as attuned to the world around her as if she and it were inhabiting one body, but her mind was constantly being pulled back to the dean and her upcoming—and unwelcome—obligations. And, as usual on a release day, she felt the joy of a return to freedom tempered slightly by her sadness in letting a friend go. Although she usually tried to release birds close to where they had been found, she had chosen this spot instead for the small falcon. His old haunts were dangerous, and he had spent over an hour clutched in the mouth of a domestic cat while the owners tried to catch her and extricate the bird from her jaws. Despite Bailey's protests, the owners adamantly refused to keep their three cats indoors, so Bailey had decided to let the kestrel go in this beautiful meadow. She would have been happy to call it home, so hopefully the bird would appreciate it as well.

She unsnapped the sides of the crate and lifted it up in one easy motion so the kestrel stood on the base of the crate, completely unencumbered. On her first releases, she had used normal pet carriers, but after watching birds hitting the sides of the cages with their delicate wings on their way out of the narrow openings, she had designed and built her own version. Now she unlatched the top and raised it as if she were a well-trained waiter uncovering a plate at dinner. No potential for injury, and she was able to quietly step away and let the little raptor get his bearings.

The kestrel puffed his feathers and looked around with an alert and wary expression. Bailey stared at him, memorizing the already familiar black spots on his belly and the exact shade of rust on his back. Although she wasn't likely to see him again at such close range, she wanted to *know* him as one of hers if she ever spotted him again. He hesitated for a few seconds before launching off the wooden platform with rapid wingbeats. His reddish tail fanned out as he flew, tipped with black and a thin line of white. Bailey heard his high-pitched call as he soared toward the valley and out of sight.

She used the hem of her sweatshirt to wipe away the tears flowing down her cheeks. Every release was the same, but every bird unique. She would never stop feeling the overwhelming wave of emotions as each one thrust into the air and into freedom. Loss and hope and a joy so great she didn't know how she kept from dissolving into it. She snapped the lid on the crate bottom and picked it up. The kestrel had only weighed a few ounces, but she felt the emptiness and lifelessness of the box as she carried it back the way she had come. She pushed through the snowberries again as she walked down the hill. She had other birds at home, waiting for her attention. She had to spend weeks—sometimes well over a year—feeding and changing bandages and doing physical therapy with reluctant, and often belligerent, patients before she had the chance to experience the thrill of a release. But it was worth every sleepless night, every struggle-filled day, to help her birds find their way to health and freedom. And how many more would she be able to save with the university's money and equipment to help? She'd have to find a way to work with the dean, to keep the intrusion on her space and privacy at a minimum, while using the vet school's resources for her birds. They were all that mattered.

CHAPTER SIX

Mud and blades of grass dotted the belly of Ken's car, which had been an immaculate red and pristine white only an hour before. She wasn't thrilled about driving her baby over gravel and dirt every day, but it was worth the extra time she'd spend washing and buffing to be able to live in this place. She hadn't been to the property since her breakup with Ginny, two weeks earlier. She pushed through the tall, resisting grass and headed straight for the slope leading to the bluff. She walked to the very edge and listened to the water lap against the shore below. The same sound she had heard on the ferry ride this afternoon, and the same sea water that had traveled from the Pacific, around Cape Flattery at the tip of the Olympic Peninsula, and down the Strait of Juan de Fuca toward Puget Sound. But here, where it washed over the sand and pebbles, it was *her* water.

Ken had only leased and rented before and had never owned. Had never belonged. Home had been a place to sleep and store her belongings, nothing more. She sat cross-legged on the thick grass and let the salty air move over and through her. She'd have to sacrifice to keep this place, to build a home here.

That meant she had to do what she could to keep her job at Impetus, although her first week there hadn't been promising. Her old firm was more her style. Architects and developers and sales staff had looked the same if you met them in the halls—as bland and indistinctive as the houses they built and sold. She had worked mostly alone, in her private office, and she blended in with the other suit-wearing employees. Impetus was too much of a change. Every person working there was different, and Ken had learned long ago that being different was dangerous.

Ken climbed to her feet and walked up the slope, aiming left toward the site of the home she had planned for Ginny. Between settling in her new apartment in Sequim and struggling through the days at Impetus, Ken had made it through two weeks with little sense of loss or loneliness. Her main goal had been to avoid Dougie at work—easily accomplished since she had spent her days shadowing Jessica on-site. They had wandered through the client's home, taking measurements and consulting blueprints as Jessica tried to make the owner's vision a reality. Jessica had been open to Ken's suggestions, asking for her opinion and her creative input with a collaborative spirit Ken had never experienced at her old firm. Unfortunately, Ken had been thrust too far out of her element. Instead of offering any worthwhile contribution, her mind had felt frozen and sluggish. She had been less help than a first-year intern. The stress of the week and the admittedly wearing commute from the Peninsula to Bellevue had left her with no energy to devote to missing Ginny. But she *had* missed her future home. Somehow this small patch of land had made its way into her and claimed her in a way no woman, no person, had been able to do.

Ken found the stakes-and-string outline of the house, buried in the deep grass, and followed the border to the spot where the front door would stand. Her original idea had been to put the two-story model Ginny preferred in the same place where the old double-wide had sat. Now she wondered if she'd been too hasty in getting it removed. Maybe she could get it back, even though it had been dingy and had smelled of mold and fried clams. At least it would be a cheap roof over her head and would mean she didn't have to keep the new job. But she wanted her gourmet kitchen and her bedroom with expansive windows looking out toward the Strait. Her sunny office space with drafting table and floor-to-ceiling bookshelves. Her home.

She clenched her fist, feeling the reassuring tightening of her biceps. She'd have a dedicated workout space in her new home, next to her bedroom. A place to maintain the body she'd started to build after eighth grade. When she had walked through Impetus in search of Jessica, she had seen Dougie. He looked the same as he had back then. Glasses and long, slightly mussed bangs that he kept flicking out of his eyes. An honest-to-God pocket protector in his short-sleeved shirt. She had shamefully ducked into the copy room until he had walked past, but she'd have to face him—and their shared past—eventually.

Ken picked a jagged rock out of her kitchen space and threw it as hard as she could. She didn't make it to the water, but it landed with a satisfying crack against a large boulder. She had changed, but he could have walked right back to seventh grade without missing a beat. Back to Rocket Club and Math Challenge and weekends playing Dungeons & Dragons. Back to the time when it didn't matter if Ken was a tomboy or different or smarter than the other kids in her class. But in eighth grade it had started to matter. And Ken had walked away from friends like Dougie and everything they represented.

She started pulling up the stakes, winding the string around her left hand. The site she had originally marked out for the house was level and close to the road, but now that she was no longer building for Ginny, she could create anything she wanted. She'd been drawn to the sloping center of the property from the start. The view and light were better, and the space was precisely in the center of the acre. A traditional house wouldn't look right, so maybe she'd come up with something different. She could do whatever she wanted. Build Euterpe's house and invite Bailey to visit. If she spent time thinking about it, she could imagine Bailey in this place, so she made a determined effort to stop thinking about it and focused instead on the slight weariness in her thighs as she bent to pull up stakes.

She had not only been neglecting visits to her property, but she had also missed too many trips to the gym in the past weeks. She had started working out in high school as self-defense against the other kids and their escalating violence. Small pushes and shoves had turned into after-school attacks, but Ken had managed to halt the progression by getting strong. Strong enough to beat up the leader of whatever pack had decided to come after her. Strong enough to protect Dougie and her old gang even though she couldn't call attention to herself by hanging out with them anymore. It hadn't been enough.

She jerked out the last of the stakes. She'd keep her job at Impetus because she needed it, and because she had the potential to be damned good at it. But she wouldn't return to her old geeky self. She'd work in the spacious, wall-free building, but she'd bring her own walls with her.

Ken opened the trunk of her car and tossed the string and stakes inside among the loose drawing supplies. She had left the cardboard box at Bailey's after transporting the osprey in it. She shut the trunk with a firm click and got in the car. So far, the osprey was the one positive result of her purchase of this property. If she hadn't come here after her lunch with Ginny, he might not have survived long enough to be rescued by someone else. She started the engine with a satisfying loud roar and drove down the gravel road. She'd stop by Bailey's center on her way back to her apartment. Bailey might not admit the osprey was Ken's, but he was the one tangible and hopeful sign that life was going to be good on this desolate acre of land. Ken had to see him and reassure herself they were both going to be all right.

❖

Bailey pressed the button to open the gate and went into the bathroom to run a comb through her tangled hair before the visitor made it up her driveway. Every time she had heard the buzzer this week, she had wondered if Ken had come back to check on the osprey. She wasn't sure why she kept picturing Ken's long legs emerging from her sporty little car, but she didn't like to dwell on the fantasy too long. Because it was nothing more than a fantasy created by the rambling imagination of someone who had spent too much time alone in a bird-filled house. Bailey needed to get out of town, go to a rehab conference, and find some female companionship. A weekend of no-strings sex was all she needed to banish the thought of Ken knocking on her door and taking her up to the bedroom, or right there on the living room couch, or on the porch...

She hurried to the door and opened it. Ken. As if conjured up by Bailey's desires. Bailey had liked the imagined visits from imaginary Ken, but she had mixed feelings about seeing the real woman. She was busy enough today, without adding her unhelpful libido to the mix. Ken was leaning against one of the porch railings, staring at the sky. Bailey followed the line of her gaze and saw a hawk circling overhead.

"Redtail," Bailey said.

Ken turned toward her with a smile. "One of yours?"

Bailey couldn't help but return the smile. "Maybe. I've released a few in the woods behind the house. I'd have to see it up close to be sure."

"You could tell?"

"Of course. They each have unique markings. Individual birds are as easy to tell apart as humans are." Easier, actually. Probably because Bailey rarely paid as close attention to people as she did to her patients, although after only one meeting she'd have been able to describe the exact blue-green shade of Ken's eyes. And the way her dark brown hair shimmered with chestnut tones in the sun. Bailey lowered her gaze, searching for a way to distract herself from the discomfiting path her mind was taking.

"I suppose you're here to see the osprey?" Bailey avoided possessives when she could, not wanting people to become too attached to the wild birds they had rescued, but for her own sake she needed to keep Ken and the osprey linked in her mind. Both were visitors in her life, and they'd both eventually need more flying space than she could provide. When one left, the other would follow. But not yet. She held the door open in invitation.

"Where is…" Ken's voice faltered to a stop when she walked into the living room and over to the large, empty cage where the redtail had been living.

"I moved her to one of the outdoor flight cages," Bailey said. She saw the relief in Ken's expression. "I was planning to put the osprey in here today, so you picked a good time to visit him."

"I can help?"

Bailey usually preferred to work on her own, but she couldn't resist Ken's eager expression. Besides, the transfer would be easier with two people. "Sure, but first I have to feed— wait, let me get that."

Bailey went into the kitchen to answer the telephone. She winced and held the phone away from her ear when the loud *Good afternoon, Dr. Chase!* greeted her. The voice of WSU's dean rang with the contented cheeriness of someone who had slept in before spending a leisurely morning reading a newspaper and drinking coffee, not someone who had been up since dawn nursing birds.

"Hello, Dean Carrington," she said, trying to sound reasonably friendly as she tucked the phone against her shoulder and picked up the food she had prepared for the owlet. She handed the bowl to Ken as she walked back through the living room and gestured for her to follow.

Ken took the container from Bailey, stifling the urge to shriek and fling it away. She wasn't normally squeamish, but she hadn't been expecting to be handed a bowl of mouse parts. She kept her attention off the unappetizing mess in her hands and focused instead on the way Bailey's expression changed from relaxed to closed and tense as she talked.

"No, I haven't had a chance to look through the applications yet," Bailey said as she went into the bathroom and knelt next to a cardboard box filled with downy blankets and a fluffy, cranky owlet. The baby owl clicked his beak impatiently and shook himself so his feathers puffed out. Ken barely registered the exasperation in Bailey's voice as she watched what looked like a wad of cotton balls strut around the small space. Bailey waved her over and picked a piece of mouse out of Ken's bowl with a pair of tweezers.

"No, I haven't done that, either," Bailey said as she fed the small owl. "It's been very busy here lately."

Ken cringed as the cute little creature ravenously devoured the disgusting food. She was torn between being charmed by the soft- and sweet-looking owl and being appalled by his table manners. Bailey's sudden outburst made both her and the owlet startle in surprise.

"*What?*" Bailey almost dropped her phone and she juggled it and the tweezers for a moment before she continued. "Are you serious? I don't have time to be a tour guide for a bunch of architects and designers."

Ken watched Bailey struggle to keep control as she rushed through the rest of her call.

"Yes, of course. Okay. I will. Talk to you then. Bye." Bailey ended the call and tossed the phone onto the rug behind her. She continued to feed the owlet while muttering half-heard phrases about intruders tromping around and disturbing her birds. Her ferocity matched the owlet's appetite, and Ken watched in detached awe as the two displayed more intensity and passion than she was accustomed to seeing in human or creature.

"Bad news?" she asked once the atmosphere had calmed down.

Bailey sighed and held another piece of mouse out for the owlet. He snapped it up and swallowed it in one gulp. "My clinic is about to become a field research center for Wazzu's vet school. The dean calls me every day with more ways to expand and change everything. Now he wants to send some damned architects out to design an addition for *my* house. Can you imagine?"

"Well, sort of," Ken said. She had a feeling Bailey's irritation wasn't aimed at her profession, but at some other cause. Still, she wasn't about to remind Bailey that she was one of those damned architects. "But won't it be helpful to have more room for your birds? And some updated equipment? I saw that X-ray machine you're using, and you'd probably appreciate a newer one. I hear they've made great strides in that technology since the nineteenth century."

Bailey laughed and took the empty bowl from Ken. The owlet had eaten his fill, and he crawled under one of the soft blankets in his box. Interns, class visits, student projects, and now architects. It was easy for Ken to encourage her to accept the changes without protest, but in a way she was right. The expansion was going to happen—it *had* to happen—so Bailey needed to focus on the positive side of it, or at least on the avian side. "It's not *that* old," she said. "But yes, it'll be good to have modern equipment for a change. I've always wanted an ultrasound machine, but I haven't been able to afford to buy anything new for ages."

She got up and covered the box with a large towel before they left the room and returned to the kitchen. She washed the owl's bowl while trying to find a way to explain her reluctance without revealing too much about herself to Ken. "Most of the raptors I have here are very shy of people," she said. She knew exactly how they felt. "They are sick or injured, and I can't allow them to be disturbed."

"And those damned architects can't be trusted to be quiet?"

"They won't understand. They'll make the changes the dean wants and ignore the way I do things."

Ken shrugged, and Bailey watched her face change and settle into an unreadable expression. She had been expecting Ken to go away once the osprey was healed, but now it was as if she'd already left the room.

Ken leaned against the kitchen counter and watched Bailey dry the bowl and add it to a stack of dishes beside the sink. She recognized the defensive notes behind Bailey's angry tone, but she wasn't about to give in to her curiosity—not concern, merely curiosity—and untangle the defiance from what was really hurting Bailey. She'd offer a scrap of reassurance, and then she'd change the subject or walk out the door. Anything to avoid falling prey to Bailey's claws as she struggled to hide her vulnerability.

"Architects can only design the shape of a place. You're the one who's filled this house with life and hope. No matter what the new expansion looks like, you'll make it your own."

Ken echoed the words Joe had spoken to her a few days ago, but her tone didn't match his at all. She had come here expecting to feel renewed and reassured, but she felt as impotent as she had all week. Bailey had created a world within these walls, but she had made herself vulnerable by doing so. Ken couldn't create more than a simple outline of a house. She had long ago doused the ability to put herself out there like Bailey did.

"I'm doing the same thing on my new property," Ken continued. The visceral need to protect the obviously upset

Bailey was stronger than she'd anticipated. The urge to hold, to stroke, to comfort. And to be comforted at the same time. She had to use words, not touch, and change the subject away from Bailey's troubles—and reassure herself at the same time. "The house I build might look exactly like someone else's, but the way I use it and live in it will be unique to me."

"But you won't have an entire vet school looking over your shoulder and telling you what to do." Bailey pushed away from the counter. "You'll be able to make your own decisions. Let's move the osprey now."

Ken trailed behind her. Bailey, unknowingly, had rooted out Ken's deepest insecurity. Even complete freedom didn't guarantee originality. Still, she decided to keep the conversation focused on her land so it didn't revert to Bailey's worries about WSU. Dealing with her own inadequacy was preferable to watching Bailey's distress without being able to physically touch her. "I'll probably use some existing blueprint and make modifications, instead of designing something new from scratch."

Bailey went into the surgery and got two pairs of heavy gloves out of a drawer. "You should wear these just in case," she said. "We won't be handling him directly, but you never know when a talon or claw might catch you. Maybe I should have you sign a release or something…"

"Don't worry. I'll survive a scratch or two," Ken said. She watched Bailey put on her own gloves, hiding delicate hands under a thick layer of leather, before following her example. She felt a little safer with Bailey's enticing hands out of sight. Ken couldn't see them without imaging them on her. In her.

"I'm sure whatever you decide will be wonderful," Bailey said as she led Ken into the recovery room. "Has this always been a dream of yours?"

Ken, distracted by the blanket-covered cage in the middle of the room, took a moment to realize Bailey had returned to their previous topic. Her land.

"Um, no, not really," Ken said. At least, the dream had been so long buried that she'd forgotten it was there until she stood on her wild acre. Those rare moments when her desires burst out of hiding—with her car, her land, with Bailey—shocked her system every time, leaving her nearly powerless to resist. Nearly. She ignored the adorable way Bailey was trying to blow a lock of hair out of her eyes while both hands were occupied, and groped under the blanket for the cage handles, careful not to put her fingers through the wire grate. She'd seen the osprey's beak close-up, and she figured he could do serious damage even through the thick glove.

"Lift on three," Bailey said, her face only inches from Ken's as they bent over the cage. "One, two, *three*." Bailey shuffled backward through the bedroom door. "What made you buy out here, then? The Peninsula can feel very isolated, and not everyone likes the solitude."

Ken searched for some tone of condemnation or condescension in Bailey's words—something to extinguish her desire to kiss Bailey—but none was there. She was stating a simple fact, with no judgment. Everyone had different tastes. "I was planning to buy a condo in Seattle. Then I decided to look for a house just outside the city." Ken concentrated on keeping the plastic and metal cage steady, focused more on protecting the osprey from bumps and jostling than on her own words. She had moved inch-by-inch away from her plan to live in Seattle, peeling back the layers of urbanity she had labored to put in place. "I guess I kept looking farther away from the city until I found myself in the new housing development just outside of Port Orchard."

"Ugh, what an eyesore." Bailey delivered another well-placed blow to Ken's ego. Unintentional, of course, since she had no idea what path Ken's career had taken, but painful nonetheless. Bailey used her foot to kick open the living room cage's door. "We'll put him down right here. Those houses all look the same. No imagination or individuality. I'm surprised people don't have trouble telling which one is theirs when they come home at night. Hang on while I get some cardboard to cover this gap."

Bailey went into the kitchen, sparing Ken the necessity of commenting on her assessment of the development. Ken hadn't designed any of those houses in particular, but her own would be indistinguishable from them. She wanted to defend the box houses, to describe the small details she added to each design, but her arguments felt weak in her own mind. They'd be even worse spoken out loud. Bailey was right—about the houses and about Ken's abilities.

"Here, hold this over the cage so he doesn't jump out." Bailey handed Ken a large square of cardboard. Ken fitted it in the space left in the flight cage's doorway above the osprey's shorter one while she watched Bailey ease her arm under the cardboard. Her face twisted in concentration as she fumbled for the osprey's latch.

"There," she said with a smile of triumph, her eyes opening and meeting Ken's. Ken looked away, in case her second skirmish with the desire to kiss Bailey's pursed lips was somehow visible on her face. "I'm going to tip the cage a little. Once he's out, we'll move everything out of the way so I can shut the door."

Ken heard the osprey's claws scrabbling for purchase on the plastic floor of his crate before she saw him hop out. He crossed to the back of his new home with a slow, strange galloping gait and jumped onto a thick tree limb. As if performing a rehearsed movement, she and Bailey removed the cardboard and small crate from the opening and shut the door with a click. The osprey stood still, seemingly carved from the limb, and stared at them.

"Let's give him some time alone. He'll be more likely to explore if we're not watching him."

Bailey opened the front door, and Ken followed her onto the porch. She thought Bailey might be unceremoniously sending her away, but Bailey went over to the railing and perched on it, leaning back against the beam. Her expression had softened since the dean's call, and her relaxed hint of a smile and casual clothes made the chipped paint of the railing look homey and comforting. Ken's change in subject had started the transformation, but most of it had been accomplished by the osprey. She guessed Bailey must feel the satisfaction of seeing improvement in her patient. The move from crate to cage was one step on his path to recovery. Ken sat in a cheap plastic chair across from Bailey and tried not to seem too out of place in the peaceful scene.

"How did you get from that god-awful development to your property?" Bailey asked. "They seem like two extremes."

Ken rested her hand on her right ankle, propped on her other knee. She felt a slight twitch, an urge to fidget with the hem of her slacks, but she kept her hand still. She hadn't even told Ginny about the day she saw her piece of property for the first time. Why was she about to tell Bailey? She'd introduced the subject of her land to keep from probing into Bailey's personal life, and now she was sharing her own. Maybe she sensed that Bailey would understand, when she had been certain Ginny wouldn't. Whatever her reason, she felt her story heading toward its inevitable—and too intimate—conclusion.

"I was convinced buying a condo was the right move. I'd done the financial calculations, researched market trends, and mapped out the ideal location. But when I was walking through the rooms, I felt confined." Ken shook her head at the memory, shaking off the remembered feeling of claustrophobia. "The feeling eased a little with every place I checked out afterward, as

I slowly worked away from the city and out here to the Peninsula. I was driving around this area, trying to decide whether to make an offer on the Port Orchard house—which had nothing I'd originally wanted in a home—when I followed some signs advertising lots for sale. I walked out to the bluff and all of a sudden everything loosened inside me. I could—"

"Breathe," Bailey finished Ken's sentence. She looked up at the empty sky, seeing in her mind all the birds she'd released over the years. "I felt the same way when I found this place. I'd been working at a small animal hospital in Bremerton, but I'd always dreamed of having my own space, where I could concentrate on wild birds. Somehow, the air on this property filled my lungs better than any other air seemed able to do."

Bailey turned back to Ken and watched another unreadable expression shift over her features. She felt, rather than saw or heard, Ken inhale and exhale with a deep breath. Somehow, sharing their stories of connecting to the land seemed too intimate. Bailey was being forced to share her center with strangers—otherwise she risked losing the property and her chance to help so many more birds—but she couldn't let Ken too deep inside. She had been worried enough about her physical attraction to Ken. Adding personal confessions to a brief, casual relationship—if it turned into any relationship at all—was too risky. She could withstand the onslaught of WSU, but Ken's quiet understanding was too great a force to battle.

Bailey pushed away from the railing and stood up. "Thank you for helping me move the osprey," she said. She saw Ken's frown as the mood changed with her obvious dismissal, and she tried to soften the transition between their conversation and her good-bye. "I'll contact you if there's any change in his condition, but he seems to be recovering nicely. Thank you for… for reminding me why I moved here, and that it's worth doing whatever it takes to stay."

"I needed some reminding myself," Ken said. She stood and walked off the porch, giving Bailey's hand the barest brush with her own as she passed. "See ya, Dr. Chase."

Bailey stood in her doorway and watched Ken drive away. Once the dust had settled, she looked at the hand Ken had touched. Surprisingly, it appeared unchanged, although the brush of skin had felt potent enough to alter it somehow. She should have kept the gloves on after she'd moved the osprey—she needed every defense at her disposal where Ken was concerned.

CHAPTER SEVEN

Ken sat on a bench in the large plaza, a crossword puzzle book open on her lap and a thermos of coffee at her side. The bronze-tinted glass skyscraper that housed the Impetus offices was at her back, and all around her the business district in modern, urban downtown Bellevue was seething to life. She had made light of the long commute when she and Ginny had discussed the move to the Peninsula, but she had to admit it required plenty of time and planning. She was trying different combinations of driving and ferry rides every day in her search for the most efficient route, but ferry cancellations and traffic patterns were unpredictable. She felt safest when she gave herself an extra hour to get to work, and she'd much rather arrive early and sit in the bright morning sun than pace back and forth on a delayed ferry.

Five Across: Whistler's Mother, in the kitchen. Ken used her green Sakura Micron pen to print *off her rocker* in the tiny squares. A large gray city squirrel scampered over to her with an undulating stride and hopped onto the metal arm of Ken's bench. He stared at her, barely blinking and obviously unafraid. She capped the pen and reached into her messenger bag for her lunch, popping open the plastic sandwich carrier and ripping some bread and lettuce off a chicken salad sandwich. She tossed the offering toward the squirrel and put the remainder of her lunch away while he nibbled the grainy bread. She had spent most of the weekend on her property, eating her homemade meals there and reading or drawing in the shade of a pink-flowered hawthorn tree. She had discovered her new neighbors included chipmunks and the small brown squirrels she had identified as Douglas squirrels—far different from the fat gray ones she was accustomed to seeing in the cities, like the fellow sharing her bench.

After her unimpressive start at Impetus with Jessica last week, Ken worried her time at the lucrative job might be limited. As much as she'd be relieved to be let go, she needed the money. Until her house was built, and while she was paying rent on an apartment along with land payments, she would save as much as possible. Instead of movies or dinners out, she had picnics on her bluff with simple sandwiches and fruit. No complaints. She had made not only her own school lunches, but those for her working parents, from the time she was tall enough to reach the kitchen counter. She had enjoyed creating sandwiches as if she were designing a building, combining textures and shapes as much for the finished appearance as for taste. As she got older, she had fallen out of the habit of making lunches, since doing anything besides buying bland fries and pizzas in the school cafeteria was yet another sign of difference and another reason for ridicule by the more popular students. So Ken had bought her lunch as well, looking like everyone else on the outside while hiding her real self deep inside.

But no one saw her on her property. She was safe to relax, be herself, and eat her unique creations. She'd carried the habit through the work week also, since she didn't think anyone cared what she ate at Impetus. Besides, saving money was more important than saving face. She had a single goal in mind— to have her house and her privacy. Then she could tackle goal number two and find a workplace better suited to her.

Any workplace, as long as Dougie wasn't there, she amended when she looked up and saw him standing by her. Ken's squirrel snatched up the remaining hunk of bread and scampered away.

"Hey, Ken. I thought that was you." He shaded his eyes from the bright morning sun with his hand. "I was hoping to catch up with you last week, but Joe said you were out on a site with Jess. Mind if I join you?"

He sat down without waiting for her to answer, resting his arm along the back of the bench and peering at her crossword. "Thirty-two across is *lithium*," he said.

"You know I hate it when you do that," Ken said as she closed her puzzle book. She felt her cheek twitch as she fought to keep from smiling. She didn't want to see Dougie or to be reminded of how close they had been. He wasn't part of her life anymore. "I suppose I have you to thank for my job at Impetus."

Dougie shrugged and pushed his sandy brown bangs out of his eyes. "We lost a couple of good architects recently. One retired and one moved out of state. Joe asked us to let him know if we knew of anyone strong enough to replace them, and I thought of you. You were the most talented artist I ever knew. Well, except for—"

"Stop," Ken said. Any sentimental feelings she had been having about Dougie were cut dead by his obvious allusion to Steve. "I won't talk about him."

"It's okay, I understand," he said, giving her a quick squeeze on the shoulder before dropping his arm along the bench again. She managed to keep from jumping away from his touch, but she knew her reflexive cringe was visible.

"How did you know I was working as an architect?" She had to change the subject. He didn't seem prepared to leave her alone, no matter how brusque she was, and she clearly couldn't let him pick their topic of conversation. Even sitting in silence until he left was no longer an option for her because now Steve's presence was too palpable in her mind. She needed to talk about anything else—if she had to talk at all.

"Vanessa had a bulletin board at our high school reunion, with all the students and what careers they were in now. But I never expected you to be anything else," he said. He pushed his bangs aside again and Ken wanted to pin him down and cut them off. The gesture was too familiar, and every time he repeated it, a different shared memory resurfaced. They were studying or throwing D&D dice or calibrating a telescope. "You were always drawing. I remember when you and Steve…I remember when you designed that entire fantasy kingdom, with houses for the gods and even stables for the mythical creatures. You were the one who got me interested in architecture, so I guess I wanted to repay the favor by recommending you for Impetus. You're perfect for this place."

Not perfect. Not even interested. Ken vaguely remembered the phone call from class president Vanessa several years ago. She had declined the bubbly offer to attend the ten-year reunion, but Vanessa had kept her talking for over an hour. So that uncomfortable conversation was the indirect cause of the recent turn of events in her life? Ken was going to be more careful about screening her calls from now on. "I thought you'd be working for NASA someday," she admitted. Dougie's love of space and stars and science fiction had rivaled her own fascination with buildings and design.

"Me, too." He shrugged. "I still love astronomy, but I took a couple architecture classes in college, sort of as a way to relive old memories, I guess, but I found out I had a real knack for it. I was planning to get married, so when my guidance counselor suggested it as a career, it seemed like a good idea."

"You're married?" Ken asked. Focus on his present, not on their past. Funny how she fought to keep memories out of sight, but Dougie actively sought ways to keep them alive.

"Yeah." He fished a phone out of his pocket and handed it to her. "Her name is Marcia, and we met freshman year at Princeton. We have two girls. Betsy is nine and Sarah is five. I've told them all about you, and I'd love to have you meet them sometime. Maybe at the company picnic next month?"

Company picnic? No way. Besides, Ken wasn't sure she'd last a month at Impetus. She looked at the picture of two smiling brown-haired little girls. The older one wore round glasses and looked like a female version of Dougie when Ken had first met him. She had been the new kid—a familiar but uncomfortable position for her—and had sat at her desk, bewildered and nervous, when the teacher told them to split into groups for a class project. But Dougie and Steve had scooted their desks next to hers, drawn by her Spider-Man lunchbox, and their immediate and unexpected acceptance had made the three fast friends. Over the next years, they had gathered other kids into their group—usually misfits who didn't quite fit in the mainstream—but the three of them had been the core. Dougie had been friendly and intelligent, perpetually curious. Steve, even at ten, had been sensitive and introspective. Ken had been the leader, dragging her new friends along every time she came up with a new scheme.

"Cute kids," she said, returning Dougie's phone. In a different life, she'd probably be known as Aunt Ken to these girls. But not in this one. She glanced at her watch. "It's time for work," she said, putting her crossword book into her messenger bag and closing the flap. "Don't we have a meeting this morning?"

"First thing every Monday," Dougie said. He stood up when she did. "You'll enjoy them. We share information on the various projects we have going, and everyone helps brainstorm to solve problems. It's a collaborative, creative space. I've never experienced anything like it at my other jobs."

Great. Nothing like being put on the spot in front of the entire firm. She hadn't been able to come up with a single interesting suggestion during her entire week with Jessica, and she doubted her dry spell was likely to disappear when she was confronted by the room full of architects and designers.

"I'm not familiar with any of the projects yet," she said as they walked through the revolving glass door and headed to the elevators. "I don't think I'll be much use in a meeting like that."

Dougie pushed the button for the twentieth floor. "You won't be expected to take part right away unless you want to. Take your time to observe and get comfortable, but if I know you, it won't be long before everyone realizes how creative you are."

You don't know me. Not anymore. At fourteen, she would have been right in her element, bouncing ideas back and forth with excitement. Now, twenty years later, she had become so adept at keeping her thoughts to herself that she doubted she'd be able to share a good one even if one smacked her in the head.

"Good morning, Kendall. Morning, Douglas," the receptionist, Marty, greeted them as they walked off the elevator and into the silver, gray, and black world of Impetus. Hushed and elegant, the twentieth floor was as far removed from the bustling city of Bellevue as if it were on a different planet. "Kendall, you need to check in at HR before the meeting. There are a few papers for you to sign."

"Thanks, Marty," Ken said, turning to the left while Dougie paused at the desk to chat.

"See you in the conference room, Ken," Dougie called after her. "And don't worry about the meeting. You'll have a blast."

Ken walked to the HR office, relieved to have a few minutes to herself and away from Dougie's relentless faith in her. He persisted in seeing her as someone strong and capable, but his presence reminded her of the real weakness at her core. If he ever needed to depend on her strength, she'd be certain to fail. She signed the tax forms and walked back through the now-empty office space. Her plan for the meeting was to sit in the back, stay as far under the radar as she could. Hopefully, as the weeks wore on and she studied the different projects Impetus had going, she'd be able to contribute something worthwhile. But today, she'd be a fly on the wall.

Or so she thought. Instead, once she came through the door into the conference room, everyone turned toward her and started clapping.

What the fuck? Ken fought against her desire to turn around and walk out the door again, not stopping until she was on the ferry and aimed toward her land. She managed a tight smile in acknowledgment of the applause and slid into the empty chair next to Dougie. Part of her original plan was to sit on the other side of the room from him, but the jarring reception made her feel awkward. She hated seeking the comfort of someone familiar, but she had no choice. Was this some sort of welcoming or hazing ritual?

"Everyone, this is Ken Pearson," Joe said. He was at the front of the room, perched on the edge of a bare table in much the same posture he had used during her first meeting with him. "Ken, I was just telling the group about your weekend when you saved the bird. Sorry to startle you with the applause, but we're impressed by what you did."

She had shoved an injured bird in a box. Hardly worthy of a public commendation. Still, she relaxed fractionally once she found out why they had greeted her in such a boisterous way. "Um, thanks. But Dr. Chase did the work."

Even in this nerve-racking environment, just the act of saying Bailey's name distracted Ken. She pictured those miracle-working hands, seemingly able to heal any injury. Ken imagined them resting on her chest. Would they be able to heal her heart?

She couldn't tell because every time she thought about them, they refused to stay put and started to roam over the rest of her body. Ken rubbed a spot under her left collarbone and brought her attention back to the meeting.

"Why don't you come up here and tell us about it," Joe said. He moved to a chair in the front row and gestured at the space he had vacated. "Did you say it was an eagle?"

"An osprey," she said, after a pause. She didn't want to stand up and give a report, like she was back in school doing show-and-tell, but Joe didn't seem prepared to go on with the meeting until she spoke. Dougie prodded her in the side and she got up with a sigh. She'd give the bare details of the afternoon and be done with it.

But once she started talking, she lost track of her intention to state a few facts and sit down again. The wild beat of the osprey's pulse as she had held him in her arms, the fierce concentration on Bailey's face as she had assessed and treated the injury, the dreamlike feeling of being caught in some transition point between the world of nature and of humans. The experience had been magical to her, rare and special. Even though she wanted to remain distant and aloof, she could hear her voice change as she took on the role of storyteller. The rapt attention of her audience—most of whom had probably seen but had never had actual contact with wild birds—and their laughter as she described her clumsy attempts to capture the osprey made her give a more dramatic than necessary rendering of the story. She didn't want to drool in front of everyone, so she carefully edited her descriptions of Bailey, making an effort to talk more about the procedure than the woman performing it. She had been mesmerized by Bailey in her role as rehabber, not as a person, and she didn't want to give the wrong impression to the group.

When she finished her monologue, she felt a sense of relief. She had been caught up in the telling but now was happy to slide back into anonymity. Joe had other ideas. He went back to his position at the front of the room, and Ken half listened to him talk as she returned to her seat.

"I spoke with Vonda Selbert again yesterday. She's been instrumental in making Dr. Chase's center an adjunct to the WSU veterinary school, and they're planning to upgrade and expand her facility. Vonda had originally planned to hire a WSU alum to do the architectural designs, but I told her we'd be glad to make this our quarterly volunteer project. If we do the design work for free and use our connections with builders and suppliers, the money will stretch so we'll be able to build an annex on Dr. Chase's property—a surgery and classroom devoted solely to the center—instead of just making an addition to the existing house. I think Ken would be the perfect person to head the project and be chief designer. What do you say, Ken?"

Ken stared at Joe while the rest of the people in the room added a chorus of approval to his suggestion. She felt herself nod in assent, but her mind was already working on ways to get out of the assignment. She had been planning to call Bailey in a week or so and check on her osprey, but see her again? No. Well, not until the osprey was released on Ken's property. She *did* want to see that. Showing up at Bailey's in the role of "damned architect" wasn't going to improve her chances of witnessing the release.

Ken occupied herself by taking thorough notes during the meeting, although she was barely aware of what she was writing. Dougie gave a presentation about the project he was managing. Ken was going to be on his team, and she thought he said something about the house being commissioned by one of the Seattle Mariners, but she wasn't sure. She'd have to corner him later and find out what she'd missed while she had been mentally preparing her thank-you-but-no-thank-you speech for Joe.

Once the brainstorming and sharing had mercifully ended and everyone went off to do actual work, Ken walked to the front of the room once again, just as reluctantly as she had at the beginning of the meeting. Joe was perched on the desk, as if waiting for her.

"Thank you for suggesting I take point on this Raptor Center project," she said. Start with the gratitude and work toward the refusal. "But I was hoping to devote all my time and energy to working with Douglas and his team. Once I'm more settled here at Impetus, I'd love to help with a community project, but maybe the timing on this one isn't right for me."

"That's a logical reason for turning down the assignment," Joe said. "You're new here, and you need time to acclimate. But let me counter it with some logic of my own. You live on the Peninsula, so it would be convenient for you to be on-site during both the design and construction of the new center. Plus, you've met Dr. Chase and you've actually observed her at work."

Ken couldn't argue with that. Her mind constantly replayed Bailey's movements, the way her talented hands had tended to the injured osprey. Ken hadn't only observed Bailey, but she couldn't get her out of her mind. So it was best to keep her out of sight. She had given in once, and she didn't think she could handle doing it again. "I don't want to spread myself too thin, so I'm not doing good work—"

"Have you wondered why a firm that designs static buildings is called Impetus?" Joe interrupted her. "Think about it sometime. Ken, I believe you have passion inside you. I saw it in those nine houses you hid in the back of your portfolio, and I saw a hint of it today when you were talking about your experience with the bird. But there isn't a sign of it in the work you've done professionally before coming here. This project is small compared to our regular work, but it will give me a chance to see what you can do when inspired. Don't think of it as a test…well, yes, think of it as a test. Find what moves you, Ken, and follow it without fear."

Yeah, right. Without fear. As if her job didn't rely on the outcome. Ken had wanted to get out of the project because she didn't want to work so closely with Bailey, because she didn't have the time to devote to volunteer work when she was consumed by work and her long commute and when she was afraid she didn't have the fresh and creative concepts her new boss expected her to produce. Now, she realized her position at Impetus depended on the work she did at Bailey's center. Great.

"I'll get to work on the plans tonight," she said. She felt defeated. One more stressful hurdle to cross in order to keep a job she didn't want. Add prolonged contact with Dougie at this afternoon's team meeting, and she'd be surprised if she made it through the ferry ride home without jumping overboard.

"Good. I'll put together a packet of info about the budget and the university's needs. Stop by my office for it before you leave tonight."

Ken nodded and left the conference room. Joe had said to find what moved her. Bailey moved her, but in uncomfortable ways Ken didn't want to examine too closely. She was attractive, yes, but not the type of woman Ken needed. Plus, she was overbearing and intense as she overcompensated for an undefined yet undeniable vulnerability that tugged at Ken's long-dormant need to protect. Ken didn't have a chance of impressing Joe unless she got Bailey's approval of the new building, and after hearing Bailey's conversation the other day, Ken knew she wouldn't be easy to please. Her boss expected fresh and innovative ideas, but Bailey would resist any sort of change. Ken had no idea how she'd please them both without giving in to the dangerous urge to get more emotionally involved with Bailey and her secrets, but she had to focus on her own house, her land. The dream—no matter how distant the reality—of having her own place made the momentary struggle worthwhile. Home. *That* was what moved her.

CHAPTER EIGHT

After answering the gate's buzzer, Bailey stood at the window with her hands wrapped around a mug of cappuccino and watched an unfamiliar and battered VW Jetta, not Ken's Corvette, come up the driveway. Another bird and not another disturbing visit from Ken, thank goodness. As much as Bailey enjoyed letting her mind wander at times, she didn't need the reality of Ken intruding on her life. Bailey had been left feeling too raw after Ken's last visit. Ken had seemed to understand Bailey—her distress over WSU's intrusion and her overwhelming connection to her land. Being understood might be comforting to some people, but to Bailey it meant she had let Ken get too dangerously close to her, to see things better kept private. Showing people what she loved, how much she cared, meant giving them weapons they could use to hurt her at her deepest level. She'd been weak for a moment but had worked to shore up her defenses since then.

Unfortunately, she'd had too much time alone to think, since the week after Ken had come had been relatively slow for the center. Two people had brought songbirds to her, both in shoe boxes and both stunned after hitting a window. Bailey had given her standard lecture about keeping a stunned bird safe from predators while letting it have time to recover, but only one of the men had listened. He had taken the little chickadee back to his house and called her a few hours later to say the bird had regained consciousness and flown away. The other guy had only wanted to drop off the wren and be done with it. Bailey had put the nondescript brown bird in a sheltered spot in her yard, and soon it had woken up and disappeared into the brush behind her house. Both results were successful, and she had one more lovely voice serenading her from the bushes. A good week. Simple and positive.

So why had she found herself longing for the complexity and inscrutability of Ken's company?

Hopefully, today's case would be just as easy as the others. She answered her door before the person outside could knock and found a woman in her twenties standing on the porch, wearing low-rise jeans and a sweatshirt with the WSU cougar on it. Her blond hair was pulled into a high ponytail, and she wore glasses with heavy silver frames.

"Can I help you?" Bailey asked.

"I'm Danielle Lawrence. Your summer intern." She shifted her maroon backpack to her left shoulder and held out her right hand.

Bailey stared at Danielle's hand for a moment before she reached out and shook it. "I haven't picked an intern yet," she said, in case Danielle misconstrued her handshake as an endorsement or binding contract of some sort.

"Dean Carrington said you've been busy with the renovations and preparing for your seminar, so he wanted to help out. He chose me because I've done some volunteer work in a wildlife rehab center before. And I live close-by, so I can commute. I'm really excited to have this opportunity to work with you, Dr. Chase."

"Yeah, yeah," Bailey waved off the sweet talk. So Dean Carrington had gone behind her back and assigned an intern to her? And apparently he was too much of a coward to tell her himself, but instead sent this young woman to break the news. Bailey had hoped she'd be able to put off having an intern until next year if she kept delaying her decision making. Apparently she had been wrong. Her resolve to do whatever it took to help the center flourish—a resolve made more firm while talking to Ken—faltered in the face of a real live intruder.

"Can I come in?" Danielle asked, shifting her backpack again.

"Oh, okay," Bailey said. She motioned toward the couch. "Have a seat."

Danielle dropped her backpack on the couch and went over to the osprey's cage. He'd settled in quickly, moving step-by-step toward release.

"Wow, he's beautiful," Danielle said. "Broken wing?"

"Yes, I think he was hit by a car." Bailey wanted to stand between Danielle and the cage, to protect the osprey, but she stayed still. Although Danielle spoke quietly and didn't go too close to the cage, Bailey watched her patient for any sign of distress. The osprey seemed fine, but Bailey felt her own anxiety rise at the thought of entertaining Danielle for the entire summer. She had been intimidated by the prospect of spending two hours a day with students during a two-week seminar. How was she supposed to carry on entire days' worth of conversation with this stranger?

"What's his prognosis?"

"Good," Bailey admitted. She had been careful about being overly optimistic since she had been disappointed too many times before, but the osprey seemed to be recovering well. Even now, he was calm while she felt prickly with the need to defend her space. Her visit with Ken had proved she was too susceptible to spending time with someone sympathetic. Either she wouldn't be able to think of anything to say to Danielle, or she'd start sharing personal information. Being alone was much easier.

"Will you need to overwinter him?" Danielle seemed undeterred by Bailey's short answers. She left the osprey's cage and walked over to the couch.

"Probably." The osprey wouldn't be healed soon enough to be released before autumn. Since he wouldn't be strong enough to migrate, Bailey would keep him in one of her flight cages until the following spring.

"I'd love to see your flight cages," Danielle said. "Unless you have something else you need me to do now?"

"Oh, um…I'm not sure," Bailey said with a frown. She had convinced herself she wouldn't have an intern this year, so she hadn't planned any inconsequential tasks to keep one busy. *Can you make me a grilled-cheese sandwich for lunch? Empty the dishwasher?* "I have an owlet that needs to be fed. You can watch, if you want to."

Danielle smiled brightly. "Great! I love owls."

Bailey took a small step back from the force of Danielle's enthusiasm. "Okay, then. I'll go prepare his food. Be right back."

Danielle interpreted this statement as permission to follow Bailey into the kitchen. She watched while Bailey made the owlet's meal, asking question after question until Bailey wanted to walk out the door and into the woods for some peace and quiet. She figured Danielle would just follow her, anyway, so she stayed put and did her best to answer. Danielle said she had been chosen because of her experience and where she lived, but Bailey quickly learned she was also very intelligent. Maybe a little *too* smart. She seemed to have a strong base of knowledge about both rehabbing and raptors. Bailey would have her hands full keeping Danielle occupied without letting her get involved in caring for the birds. They were Bailey's responsibility.

Bailey walked to the bathroom with Danielle trailing behind. She had a ridiculous desire to hurry inside and lock the door, but Danielle was too close on her heels. This was Bailey's inner sanctum. Not so much a private place for her, but a safe haven for the fragile and easily disturbed youngster. She felt as fierce and protective as any mother would feel, and she was prepared to evict Danielle at the first sign of trouble. She knelt on the bathroom floor with Danielle close beside her and was relieved that the owlet's appetite didn't seem to be suffering due to his doubled audience. Unfortunately, she wasn't nearly as unruffled since her mind and body remembered being in this same position with the spicy scent and electric feel of Ken close beside her.

Danielle quietly watched the feeding process for a few minutes. "Can I try?" she asked, taking the tweezers out of Bailey's hand before she could protest. The traitorous owlet greedily accepted food from Danielle. If he had shown any sign of hesitation, Bailey would have had an excuse to dismiss her intern, but he didn't seem to care who held his meal, as long as he was on the receiving end. Bailey hugged her knees to her chest and took over the role of onlooker. She had been too distracted by thoughts of Ken to keep up her guard.

"Will he be able to go in the flight cage soon?" Danielle asked, her eyes on the small ball of feathers she was feeding.

"No. A friend who runs a rehab center near Olympia is coming tomorrow to take him. She has two barred owls about his age, so he'll be introduced to them. He needs to be with other nestlings of the same species."

When the owlet had eaten his fill, Danielle followed Bailey when she returned to the kitchen. She offered to wash the bowl and tweezers, and Bailey gave up that responsibility happily enough.

The small dishwashing chore took up all of one minute, but Bailey needed to keep Danielle occupied long enough for her to call Dean Carrington. He had hired Danielle, so it was his job to fire her. Until then, Bailey needed to find something harmless for her to do. Luckily, a quick scan of the kitchen gave her several ideas.

"These towels and blankets need to be washed," Bailey said. She pointed at a pile spilling out of the laundry room. "I use them for bedding in the cages," she added, in case Danielle mistakenly thought she was doing Bailey's personal chores.

One assignment made, but there would be plenty of downtime during the washing and drying cycles. Bailey separated a stack of notebooks from the pile of paperwork on her table. "And these treatment notes have to be entered into this ledger, exactly as written. They're cross-referenced by bird and by number. My handwriting isn't neat, so ask if you have any questions."

"Great!" Danielle's voice was as enthusiastic as if she'd been handed tickets to a concert instead of a mountain of work. "I'll get started."

Bailey was starting to wonder if she'd been too hasty in her decision to get Danielle fired. The monotonous chores took up a huge part of her day, and she had more important work waiting to fill the newly freed-up time. Like cleaning the flight cages.

Bailey busied herself in the outdoor cages for over an hour before she heard another car coming up the drive, reminding her that in her confusion over Danielle's disruptive arrival, she hadn't closed the gate again. Two visitors in one day. Exhausting.

She carefully latched the cage door behind her and paused when she saw Ken getting out of her car, a large sketch pad in her hand. Bailey walked over to meet her. To send her away. Anything to keep from losing her composure again. She'd let Ken see how upset she was over the dean's call last week, and

Ken had somehow known the right things to say and had steered the conversation so Bailey found the answers and comfort she had needed. All very nice, but not something she could rely on. She'd be left on her own to face life when Ken got tired of visiting the osprey and moved on, and Bailey needed to stay focused and not allow herself to get used to Ken's companionship.

"Why are you here? Are you planning to draw the osprey?" she asked.

"No. I'd love to see him if you think I won't be disruptive, but I'm here about something else. Can we go inside and talk?"

"Oh, okay," Bailey said. Not the most hospitable response, but it seemed all she was capable of offering today.

Ken followed Bailey into the house and went directly to the osprey. He was center stage in the room, something powerful and awe-inspiring in the midst of shabbiness. Ken slowly approached the mesh cage where the bird, his wing in a light bandage, was sitting in one corner, perched on a limb set low enough for him to hop on without needing to fly. Bailey watched Ken walk closer until she noticed the bird tense up as if ready to move. She was about to tell Ken to stop, but Ken took half a step back on her own and watched him from a distance.

"He looks great," she said to Bailey. "He seems content in his new home."

"He's doing well," Bailey said. His yellow eyes were bright and clear, and his body language was alert and active. Even after all he'd been through, there was nothing listless or dull about him. Bailey had been watching him—partly because he was connected to Ken, and Ken had never been far from her mind, but also because his mere presence was something of a miracle. How easily this feathered soul might have been lost if Ken hadn't stepped in to help. "He's lucky you found him." Bailey swallowed around a suddenly tight throat. She was accustomed to sending out thoughts of gratitude to the people who helped her save birds, but she rarely had chances to thank people face-to-face. "And that you cared enough to bring him here. He wouldn't have survived long the way he was."

A grounded bird, on the edge of a wooded area. Bailey shut out the images of the osprey's fate if he had been left there alone. She was glad when Ken turned away from the cage.

"I just did what anyone in my situation would have done," she said.

Danielle appeared in the doorway leading to the kitchen. She was holding one of Bailey's notebooks in her hand.

"Ken, this is Danielle, from WSU," Bailey said. She wasn't about to introduce her as an intern when she hadn't yet decided whether Danielle was going to stay. "Danielle, this is Ken. She's the one who rescued the osprey."

"Nice to meet you, and please, call me Dani." She came over to shake Ken's hand. "Awesome job with the osprey. He's beautiful. I hope I'll be able to help with his rehabilitation while I'm here."

"Thanks, Dani. I'm proud of him," Ken said. "Do you work with Dr. Chase?"

"Yes, as of today," Danielle said. "I'm a student at WSU, but this is my summer job."

"I'm sure she'll keep you busy."

"Laundry and paperwork, so far," Danielle said with an easy smile. "The exciting life of an intern. But I did get to feed an owlet earlier."

"Really? I got to watch the disgusting process, but I wasn't allowed to participate." Ken winked at Bailey. "Not that I wanted to take part…"

Bailey watched the interchange between the two as Ken asked about the baby owl and Dani recounted her feeding experience, making it sound much more interesting than Bailey remembered it. She envied the easy way Ken had with someone she'd just met. Bailey had been struggling to come up with complete sentences to use with Dani, and she had a shared interest with the vet student. Ken didn't seem to need the common bond to be able to converse as if she and Dani were old friends. Even if Bailey had been warned about her imposed intern's arrival ahead of time, and had written down topics to cover, she wouldn't have been able to chat with her like Ken did.

"Did you have a question, Danielle?" she asked, when there was a brief pause in the conversation.

"Oh, yes," Dani said. She held out the notebook and pointed to a paragraph. "This entry doesn't have a number."

Bailey scanned the short treatment note. She could picture the raptor that had spent only a few days at her center before being released. The falcon's injuries had been minor, and she hadn't required much care beyond transport to a safe release site. "A peregrine falcon. She was here in the beginning of April, so you should be able to find a form with her number in the filing cabinet next to the sink. They're filed by species, and then by date."

When Dani had left the room, Ken sat down on the couch. She crossed her legs and leaned back, as if she felt at home here. She was wearing creased black jeans and a green pin-striped shirt, and Bailey couldn't tell if she'd come from work or from a day off. Either way, even in casual clothes, Ken managed to look comfortable and composed. Her elegance made Bailey feel even more out of sorts in comparison, and she perched on the edge of a chair next to the couch.

"What brings you here?" Bailey asked again. Was Ken here to emphasize her social ineptness with Dani? Or to make her feel unkempt and awkward? Bailey knew she was being foolish. Barring psychic power, the first was impossible, and so was the second—Ken wasn't cruel. But whatever the reason, Bailey was growing less and less interested in hearing it.

"I'm not sure if you saw this on the form I filled out when I brought my osprey here, but I work for an architecture firm called Impetus. Long story short, my boss designed Vonda Selbert's house in Poulsbo," Ken said. Her sketchbook rested on her lap, but she kept one hand firmly on top as if keeping it closed. "And now she wants my company to work with you and the university on the expansion of your clinic. I'm the architect you've been dreading."

"What?" Bailey asked. First, an unexpected intern, and now an equally undesirable architect. Well, desirable, maybe. But definitely not welcome. Bailey's intention of putting off decisions until the dean gave up and went away had backfired in ways she hadn't anticipated. Now, it seemed all control was being taken away from her. And her dignity, as well. She'd known it was a mistake to share so much with Ken, but she hadn't realized Ken had been laughing inside while Bailey went on and on about her privacy and what it meant to have strangers overrun her center. Ken had actually made Bailey believe that she cared. "Why didn't you tell me when the dean called? Did you think it was funny to let me ramble on about not wanting architects here when you knew—"

"I didn't know then. I wasn't given the assignment until Monday. But this is good news," Ken said. She was frowning, as if she hadn't expected Bailey to do anything but quietly acquiesce and let other people take over her home, her life. "First, I'm familiar with your clinic, so I'll be less likely to disturb your birds. Second, since we're doing this pro bono, there's more money available for construction. We'll be able to build a separate annex for the surgery and classrooms, plus two new flight cages. You'll have your house to yourself, instead of sharing it with birds and interns."

They were kicking her out completely. Bailey was speechless. She had spent her life trying to get to this place of solitude, where she was able to help her birds and live in her own way. It was a chaotic life and often a lonely one, but it suited her. Now, Ken was planning to design her right out of her center. The new annex would be filled with interns and students. There wouldn't be room left for her.

"I made up a few plans earlier this week," Ken said. She opened the sketch pad and Bailey tried to concentrate on the heavily penciled lines that intersected the soft blue grid pattern of the paper.

"You already..." Bailey frowned. Aside from two visits here, Ken didn't know the first thing about bird rehabilitation. During the osprey's procedure, she had done what Bailey asked her to do. Now Ken was taking the initiative and making plans behind Bailey's back. She took the pad off Ken's lap and stared at the rooms. Empty spaces that would be filled with the university's equipment and students. With other people.

"You drew a square," she said, flipping the pad closed and handing it back to Ken. "I don't see why they needed to send an architect to my house when I could have done *that* on my own."

Ken caught the pad before it slid off her lap. Bailey's comment left her feeling physically bruised. She had been trying to maintain a pleasant expression since Bailey was essentially a client, but she felt it shift once more into a frown. The only reason she didn't storm away and let Bailey design her own fucking building was because she had no option but to *agree* with Bailey, damn it. Ken had been searching for inspiration for four days, since she had been given this assignment. She had sat on the ferry and stared at the seagulls, had sat on her property and searched the sky for another osprey, had tried her best to come up with an idea that was more useful and attractive than a box with separate but uniform spaces for an examination room, a classroom, a laundry room...Ken hadn't been any more successful in her meetings with Dougie and the rest of their team.

She was beginning to believe the evidence in front of her. She couldn't design anything more interesting than a box. Bailey's words hurt because they collided against the places where Ken had been beating on herself all week.

Ken rubbed a hand over her eyes. The only thing she had been sure of this week was how much she loved going back to her property every night after work. There was nothing on the lot except a chair she used either on the bluff or in the natural arbor at the edge of the woods. She'd sit there, battling with the wind for control of her drawing paper, until the sun had dropped below the horizon and the world was lit only by its memory. Then, only because she had no choice, she'd pack her supplies in the car and drive back to her small apartment. She thought she'd miss her active social life and the busyness of the city, but she felt only relief at being away. No observers, no danger of not fitting in or being the person she was expected to be. Every mask slipped away as she sat on her bluff. At the moment, Bailey—the one person who had seemed to truly understand what a person would sacrifice for a sense of place, of belonging—was the main obstacle in her path to building a permanent home there.

"Okay, you're the expert here. Why don't you tell me how you want the annex to look?" A more polite phrasing than *let's see you draw something better, know-it-all*. She opened the sketch pad to a clean page and sat with her pen poised above the empty paper.

Bailey paused, her forehead scrunched as if she was searching for what to say. "Oh, I don't know," she said with a dismissive gesture. "I can't think of anything besides a big square, either. I don't even want the damned annex."

Ken frowned again. She was going to need Botox injections when she finally finished this project. "So you'd prefer to go with the original plan of building an addition on the house?"

"No." Bailey sat still for a moment, and then the words sort of exploded out of her in a forceful whisper, as if she had been bottling them up too long. "What I'd *prefer* is to have you and the dean and that blasted intern go away and leave me alone."

Ken was worried Bailey might add tears to her outburst, so she hastily started to sketch. Bailey was angry with the dean, with the university, just as she had been last week. Ken pushed aside her own fears and awkwardness over the assignment and focused on calming Bailey and dissipating her helpless fury. Comforting Bailey by talking about her own life was a weakness, and it had drained Ken, but she had other resources. She tugged on a distant memory of castles she and Steve had drawn. "Hey, I can work with that. I'm picturing a moat around the house. Maybe a crenellated roof so you're protected while you shoot at intruders through the notches..." She heard Bailey's muffled laughter, but she kept drawing as she outlined Bailey's house and outfitted it for battle. "We can design some sort of pulley system with a basket, so people can deposit birds and you can tow them across the moat without having to actually talk to anyone."

Bailey tapped on the picture of her roof with her index finger. Ken wanted to grab hold of her hand and squeeze, but it was only because she felt a sense of relief as the tension between them eased.

"Can we put one of those catapult-things up here?"

"Good idea," Ken said with a solemn nod as she drew. "It'll be an effective defense against interns with battering rams."

Bailey grinned when Ken ripped the drawing out of her book and handed it over. "Thank you," she said. "I like this much better than the square you originally drew."

"So do I," Ken admitted. She slowly screwed the cap onto her pen. She wanted to keep the truce between her and Bailey, but she had an obligation to fulfill. Her first loyalty was to Impetus and Joe, not to Bailey, but she needed to play both sides if she wanted to keep everyone happy. And for some reason—even beyond her house and her job—Ken wanted to keep the smile and lightness on Bailey's face. "I thought you were working *with* the vet school. I didn't realize this was a hostile takeover."

Bailey shrugged and leaned back in her chair. She stared at the sketch Ken had made, with its battlements on the roof and snapping crocodiles in the moat. She had been opposed when she first thought Ken wanted to draw the osprey, but now she was reconsidering. Ken was clearly talented, and Bailey would love some sketches of the different birds in her care for her room. On second thought, she didn't need more reminders of Ken in her bedroom. Bailey was already growing too skilled at picturing her there, and Ken's ability to make her laugh and to reorient her when she was stressed was making her even more appealing. If Bailey didn't get herself together, she was going to fall apart when Ken eventually walked away.

"I suppose I agreed to it somewhere along the way," she said. But only because she hadn't realized how much the intrusion would affect her. She had been concerned about her patients being disturbed, but she was the one who seemed most upset by the changes. "I really do want to help as many raptors as I can, but I'd rather Vonda had donated money or equipment directly to me. I don't want the students and the interns and the researchers moving in with me."

Tread carefully, Ken warned herself. She saw the flaw in Bailey's logic, but it wasn't *her* home that was being invaded. "That's why I'm here to design the new building. You'll have your home to yourself, with all the privacy you want."

"It's almost feeding time," Bailey said. She stood up, and Ken did the same, uncertain what had precipitated the change in subject and obvious end to their conversation.

"It is?" Dani asked from the doorway. "I finished the laundry and half the ledger entries. Can I help you feed?"

"No," Bailey said abruptly. "I mean, I was hoping you could go to the post office in Sequim for me. I have a package of crickets there, and it needs to be picked up today."

"The adventure never ends," Ken said with a wink as Dani dug her car keys out of her backpack.

"Are you going to let her do anything significant while she's working for you, or is she going to be an errand girl all summer?" Ken asked once Dani had left the house. Bailey frowned at her.

"She's supposed to be making my life easier. It's easier if I don't have to go to the post office."

"Huh. I thought interns were supposed to be learning." *My God, shut up!* Ken was losing what little accord she had gained with Bailey, but she couldn't understand why Bailey was being so pigheaded about everything associated with WSU. And Ken couldn't understand why she—instead of smiling and nodding along with Bailey's insanity—was continuing to aggravate the situation.

"I didn't want her here, so save your lectures."

Ken held up her hands in surrender. "I can tell you don't want her here. But she *is* here, so why not take advantage of it? You'll have someone to help you take care of all these birds, and she'll gain valuable experience by shadowing you. Everybody wins."

Bailey shook her head. "Do you have any idea how hard it is to train someone to do this job? And what if she makes a mistake? She could do serious damage if she's careless with one of my birds."

"I thought they weren't *your* birds," Ken said before she could stop herself. Bailey and Dani's relationship wasn't any of her business, but she saw how tired Bailey looked, and she could only guess how difficult it was for her to feed and treat and clean up after her patients. If she hadn't stuck around to help with the osprey, she didn't know how Bailey would have managed to do the whole procedure on her own.

"They're not. But they're my responsibility. I can't let just anyone in here to mess up my system. To *change* things. And now you're here, too, trying to tell me what to do."

"Look, Bailey, I didn't ask to be assigned to this project, but I'm here now," Ken said. Might as well be honest about it since obviously neither she nor Bailey was happy with the situation. She had tried to connect with Bailey without resorting to personal confessions, but she didn't see any other way to salvage the project. "My job depends on this annex of yours. I didn't want the assignment, and I don't even know if I'll be able to do it well, but if I fail, I'll be let go. And without Impetus, I won't be able to build my house. I need to do a good job to impress my new boss, and you want things done your way. Why don't we work with each other instead of fighting against each other?"

"What do you propose?" Bailey asked, her arms crossed tightly over her chest. She looked as bound as if she were wearing a straitjacket, and Ken lowered the tone of her voice.

"Let me tag along with you this weekend so I can see what you do day-to-day. I won't interfere or touch anything," she said when Bailey opened her mouth as if she was about to protest. "Together, we can come up with a design for the annex. So it works well for you and your raptors. If the university is giving you money, why not use it the way *you* want?"

"I guess we can try…"

"Good," Ken said. Part of her job was pleasing temperamental clients, and she had often needed to compromise and bear with indecision or obstinacy. Bailey was being stubborn about this annex, and Ken's job depended on making her happy. It should have been as simple as finding out what Bailey wanted her building to look like, but Ken was getting too interested in the *whys* behind Bailey's genuine reluctance to have WSU help her expand the center. "I'll be back Saturday morning."

Bailey watched out her kitchen window as the clouds of dust from Dani's and Ken's departures settled, and then she sat at the table and rested her head on her crossed arms. She needed to calm her thoughts before handling her patients. After spending most of her time alone with only birds for company, she was overwhelmed by the activity of the day. Ken, Dani. Demanding time and compromise from her.

Ken confused her in too many ways. She was damned attractive, which was disconcerting enough, but she was an enticing enigma besides. She appeared as straitlaced and conventional in dress and bearing as the popular kids in school. As boring and bland as the square annex she had designed. But there were hints of depth beyond the unruffled calm of her surface, in the whimsical drawing she had made for Bailey and the brief expression of hurt when Bailey thoughtlessly criticized her original sketch. She sat up and frowned. She had been so focused on the disruptions in her own life, she had been unintentionally rude to Ken. She'd need to apologize for her remark, even though she really hadn't been impressed by the design. Ken obviously had talent reaching far beyond the uninspired plan, but Ken's abilities as an architect were only of interest to Bailey for as long as it took to design and build the annex.

Bailey had been reluctant to have a stranger, some unknown architect, traipsing around her property and designing her future. Ken would be more respectful, and she seemed interested in staying true to Bailey's vision without imposing her own. Why, then, was Bailey so much more disturbed to have Ken assigned to her project? Ken was right, the expansion was going to happen—Bailey herself had helped set the process in motion—so Bailey might as well make the best of it and work with Ken to create a safe refuge for her birds, no matter how much Bailey worried about the prospect.

She'd try to cooperate with Ken for the sake of her raptors. And she'd try to ignore her physical attraction to Ken for the sake of her own sanity. Bailey couldn't even look at her without imagining her naked, stripped bare so her elaborate tattoos were available for Bailey to explore and trace with her fingers, with her lips. Bailey rubbed her eyes. She had given up the search for something permanent and had settled for occasional and temporary connections. No one seemed to understand her passion for rescuing birds, let alone share it. Bailey had learned that lesson early in life and had faced it again every time she took a chance on dating. Even women less image-conscious than Ken seemed to be soon tired of her lack of interest in how she looked and the weird things she kept in her fridge, let alone the missed dates and her girlfriends' second-place priority in her life. Ken was like the osprey. She added a touch of rugged beauty and elegance to Bailey's house, but her stay was only temporary.

Still, she and Ken seemed destined to be partners for a short time. Bailey had to protect herself so she wouldn't be disappointed when Ken inevitably flew away. Easy enough, because although Ken was gorgeous, she was also pushy, criticizing the way Bailey treated Dani, even though Ken had no idea how difficult it would be to properly train an assistant and oversee her every move, only to have her leave at the end of summer.

Yes, Ken had overstepped when she lectured Bailey on her intern. Dani hadn't seemed to mind the work, and she willingly had done the menial tasks Bailey had given her. Bailey looked around the kitchen. Dani had not only cleaned the bowl they'd used for the owlet, but she had washed the dishes Bailey had left in the sink after breakfast. Freshly washed towels and blankets were folded neatly and stacked on the counter, and Bailey's notebooks were just as tidily arranged on the kitchen table.

She got up with a sigh, stretching her back in a deep arch before she walked over to the fridge and started pulling out bags and pouches. For a brief moment, Ken had opened up to her. Admitted her concerns about her abilities and how important the project was to her. She was struggling through changes and self-doubt and the need to sacrifice for something she'd made a priority. Just like Bailey was, as she let the university into her life, inch by inch. And just like Dani, as she faced Bailey's unwelcoming attitude with a cheery smile and a clear devotion to hard work. Bailey set out a line of bowls and plates. She'd get the meals ready for her charges, but she'd wait until Dani got back and let her help feed.

CHAPTER NINE

Ken sat at her massive steel and black laminate desk and unpacked her messenger bag. A laptop, several notepads, her favorite pens, a small plastic box with compartments for paper clips and sticky notes. She sat in her ergonomically designed chair and swiveled around, checking out the rest of the office. Her desk was the most impersonal, and she took everything with her when she left at night as if she never really believed she'd come back the next day. Everyone else appeared settled in place, at desks as different as the people sitting at them. Action figures and photos and interactive toys like Rubik's Cubes and Kohs blocks were as commonplace as in-boxes and vertical filing cubbies. Each employee had a personal desk in the huge open-plan office space, but most of them—besides Ken—spent hours of the workday in the public spaces, at the upright drafting tables near the windows or holding impromptu brainstorming sessions at the tables near the kitchen area. Nerdvana. Perfectly acceptable here, but how would these people function in real life? How would they manage to navigate the streets of Seattle without getting beaten up or having their lunch money stolen? This environment might work for them, but it didn't work for her. Too risky. Too *different*. She longed to be back in her tiny, utilitarian office at her old firm.

Ken clicked a mechanical pencil until the lead appeared. She opened a notepad and started to sketch. Her osprey floundering in the grass and later resting on the surgical table while Bailey's hands stretched and set his injured wing. She was drawing him as he had been yesterday, regal and composed even as he perched on a little stump in a cage, when Dougie stopped by her desk. He was wearing new and stiff-looking dark denim jeans and a T-shirt with an alien from Space Invaders on it. She closed the notepad before he had a chance to comment on her drawing.

"We're having a team meeting in the conference room in ten," he said.

"I'll be there." As if she had a choice. Teams, group projects. So different from her accustomed way of working, where architects and executives looked interchangeable, but worked on their own. Here, the people looked like individuals, but the emphasis was on collaboration. She preferred to appear like everyone else while keeping her insides and her work private.

She sat at her desk, her drawings pushed to one side, for nine and a half minutes, and then she went to the conference room. Four desks had been arranged in a square. Ken sat in the empty chair, between Dougie and Angela, the interior designer. Randy, the landscape architect, waved in greeting from his seat facing hers. Ken had been dreading this meeting because she still wasn't sure what to expect, even after she had been to two already. She had gotten up before sunrise this morning and had driven to her property, sliding down the bluff in the semi-darkness and jogging a few miles down the beach. The sand had shifted underfoot, and the waves kept a rhythm with her breath as she ran to connect herself with the place and to chase away her nagging doubts about this project. She had been successful in the first case, not so much in the second. Except for the fantasy worlds she and Steve had created together, she had never worked on a team like this, with all aspects of the house coming together at once. In her old job, she had designed a basic floor plan on her own. Later, well after she had moved on to other projects, the house would be built, painted inside and out in neutrals, and decorated with a simple yard and handful of bushes. Now, her every suggestion and every drawing would be scrutinized by the group. Failure would be public, not private.

Dougie tossed a deck of cards to each person. "Let's start with a little contest," he said. "Ten minutes to build a house of cards. Winner gets a candy bar, and time starts now."

Oh, goody. A game. Dougie must have read some new-age project management book. Even as Ken was sneering at his ridiculous idea, she started to carefully build a foundation for her card house. What the hell. She hadn't packed any dessert in her lunch, so a candy bar would be a nice treat. She glanced around the room and saw the other three seemed to be concentrating on wide bases. Dougie hadn't said what the criterion was for winning, so she decided to go for height instead. Her house might be more precarious, but she'd risk it.

She held her breath as she added a fifth story to her narrow tower. She checked the clock and managed to balance two cards together to create a little lean-to on the sixth level before Dougie called time. She looked at the other houses. Randy's was low and sprawling, taking up most of the table in front of him. Dougie and Angela had both finished three levels, twice as wide as Ken's.

"The winner took the most chances." Dougie tossed a Milky Way toward Ken, and she knocked over her flimsy construction when she caught it. "Hmm. I think there's a lesson to be learned there," he said with a laugh as she gathered up the cards and tapped them into a neat pile.

Ken set the candy bar aside and took out her notebook, ready for Dougie to start the informational part of the meeting. Playing with cards was fine—admittedly fun—and Ken felt inordinately pleased with her win, but she was ready to get to the details of the project. No such luck.

"Ken, what does *home* mean to you?" Dougie asked.

Ken stifled a sigh. She wasn't ready to work with these people, let alone share her feelings with them. What would be next? A group hug? She was about to throw out some ordinary definition, maybe *security* or *family*, but she hesitated. Her house of cards hadn't been formed by those words, and her unbuilt future home certainly didn't offer either at the moment. She thought of Ginny's car as it drove away from her and onto the ferry. She thought of sack lunches and Impetus, with its uncomfortable meetings like this one, of Bailey and her inexplicable obstinance.

"Choice," she said. She had been about to say *sacrifice*, but the word was too revealing.

"Excellent," Dougie said. He got out of his chair and came around to the front of his desk, so he was standing in the center of their square. "When you built your house of cards, you made the choice to go high instead of wide. To go in a different direction. As architects, we make choices that are in accord with our clients' needs and desires when we create our designs. What about you, Randy? What does home mean to you?"

Ken tuned out the rest of the discussion. Dougie's question had been meant to get her thinking about the project and the client, but she was still focused on her own home and the sacrifices she was making for it. She was confident in them at the moment, and willing to continue with the commute and the unsuitable work environment for as long as it took to build her house. She had always believed in the importance of making sacrifices *for* home and family, but now she was making choices *between* the two. She had made the decision to be alone since she couldn't compromise enough to satisfy Ginny, or any girlfriend who had come before. How long would she be content living on her own? Working toward an empty home and an empty life?

Bailey seemed satisfied with that kind of existence. In fact, she was fighting to keep everyone *out* of her life. Ken remembered Bailey's laughter when she was transforming Bailey's home into a castle. Laughter, but with a hint of longing, as if she really wanted the stone walls and deep moat around her aviancentric world. But Ken had felt a little of Bailey's loneliness, too. She didn't want the dean and his interns taking control of her center, but she also had the drawn and weary look of someone who worked unwaveringly for a cause without giving much thought to her own needs. And without someone to take care of those needs for her.

When Dougie finally got down to business, Ken clicked her pencil several times and concentrated on copying down the long list of requests the client had given him. Halfway through, her too-long lead snapped off and left a trail of black powder on her notepad. She blew on the paper to clean it. She and Bailey had something in common—the unwelcome presence of people making demands on their lives under the guise of helping them. Joe was giving Ken a chance to prove herself with the raptor center project. Dougie, although he had made light of recommending her for Impetus, had most likely staked his reputation on her unconfirmed talent. Both put unwelcome pressure on Ken, just like the university was doing to Bailey.

Yes, Ken was making the right choices. Even if she had to live alone, she'd be free on her own property. No need to be what her circle of friends or her employer wanted. And she'd try to have more respect and understanding for Bailey's reluctance to work with WSU. They'd both be better off living their lives without interference. Ken wondered briefly who she'd be once she escaped all the expectations and demands of other people. Right now, she wasn't sure, but she'd find out soon enough. She exposed a more reasonable amount of lead and started taking notes again, forcing her attention onto the meeting's agenda.

CHAPTER TEN

Ken maneuvered through the obstacle course of potholes and berry bushes on Bailey's driveway before six the next morning. She was going to need a beat-up old commuter car so she could keep her Corvette in a safe garage. These unkempt roads and the abrasive salt air from regular ferry crossings were going to damage the careful restoration and paintwork she'd done. She needed something more like the ancient Honda parked in Bailey's yard.

"Were you trying to pack up and get out of town before I got here?" Ken called out as she climbed out of her car. Bailey was shoving an armful of nets and poles into the back of her rusty, dented Civic. "I know you weren't looking forward to my visit, but this seems a little extreme."

"I'm not going...wait, were you joking?" Bailey asked. She shoved one of the poles, but it was too long to fit in the car.

Ken walked over and rolled down the back window so the pole stuck out about a foot. "Yes, I was joking," she said. Bailey appeared more harried than usual, and Ken traced her finger along the collar of Bailey's sweatshirt before she could stifle the urge to touch her. She felt Bailey's collarbone and the warmth of her skin in the brief contact. Bailey looked as if she'd been recently and jarringly roused from sleep, and the image of her in bed was disconcerting. "Your shirt is inside out."

Bailey blinked, snapping out of the trance caused by Ken's momentary touch. She was unprepared to be awake, and the added stimulus of Ken's presence was overwhelming. She looked down at her front and saw the matted pile of her blue sweatshirt. "You're right," she said. She'd fix her clothes later. "I need to leave a note for Dani, and then we can go."

She jogged back to the house with Ken on her heels. "Where are we going?" Ken asked.

Bailey slowed down as she walked past the osprey's cage and into the kitchen. "I just got a call from a ranger at Dungeness about a trapped bird. Here, carry this out to the car, will you?"

Ken took the small pet carrier from Bailey's hands and went back outside. Bailey hastily scribbled a note for Dani, listing each bird's meal and dining habits. Dani had been helping her feed for two days, but Bailey didn't expect her to remember everything. At least she had grudgingly let her intern share the feeding responsibilities, because otherwise she would have had to choose between getting out to Dungeness quickly or feeding her patients on schedule. She had already sent Dani a text asking her to come early, but she felt better with every detail she added to her long list.

"Are you writing a memo, or a Russian novel?" Ken asked. She stood close behind Bailey and was reading over her shoulder. "Do you really need to tell her to be careful not to let the birds fly out of their cages? I'm sure that was covered in her Birds 101 lecture, These Things Have Wings."

Bailey tried to ignore Ken as she skimmed through her note one last time and added a warning about the sticky latch on the smaller flight cage. "There," she said, satisfied for the moment. She'd send Dani another text if she had forgotten anything. "Come on, we need to go."

"Hey, I've been ready for ten minutes," Ken said as they returned through the living room. The osprey watched them go, motionless except for his turning head as he tracked their movements.

Bailey peered through her car's rear window and did a quick inventory of her equipment. Nets for catch-up, a carrier for transport, and an emergency kit in case she needed to stabilize the bird before moving it. "I think we have everything," she said as she and Ken got in the front seat and fastened their seat belts. Plus an assistant. She'd have to wait and see whether having Ken along was an advantage or not. She had never done an emergency callout with a helper—besides the person who called her in the first place. Ken wasn't trained or knowledgeable about rehabilitation beyond her short experience with the osprey, but she had proved herself to be calm in an emergency and respectful around the wild birds. And if she got in the way, Bailey would make her stay in the car.

"So, what's the story?" Ken asked once they were on their way.

"Mike, one of the rangers at the Dungeness refuge, saw a bird wrapped in a plastic grocery bag, so he called me."

"What kind of bird? Why doesn't he catch it himself?"

"He couldn't tell what species," Bailey said, signaling to merge onto Highway 101. Luckily, the route was familiar, because she was driving on autopilot. Most of her mind was thinking about Dani and imagining all the possible problems she might encounter while feeding alone. The small part of her brain that wasn't conjuring up visions of Dani chasing injured escapee raptors around the house was debating whether or not she was happy to have Ken sitting next to her. She was oddly comforted by her presence and aware of Ken's leg only inches from her own, but happy? She wasn't sure. A third, and very small, part of her mind was longing for the steaming cup of espresso she would normally be brewing about now. "If the bird panics while he's trying to capture it, it could be seriously injured. I have the proper equipment, so he's right to wait until I'm there."

Ken pulled her brown fleece jacket tighter around her body. The early morning was cool and drizzly, and the open window wasn't helping. Watching Bailey at work in the field might be interesting, but it wasn't the reason she had gotten up with the proverbial birds this morning. She was supposed to be observing Bailey at home, so she'd be able to design a building to meet her needs. All she had learned so far was that Bailey needed a bigger car with a better heater. "You're going to capture him with one of those long poles?"

"Yes. And then…I'll see what I can do."

The slight catch in Bailey's voice caught Ken's attention. She had been thinking of how cold and tired she was, and how this trip would delay her real purpose this weekend. Now she thought of Bailey holding the end of a long pole with a net. What would she find when she lifted it off the bird and did her examination? A wing fractured beyond repair or a neck lacerated by the twisted handle of the bag? Ken put her hand on Bailey's shoulder and felt the nubby texture of the still inside-out sweatshirt. Bailey flinched slightly at the contact, but she didn't pull away. Instead, she bumped Ken's hand with her chin, never taking her eyes off the road ahead.

"I'll help however I can," Ken said. A weak promise, since she had no idea what she was doing, but it was all she had to offer. She couldn't tell Bailey everything would be all right since she didn't know if it was true.

They drove the rest of the way in silence. Once off the highway, they passed through a sleepy farming community with pastures dotted with dozing horses and vegetable gardens filled with neat and lush-looking rows of plants. Cherry blossom trees were bright and vividly pink against the gray, overcast sky. Bailey drove over the speed limit on the unbending country roads and turned into the Dungeness Recreation Center and Wildlife Refuge. Ken had seen the signs for the place, but she hadn't had a chance to visit yet. She had been looking forward to the miles of hiking trails she had read about, but she hadn't expected to come here on a bird rescue mission.

Ken felt as drawn to the rugged scenery as she had been to her property. The refuge looked wild and abandoned, except for the occasional flutter of bird wings in the morning mist. Seagrass-covered dunes rolled alongside the pavement, and several cutoffs led off the main road and toward the ocean. Ken would be back to explore the side roads another day, but now Bailey drove to the trailhead for Dungeness Spit and parked in the empty lot.

A golf cart rolled up as soon as they got out of the car. The heavily bearded driver climbed out and helped Bailey unpack her car as if he'd done the job plenty of times before.

"The name's Mike," he said as he passed by Ken with the poles in his arms. Bailey was too busy muttering to herself as she pawed through her first-aid kit to do proper introductions, but Ken didn't care. Now wasn't the time for social niceties.

"I'm Ken. Nice to meet you." She picked up the carrier and a pair of heavy leather gloves and stowed them in the back of the golf cart. Between the three of them, they had the contents of Bailey's car transferred in less than a minute. Ken wedged herself into the small space on the backseat beside the carrier and first-aid kit, and she held on to the side of the cart as Mike sped along the packed-dirt path leading to the spit. Mike and Bailey talked about the bird as they careened through the forest, but Ken didn't pay any attention to them. She concentrated on keeping herself and Bailey's equipment from being jettisoned as the golf cart slid around corners and down an alarmingly steep slope to the beach. She'd enjoy hiking these trails someday, but she'd have to remember not to accept if Mike offered her another ride.

Bailey caught the first-aid kit as it slid out of Ken's hands and into the front seat when Mike skidded to a stop. She stepped out of the cart and walked over the sand and large, flat rocks to the ridge of the spit. The dense clouds on the strait felt as tangible as a wall, pressing her in this isolated space between the water and the steep ridge behind her. There were islands across the strait and most likely huge tankers and shipping vessels passing by, but Bailey couldn't hear or see anything beyond the base of the long, narrow arc of land, jutting into the water. She lifted the binoculars she wore around her neck and scanned the inlet between the strip of sand bar and the mainland.

She saw the plastic bag lying in the shallow water. Too still. She swallowed hard and turned away, grabbing one of the poles with a woven net attached to its end.

"Hey, it moved," Ken said. She had ducked under the yellow rope that kept the public away from the fragile inner curve of the spit and was staring at the unnatural splash of white. Bailey heard the relief in Ken's voice.

"Good," she said. "I'll go around to the right so I can stay on the sand. I should be able to be quiet enough to get close that way. Once I drop the net on it, the two of you can bring the rest of the equipment over. We can examine the bird on the flat rock over there, so we can move it as little as possible."

Bailey stared at the path in front of her, only looking up now and then to orient herself to the white bag. She felt a burst of hopeful joy every time she saw the bag flutter, but she tried to remain detached and objective. She might only be seeing movement caused by the breeze or the softly lapping water. She carefully picked her way over stones, some speckled with pinks and greens and some slate blue with thick veins of white. The bird must be exhausted, and she didn't want to alarm it more with a noisy approach.

Once she got to a small rise between her and her target, she dropped to her knees and crawled closer to stay out of the bird's sight as long as she could. She felt moisture seeping through the knees of her jeans, and the damp sand was gritty under her hands. Sand fleas hopped around her face, and she waved them away before putting her hand down again. Her palm landed on the sharp edge of a broken shell, but the flash of pain was less worrisome than the involuntary yelp she barely contained. She got on her belly and slithered the last yard, slowly lifting her head to see where she was in relation to the bird.

Close. Almost close enough. She crawled another foot forward and to the right before she inched the long pole out from its position by her side. Her muscles ached as she kept control over its movements until it hovered directly over the bird. One quick swoop, and she had the bird and the plastic bag contained.

After her achingly slow progress, the next seconds were a flurry of activity as she hurried toward the bird and pressed down on the edges of the net, keeping her quarry firmly in place. The rush of emotion as she closed her hands over the now-struggling bird was a mingled chaos of relief—because the creature had some fight left—and fear of further injury as it panicked in its double snare. She groped blindly for the bird's wings, nearly crying with relief when she finally got them folded and pressed close to its body. The steady thrum of heartbeat in her hands seemed to reverberate through her whole body with a steady pulse of relief.

"It's bleeding," she said when Ken and Mike appeared by her side with their arms full of equipment.

"Nope, the blood's yours, kiddo," Mike said.

Ken knelt and put her hands directly over Bailey's on the blood-smeared netting. "Slide your hands out and let Mike bandage your cut," she said. Bailey started to protest, of course, but Ken nudged her with her shoulder. "You can't help the bird if you pass out from loss of blood. Now, move."

Ken could feel Bailey's reluctance, but she eventually slid her hands away. Ken's joke about the loss of blood hadn't been far from the truth. The gash on Bailey's palm looked disturbingly deep. She kept her mind off the unsanitary conditions around the wound and concentrated instead on holding the bird tightly enough to keep it from flailing and loosely enough not to squish it. She was relieved when Bailey came back—her hands covered with the leather gloves—to relieve her of the burden. Ken shifted aside, ready to relinquish her hold on the bird, but Bailey stopped her.

"I could use your help," she said. "Keep your hold on the wings while I carry the bird over to that rock."

Ken nodded, standing up as Bailey reached under the bird and scooped it up along with the netting. Mike held the other end of the pole to keep it steady as they edged their way over to the rock. Bailey set the bird down and bent over to peer under the edge of the net.

"A kingfisher," she said. "Looks like it speared the bag with its beak. Can you hold the wings with just your right hand, Ken? Good. Give me your left and I'm going to have you hold its beak closed while I get the plastic off. Yes, there. Not too much pressure."

Ken followed Bailey's murmured instructions as they traded hand positions several times until the net was off and Ken was holding the soft gray body of the kingfisher wrapped in one hand and its long, knifelike beak in the other. Mike handed Bailey a pair of scissors, and she pulled off her gloves before she cut the bag away from the bird. He picked up the discarded trash and stuffed it in his pocket.

"She's a female," Bailey said as she extracted one wing, gray with tiny white spots, from Ken's hand and spread it out to check for injuries. She replaced the wing and ran the tip of her finger over a rust-colored band on the bird's white belly. "Males don't have this marking."

Bailey continued her examination, and Ken tried to keep her attention on the kingfisher's blue-gray head, with its wispy feathers that gave the bird a somewhat frazzled look. Anything to keep her mind off the feel of Bailey pressed against her side and the brush of her hands against Ken's as Bailey checked every inch of the bird. Bailey didn't smell of vulture vomit today. Instead, she smelled surprisingly of apples. Ken inhaled. Apples and something tropical, maybe guava. Enticing and fresh.

"Okay," Bailey said, stepping back and snapping Ken out of her island daydream, where she and Bailey were lounging in beach chairs and drinking piña coladas.

"Okay what?" Ken asked.

"You can let her go. She appears to be uninjured."

"Really? Let her go, just like that?" Ken hesitated as the bird twitched in her hands as if trying to take flight. "Don't you need to keep her for observation?"

"It'd be too traumatizing to stuff her in the carrier and take her home. She's better off staying here. Let me and Mike get over to the ridge before you let go, so she has as much space as possible."

Ken twisted to look over her shoulder as Bailey and Mike moved away from her. When she saw Bailey nod, she released her hold. The kingfisher tilted her head and stared at Ken, as if she was as surprised by her freedom as Ken was. Then, in a startling flurry of gray and white, she launched off the rock and landed on a rotting wooden pylon several yards away. She fluffed out her feathers with an indignant glare at Ken before she started to preen. Ken watched her for a few minutes, until the small bird flew farther down the beach, and then she turned away and walked over to Mike and Bailey.

"Awesome job, you two," Mike said. "C'mon, I'll give you a ride back to your car."

"I think we'll walk," Bailey said. "Ken hasn't been here before, so I'd like to show her the trail. You can just leave my stuff next to the car."

He shook hands with both of them and zipped up the hill in his golf cart. Ken held the yellow rope for Bailey before stepping under it and back to the public side of the spit. Bailey had once again given her a unique look behind the scenes, a glimpse into the natural world Ken had rarely seen before.

"I hope you don't mind walking," Bailey said. "I thought I'd be sick if I had to ride in that cart again."

"Are you kidding? I'm relieved. The man's a menace behind the wheel." Ken climbed over a large piece of driftwood and walked toward the strait. Bailey could easily have taken over back there, releasing the bird herself instead of letting Ken have the honor. But she hadn't. She had let Ken experience the wonder of flight and freedom. How much more wonderful must the moment of release be after she had spent weeks or months caring for the creature and living in such close quarters? She stared out at the strait and watched a dark bird disappear under the water, only to resurface again moments later. "Thank you for today."

"I should be thanking you," Bailey said. She pointed at a flock of birds several yards down the beach. They were scattered along the water's edge, some on the sand and some floating close to shore. "Pigeon guillemots. Anyway, I appreciated having you here. The whole process was much smoother with the two of us than it would have been if I'd been alone, or if Mike had tried to help."

"You're welcome." Ken squinted at the pigeon...whatevers. "How can you tell what they are? They all look the same to me."

Bailey handed her the binoculars. "See their red feet and the white patch on their wings?"

"Oh yeah," Ken said. The distinct features began to stand out once she looked for them. She searched for the bird she had seen diving.

"It's a loon," Bailey said, putting her hands on Ken's shoulders and turning her slightly. "Black head, black-and-white speckled body."

They stayed on the beach for another fifteen minutes while Bailey gave her a crash course in bird identification. Ken doubted she'd remember all the names and markings, but she enjoyed the feel of Bailey's touch as she guided Ken toward each new species she found.

"Fascinating," Ken said. She draped the binoculars around Bailey's neck again and took hold of her injured hand. She traced the bandage with her thumb. "I could stay here all day, but we need to get you out of here so we can clean this wound. You might need stitches."

"I can sew it up at home if I need to," Bailey said, pulling her hand away. She started walking along the trail leading off the spit. The first section was a steep climb up the bluff, and Bailey used the time to pull her wandering thoughts together. Working side by side with Ken had been too confusing. The quiet and easy way they had handled the bird, as if they could read each other's moves before they happened, was in direct contrast with the electric charge Bailey had felt every time her skin touched Ken's. She had shared her work with Ken, and she had wanted to share the reward as well. She had no doubt Ken had recognized the importance of the moment of release—Bailey had seen the beauty of it reflected in Ken's expression as she watched the kingfisher take flight.

But Bailey knew there was always pain mixed with joy when a wild creature regained its freedom. Ken was working with her because she had to, because she had been given an unwanted assignment by her boss. She wouldn't stay for long. Bailey had tried to hurry them to the inevitable time when Ken would decide her bird obsession was too weird or too boring. But Ken had seemed interested in the mini-lecture even though Bailey hadn't included any jokes or interesting anecdotes as she listed the identifying features of waterfowl. Ken must still be basking in the release. Soon the excitement would wear off, and they'd both return to the routine of their lives.

Once they reached the top of the hill and the path leveled out, Bailey paused next to a garbage can full of paper coffee cups and fast food bags. She took out her phone and checked the signal strength.

"I need to call Dani and make sure she didn't have any trouble feeding."

Ken snatched her phone away. "Why don't I call her and let her know the rescue was a success and we're going out to breakfast to celebrate. Then she won't feel like her boss doesn't trust her, and you'll know your birds are safe."

Bailey grabbed for her phone, but Ken used her extra height to keep it just out of reach. "I *don't* trust her. Not yet, anyway. I just met her."

"So instead of automatically trusting people until they prove themselves unworthy, you start by believing they're untrustworthy?"

Bailey paused with one hand on Ken's waist. She had been reaching for her phone with the other, but she let it drop while she struggled with a way to answer Ken's question. Automatically trust people instead of the opposite? She'd never even considered it as a viable option. She paused long enough, distracted by the issue of trust and by her reluctance to move her hand, for Ken to search through her contact list.

"Hi, Dani? It's Ken. We met a couple days ago at Dr. Chase's house...Yes, I'm with her now."

"Give me the phone," Bailey whispered.

"It was a kingfisher," Ken continued, batting away Bailey's hand. "Gorgeous. By some miracle, she wasn't injured, so we let her go."

Bailey tugged on Ken's sleeve. Apparently, she wasn't getting her phone back, but she at least wanted an update on her birds. "Did the redtail eat? She can be fussy if her routine is changed."

"So can you," Ken said to her before returning to her phone conversation. "Hey, I was going to take Dr. Chase to breakfast as long as you're coping there on your own...Oh no...Really? How many of them got loose?"

"*What?*" Bailey asked loudly.

Ken laughed at Bailey's expression. Shock mixed with resignation, as if she'd been convinced all along Dani wouldn't be able to keep the birds in their cages. "Thanks, Dani. We'll be back in a couple hours. Call if you need anything."

"You were joking? Please tell me you were trying to be funny," Bailey said, crossing her arms and glaring at Ken.

Ken smiled. "Yes, I was kidding. Your birds are fine. Dani said the feeding went smoothly and everyone was well behaved. No one escaped."

Bailey pivoted away from Ken and scanned the ground beside the trail.

"What are you looking for?"

"Something to throw at you," Bailey said, but Ken could hear the hint of laughter in her voice. It had a hysterical note to it, since Bailey had been tricked into thinking her nightmare had come true, but at least it was laughter. Ken caught her by the arm and made Bailey face her, running her fingers over the beautiful curve of Bailey's mouth. Bailey's smiles were rare, but genuine.

"I'm sorry," Ken said. "I shouldn't have teased. Your birds are safe, and Dani will be there all afternoon. At least have breakfast with me?"

Bailey tugged her arm out of Ken's grasp and started down the trail. "Okay. I have to go to the feed store for some bedding for my cages, and there's a diner next door to it."

Ken easily caught up with Bailey. She had never chosen a restaurant because of its proximity to a feed store, but she wasn't surprised by Bailey's order of priorities. Bird supplies first, human meals second. Ken was content to be an afterthought to an errand if it meant Bailey would take an hour or two away from the stress and responsibility of her center. Ken didn't know the statistics, but she was willing to bet the rate of burnout for wildlife rehabilitators was high. She had watched Bailey at work, had seen firsthand how much emotion she invested in each feathered creature that crossed her path. How long could she keep driving herself, unwilling to accept help or say no to any bird, before she broke down? Whether Bailey wanted to admit it or not, she needed rest and time away from her birds if she wanted to stay healthy. Even now, after the reassurance from the phone call with Dani, Bailey seemed less taut. She walked along the forest trail with the ease of a creature that had been born to live in the nonhuman world.

The path was marked with scattered signs identifying trees and bushes, and on a normal hike, Ken would have read each one. She might have remembered a name or two if a certain plant caught her attention, but her walk with Bailey was different. Bailey described every detail, pointed out every quality of shape and texture in the plants around her. Ken used to walk through areas she'd refer to in general as woods, but Bailey helped her separate out various forms and shapes from the homogenous whole.

Even the forest sounds stopped being mere background noise as Ken started to recognize the different voices in the chorus.

"Hey," she said, pausing in the middle of the path. She waited as a family with two children passed them going the opposite direction, toward the spit. The forest grew still as the group went by, sharing hellos and comments about the rainy weather. Once she and Bailey were alone again, Ken continued. "I hear an owl."

Bailey cocked her head and listened. Adorable. "The cooing sound? No, it's a mourning dove."

Not as exciting, but Ken filed the sound and the species away in her mind. A few moments later, she stopped once more. She stared into the branches of a massive western hemlock until she caught the red flash again. "Look," she said, pointing toward the bird. The bright color seemed exotic and out of place in the woods. She was sure Bailey would tell her it was something rare, something unusual.

"It's a robin," Bailey said. She handed the binoculars to Ken who confirmed it was, indeed, a standard robin. Ken watched the bird flit through the dense branches. She saw robins everywhere, but she had never really noticed how bright their red breasts and yellow bills were, and how delicate and sweet their song was.

Ken returned the binoculars, her fingers sliding over Bailey's, and it felt natural to take Bailey's hand in her own. The world seemed private and isolated, the sounds of the woods only occasionally broken by the discordant noise of a passing group of tourists. Ken turned Bailey's hand over and pressed her thumb along the edges of the bandage to tighten the seal. Bailey used her hands to heal, and she needed someone to heal *her*. Ken let go of Bailey's hand when she heard another group of people approaching from beyond a bend in the path. Ken wasn't strong enough to be what Bailey needed. She had proven beyond doubt that she wasn't capable of protecting someone as sensitive and unique as Bailey. Someone who lived in an internal and ideal world but seemed unprepared for the details and dangers of real life. Ken was better off with a woman like Ginny who conformed to the standards set by society. Someone self-protected and not in danger of being deeply wounded because she was different.

Bailey felt the loss of Ken's touch as keenly as the release of one of her raptors. One second she was feeling lighthearted and connected, and the next she was standing alone and empty as a trio of laughing and chatting tourists passed by her on their way toward the spit. Ken had done more than drop Bailey's hand. A touch, a bond so quickly forged and broken.

Bailey had enjoyed the feel of Ken's palm pressed against hers. She felt the same rush of energy she got when she held a wild raptor. A powerful life force, strong and sure, infiltrating her veins for a brief time. But Ken was different from her birds. Their reactions and emotions were simple and intense. Consistent. Ken's seemed no less intense, but they were complex and harder for Bailey to read, capable of change in the rapid blink of an eye. Which one should Bailey trust?

She walked in silence, still feeling the tingling progress of Ken's thumb as it had circled around the cut on her hand. She so rarely spent time walking in the woods like this, with no real purpose. She was always focused on birds when she was in the woods, but she was usually catching or releasing one, not merely enjoying the way their different calls and songs surrounded her or the way their movements among the tree branches brought life to the forest. Because these birds didn't need her. The ones back home did.

Just breakfast, just an hour or two away from home. Why stop there? Why not stay away a week or a month, since Ken and Dani seemed determined to convince her she wasn't necessary? Bailey knew it wasn't true. Young people like Dani were interested in saving the world, giving their unbounded time and energy to a cause like wildlife rehabilitation, but how many of them stuck around for the long term? Too damned few, as exhausted people like Bailey and Sue proved. Eventually, Dani would move on to a new project. Ken would finish her designs and move on to a new job. The raptors, with their injured wings and wounded spirits, would still be there, needing her.

Bailey had been caught up in the temporary and insubstantial promise of the day. She liked Ken's company, saw Ken's interest in the world around her and her joy as she started to identify and recognize patterns in sound and shape. But Bailey wanted the stability and constancy of her solitary life. WSU's interns and architects and researchers would come and go, but the core of her center—the birds of prey—would remain.

She was agitated suddenly, as anxious to get home as she had been before the phone call. Maybe more so. She was sure the cages were securely locked and the birds were fed, but she needed to be back in her world. She increased her pace just as Ken stopped to stare at a broken tree trunk. Bailey squinted at the ordinary-looking sight as she tried to figure out why Ken seemed so entranced. The deep crevices in the Douglas fir's trunk were filled with moss and tiers of flattish oyster mushrooms. The decaying log had broken in two places when it fell against the hillside, giving it a step effect as its three sections followed the contour of the ground. Interesting, and useful in an ecological sense, but hardly noteworthy. Ken must be looking at something Bailey couldn't see.

The morning drizzle had turned into a light rain. Bailey heard the drops falling, but the dense canopy above them kept the moisture from reaching the ground, and it remained dry under the cathedral ceiling of the forest. She heard the guttural cry of a raven in the distance.

"What is it? Do you see a bird?" Bailey asked. She shifted impatiently.

Ken shook her head, looking at Bailey as if she'd forgotten she was there. "No, just…do you have a pencil and paper?"

"In the car," Bailey said. Ken started walking toward the parking lot with more purpose now, and Bailey hurried to keep up with her long strides. She wanted to ask more questions, to figure out what had changed Ken's mood and made her seem so distant, but she remained silent. She thought about the time, earlier in the spring, when she had been struggling to come up with a way to help a hawk with a stubborn break in its leg. Her traditional splinting methods had failed, and she was about to accept the raptor's life sentence with a crippled leg, when she had stood in the grocery store and looked at the corkscrew-shaped pasta. The vision of a twisted splint was so clear in her mind, she had needed to drop her basket of groceries and run out of the store, unable to talk to anyone in case her inspiration disappeared before she had a chance to capture her design on paper. Ken had the same single-minded, inward-looking focus Bailey had felt then. She didn't want to interfere with Ken's vision, so she kept quiet. Besides, at least they were speeding toward the car now.

Once they reached the parking lot—where most of the spaces had filled with cars as tourists came to see the refuge and walk the spit—she hurried over to her car and dug a stubby pencil and piece of paper out of her glove compartment. Ken accepted them with a quick thank you before she sat on the Honda's scratched-up bumper and started to draw. Bailey began loading the equipment Mike had left in a neat pile next to her trunk. No matter how many times she carried the exact same equipment, it always took her several tries to get everything arranged neatly enough so her trunk lid and car doors would close. She had just replaced the first-aid kit in her trunk when Ken stood up and stretched her back.

"Thanks for this," Ken said. She handed the pencil to Bailey and took the pole out of her hand, sliding it through the still-open window. Ken felt her previous sense of lightness fading away, as if the kingfisher's release had given her a flash of inspiration on temporary loan. "Do you mind if I keep the scratch paper?"

"Well, sort of," Bailey said. "It's my car's registration."

Ken flipped over the green-tinted paper she had used for her sketch. Sure enough, Bailey's signature was scrawled across the bottom. "Oh, sorry. I guess you'll need this back, but it doesn't matter. It's not important."

Bailey took the registration from her. Ken fought her urge to keep hold of the paper, not because she wanted to keep the drawing but because she didn't want Bailey to do exactly what she did. Turn it over and look at Ken's sketch.

"Oh. What a beautiful home."

"I'm capable of doing more than drawing squares," Ken said. She heard the defensive tone in her voice, brought out by the obvious surprise in Bailey's. The house Ken had drawn was no more likely to be made real than her fanciful Muse houses, so she didn't know why she felt the need to reaffirm her skills. She had sketched the design because it was in her head and needed to get out, not as a way to prove her worth to Bailey or anybody else.

"I'm sorry for criticizing your work like I did the other day," Bailey said. "You are obviously very talented."

Ken shook her head. She wasn't being modest, but she didn't want to hear Bailey's compliments. For some reason they hurt more than the criticism had, but Ken wasn't sure why.

"Really, you are," Bailey said. She waved the drawing toward Ken. "This looks like something you'd see in a magazine or a book on famous architects. It's not for my annex since my property is flat. Is it for another one of your clients?"

"No. I was picturing it on my property," Ken admitted. Three levels, joined by interior staircases and draped over the contours of her land with a natural, low profile. A kitchen and living area on the lowest level, her master bedroom on the second. The third level—with the highest elevation and the best view and light—would be devoted to her drafting table and weight room. A private, grounding place.

"I can picture you living here," Bailey said. "Entertaining clients and guests. What a way to showcase your designs."

Exactly what Ken *didn't* want. She'd file the image away in her mind, and maybe she'd be able to use it with an Impetus client someday. She'd build something more basic for herself. "About breakfast—"

"I really should get home," Bailey said before she could finish.

Ken got in the car and fastened her seat belt, glad to be only a short drive from privacy. She needed time alone, to work out or jog until she was exhausted and had forgotten the thrill of her imagined walk through the staggered house she had designed. The distance between vision and reality was too great to overcome. The beauty of her design wasn't strong enough to withstand the transition to wood and stone. Or maybe she was the one who wasn't strong enough.

"I know I said I was going to shadow you all day, but I've had plenty of chances to see you work. I should spend the afternoon developing some of my ideas for your annex." She was lying. She still didn't have anything besides a big square in her mind. Well, maybe a rectangle. But Bailey sounded as relieved as Ken to be heading their separate ways.

"Will you do me one favor?" Bailey asked as she backed out of her parking place.

"Of course," Ken promised, surprised by her lack of hesitation when all she had wanted moments before was to be away from Bailey.

"If you build the tree trunk house, will you add more panes to the windows? You'll still get plenty of light, but birds will be less likely to fly into them than big picture windows."

Ken took the paper and pencil off the center console where Bailey had put them, and she drew crisscrossed panes on the windows.

"Better?" she asked, holding up the revised sketch for Bailey's approval.

"Whew, yes. Thank you."

Ken had to laugh at the obvious relief in Bailey's voice. Even in the fantasy world, the welfare of the birds came first.

CHAPTER ELEVEN

Bailey tucked her hands under her thighs and rocked slightly as she sat on a stool next to the examination table and watched Dani clean the wounds on the hawk's belly. She wanted to wrest the bird away from Dani and take care of it herself, but she increased the pressure on her hands in an effort to keep them still.

The small sharp-shinned hawk had been dropped off at the clinic the day before—dumped unceremoniously out of a pet carrier and onto Bailey's living-room floor. It had gotten mauled by a cat while hunting sparrows and chickadees in the woman's backyard, and she warned Bailey not to release it anywhere near her home once it was healed. She had refused to fill out any forms and had sped away, leaving Bailey and Dani to chase after the hawk with long-handled nets while it swooped and shrieked through the house. Bailey was glad she didn't have any close neighbors because the screaming sharp-shin gave an uncanny impression of someone being murdered in a slow and painful way. They eventually cornered the hawk, and Bailey had given Dani her first lesson in how to restrain a raptor and assess its injuries. She hadn't let Dani actually *touch* the bird yesterday, but she had finally given in to Dani's long-winded pleas and reasoning and was letting her treat it today.

The cat seemed to have done little besides carry the hawk around like an undignified chew toy, and it had nasty gouges near the wrist on one wing and on the tender skin of the other armpit. It would require only a short stay at the clinic while they watched for any signs of infection and cleaned the wounds, so the hawk was an ideal first patient for Dani. It was small enough to immobilize easily, but feisty enough to provide a challenge. Still, Bailey thought she might need to sedate herself if she wanted to let Dani finish the job.

Since her trip to Dungeness with Ken over the weekend, Bailey had been in a near-constant struggle with herself to give Dani more responsibilities. She had witnessed Ken's open elation as she had released the kingfisher, and Bailey had felt a corresponding sense of gratitude as she shared what was usually a private experience. And a lonely one, as she usually trekked back home after a release with an empty carrier in her hands and a swirl of accompanying emotions in her heart. Dani had worked hard at every menial task Bailey had tossed her way, and she was eager to learn. Bailey's fight was with Dean Carrington, not Dani, and Bailey had come to realize she not only had the responsibility to share her knowledge with Dani, but she— surprisingly—*wanted* to.

But Bailey's long-held desire to be self-sufficient and isolated at the clinic was proving difficult to change. She wavered between a frustrated urge to take over and do every job in her own way and a wave of sadness every time she saw Dani master a new skill. Bailey didn't want to teach herself into redundancy. Sometimes, the only reason she didn't send Dani away from the clinic for good was the vision of the new flight cages she wanted Ken to design for her.

After Ken had left last Saturday, Bailey had slowly unpacked her car, making more trips than necessary as she went through the tiring ritual of returning every piece of equipment to its rightful place. She had been about to put her registration back into the glove compartment when she turned it over for another look at Ken's design. She had sat in the driver's seat for a long time while she marveled at the way Ken had taken a broken-down, decaying tree trunk and had transformed the image into this organic and inviting home. Bailey had thought about a meadow she had found several years earlier, deep in the Olympic rain forest. It was her idea of heaven, complete with birds and the fresh scent of the lush vegetation. What might Ken be able to create if she saw it? Bailey wasn't able to describe the place in words or by drawing a picture, but she could take Ken straight to the actual spot and show her, as long as Bailey was confident in Dani's ability to run the center for a whole day. The imagined vision of her new flight cages, replicas of her meadow, made it necessary for her to let Dani take on more responsibility in the clinic, but it wasn't enough to keep Bailey from caring about her birds.

"Be careful not to use too much pressure with the swab," she said, leaning to one side as she tried to peer around Dani's arm. "You don't want to open the wound again."

"All right," Dani said in her unperturbed voice. Bailey had given the same instruction at least twice already. She wasn't sure if she was more impressed by Dani's natural knack with the hawk, or by her admirable restraint.

"Do you feel any heat on the skin around the cuts? Are you seeing any pus?"

"No. No signs of infection." Dani recapped the antibiotic cream and looked at Bailey. "Done. Do you want to look him over before I put him back?"

"Yes. No, I'm sure you did fine," Bailey said, taking her hands out from under her thighs and clasping them together between her legs. She had been watching Dani's work from only two feet away, and she knew the hawk was in good hands.

"Well, I suppose it wouldn't hurt to double-check, since it's your first time doing this."

She got off the stool and went over to the table, stifling her sigh of relief when she finally was able to run her hand over the bird's feathers and inspect his treated wounds.

"Good job," she said. She was about to pick up the hawk and carry him back to his temporary home in the recovery room, but she stopped herself. "He can go back now." She stepped back and let Dani take him.

Bailey didn't follow her into the recovery room but instead occupied herself by cleaning up the examination table and stowing the few supplies Dani had used back on the closet shelf. Even without the prospect of a hiking trip with Ken, Bailey had to make better use of her intern, both for her own sake and for Dani's. Logically, she knew the more experience Dani had with these easy cases, the more she'd learn. And the more she learned, the more help she'd be at the clinic. Dani was devoting too much time and energy to the raptor center to simply wash blankets and feeding bowls.

She'd need to entrust Dani with every aspect of the birds' care. Treating wounds, feeding, cleaning, providing emergency care if any new patients arrived. Bailey hadn't been off the property for more than a few hours at a shot in over a year, and every time she thought about calling Ken to invite her on the hike to the meadow, she managed to find some reason to put it off another day. She wasn't sure whether she was more nervous about leaving the clinic, or about being in close quarters with Ken on the long drive and in the secluded woods. She was too interested in Ken, wanting to know more about her and how she maintained such a calm demeanor when her eyes looked as wild as a bird soaring on an ocean breeze. Bailey didn't want Ken to leave her alone, but her very desire to be around someone so enigmatic as Ken meant trouble.

"I'll get back to the papers I was filing," Dani said when she returned to the room.

"Later," Bailey said. Her phone buzzed and she paused with her finger over the call button. Ken. "First, we need to catch the redtail for a checkup. I think one of the wounds from the BBs might have reopened. Be sure to bring the heavy gloves, and I'll meet you outside."

"Hello?" Bailey left Dani in the examination room and walked down the hall and toward the kitchen as she answered her phone.

"How's my injured bird rescuer?" Ken asked.

Bailey smiled as she rubbed the frayed edges of the butterfly bandage that covered her healing wound. Ken's voice became a tangible thing, and Bailey inhaled at the remembered friction of Ken's fingertips brushing against her palm.

"I'm fine, thanks. You can barely see where I got cut." There wouldn't be a physical scar to remind her of their day together, but Bailey didn't need one. Every detail—from the whisper of the released kingfisher's wings to the synchronized crunch of shoes on pine needles as she and Ken had walked side-by-side— was clear in her mind.

"I'm glad," Ken said. "Don't forget, I still owe you a breakfast."

"Yes, you do." Bailey should be suggesting they combine her hiking idea with the breakfast, not hoping for two separate outings with Ken. Somehow, though, Ken's voice made her innocent sentence conjure up sensations of whispered words and tousled sheets, and Bailey was ready to trade her hike for breakfast in bed.

"Any chance you'd accept lunch instead?" Ken asked. "Tomorrow afternoon?"

Lunch in bed? Even better. "I'd love to. Dani can bird-sit."

Ken laughed, and Bailey felt herself smiling in response. They had left Dungeness with an air of tension between them, but it seemed to have dissipated.

"Great. I'll pick you up at eleven and drive us to Poulsbo. My boss will meet us at Vonda's house."

"Oh, well..." Bailey struggled to catch up with the conversation, but the jump from breakfast in bed with Ken to lunch with Vonda was too huge. "I, um..."

"Does eleven work? I'm sure I can change the time if it's inconvenient for you."

"Yes, I mean, no. Eleven is fine."

Ken disconnected after a breezy good-bye, and Bailey leaned against the kitchen counter and stared out the window to where Dani was pulling the catch-up nets out of a small shed. Bailey realized she hadn't mentioned her idea of hiking to the meadow, but she'd bring it up tomorrow. Who knew, maybe Ken would invite Dean Carrington along for that excursion. Bailey exhaled and let go of her foolish thoughts of romance. Tomorrow's lunch would be business. Yet another battle in the war for control over her sanctuary. She went out the back door and walked across the lawn toward the flight cages.

❖

Ken tucked her phone in the back pocket of her jeans and picked up a mechanical pencil. The cold metal felt oddly unfamiliar in her hand although she had used the same brand for years. She stood at her upright drafting table with one ankle crossed over the other and stared out the tiny window of her second-story apartment at the uninspiring view of the back of a Safeway.

She couldn't blame the ugly concrete building across the parking lot for her miserable attempts to design something—

anything—for either Dougie's client or Bailey. Ken balanced her pencil on the rim of the table and leaned her head in her hands. She rubbed her eyes and shoved her fingers through her hair before she straightened up again. Her conversation with Bailey had left her feeling more distracted than usual. She gave up the pretense of working and went to the fridge for a bottle of beer.

Bailey had sounded as unenthusiastic about the lunch as Ken felt. Joe Bently had suggested the four of them meet at Vonda's to discuss the project in an informal setting, and he had managed to make the suggestion an iron-clad order. Ken hadn't even bothered to argue and had accepted the meal as a chore she had to endure, just as Bailey had seemed to do.

Ken held her bottle of Widmer Brothers Hefeweizen in the small patch of sun drifting through her little window. The murky, unfiltered beer glowed like the eyes of her osprey in the light. She might have been imagining it, but Bailey had sounded happy about having lunch with *her*, but disappointed when she found out they would be eating with Joe and Vonda. Had she thought Ken was asking her on a date? Ken shook her head and took a drink of her beer. Ice cold and hoppy, with an aftertaste of bananas. A date with Bailey had its appeal, but Ken couldn't lose sight of every one of her goals. She'd compromised with her car and property, following her foolish whims instead of careful plans, but she had to be more careful with her romantic plans. Bailey had all the heart Ken could want, but she was Bailey. No apologies, no masks. Ken admired her courage but didn't have enough of her own to live life the way Bailey did. And she definitely didn't have the strength to protect and defend Bailey when the rest of the world turned on her, challenging her right to live with such freedom and individuality.

CHAPTER TWELVE

B ailey raced up her stairs at five minutes to eleven the next day. She had been so busy helping Dani with the morning chores and writing instructional notes, she had forgotten to leave enough time to get ready. She had been fretting about the lunch, trying to decide what her tactic should be when faced with these people who were making plans for *her* clinic. The passive approach obviously wasn't working. Instead of giving up and going away, the forces of change had kept going. Ken and Dani had barged into her life and her house, and the dean was having a meaningful relationship with her answering machine.

She had opted for the aggressive approach for today's lunch—to go on the offense and take charge of any decisions about her new annex. She had pictured herself dressed for the part, confident in her business suit and dangerous-looking spiky heels. Of course, aside from not leaving enough time to get ready, she had conveniently ignored the lack of such clothes in her closet. She pulled off her navy sweats and red-and-white baseball shirt and flipped through the hangers in her closet. She was still in her underwear when she heard Ken at the front door.

Leaving Dani to play host for a few minutes, Bailey put on a clean pair of khakis and the least wrinkly shirt she could find. Instead of the elegant hairdo she had imagined, she ran a brush through her hair and left it as it was. She paused in front of the mirror. She had wanted to look good for Ken, too. She felt put out because their lunch together had turned into a group meeting about her clinic, but she had no acceptable reason to blame Ken for her temporary misunderstanding. Still, she had wanted to make Ken wish they were eating alone.

Not going to happen. Bailey turned off the light and left the room. At least she was clean and, since she had let Dani handle the vulture this morning, she didn't reek. Small victories, but sometimes they were all her demanding schedule allowed. She came down the stairs and paused when she saw Ken.

All thoughts of dressing to impress were moot now. No one would even notice if Bailey was in the room once they caught sight of Ken, with her eyes made even brighter in contrast to the fitted navy dress shirt she wore. Bailey's breath hitched when she watched lines and movement play over Ken's features—usually so composed and unhindered by emotion—as she laughed at something Dani was saying. Ken glanced in Bailey's direction, and her laughter stopped as suddenly as if a curtain had dropped over her face.

Ken watched Bailey walk down the last of the stairs. A sleeveless pale green shirt showed the edges of her farmer's tan. Her shoulders were pale in contrast with the rest of her arms, and the deep scooped neck of the shirt revealed tantalizing glimpses of a suntanned V and the tender-looking white skin of her chest. Ken had always liked seeing women with all-over tans, carefully cultivated in sterile tanning beds, but the markings on Bailey's body were so much sexier. Ken could barely keep her breathing even. Bailey's tan lines had come from being physically active outside, and Ken's response was equally physical. She wanted to pin Bailey against the wall and lick every boundary between sun kissed and pale.

Dani cleared her throat. "So, um, I'm going to go check on some birds. You two have fun today."

"Call if you need anything," Bailey said as Dani walked out of the room. "We're not far away, and I won't be gone long."

Ken took her arm and led her out the front door, using Bailey's reluctance to leave without giving Dani a hundred last-minute warnings as an excuse to get her hands on her tempting skin. She kept her fingers lightly wrapped around Bailey's upper arm until they got to the car, enjoying the feel of warm, wind-roughened skin under her palm, and reluctantly let go when she opened the passenger door for Bailey.

"It's so clean," Bailey said when Ken got in the driver's seat next to her. She ran her hand over the shiny red dash and the polished knobs and dials on the white instrument panel.

Ken laughed at the sound of wonder in Bailey's voice. "That's because I don't routinely use my car as a bird transport. Just the one time."

"I can't see you carrying sea-water-soaked nets or dirty blankets in a car like this," Bailey said. "I suppose we have to be presentable when we arrive, but maybe we can have the top down on the way home? I like the feel of wind in my hair—it feels like I'm flying."

"Of course," Ken said with a smile. She usually met with protests and threats when she suggested lowering the top of her convertible. "I love the feeling, too."

Bailey's hands fidgeted restlessly in her lap as Ken drove toward the highway. Once she had merged onto 101, she reached over and clasped both of Bailey's hands in her own.

"Your birds will be okay," she said, giving Bailey's hands a squeeze. "Like you said, we won't be gone long."

"I know." Bailey pulled one hand free and patted her shirt pocket. "And I have my phone, just in case. I've been giving Dani more responsibility lately, so I feel more confident leaving her alone."

Ken laced her fingers through Bailey's. Why not? Bailey had only pulled one of her hands away from Ken's touch. "What caused the change of heart? You were so reluctant to have her here at first."

Bailey relaxed as much as she could with Ken's hand in hers, resting on her thigh. She had been nervous about meeting with Ken's boss and Vonda, but now her agitation had a different cause. She casually rubbed her thumb along the side of Ken's and was rewarded by Ken's audible intake of breath.

"I have a plan," she admitted. "I've been looking at the drawing you made, of the tree trunk house."

"And it inspired a plan?" Ken asked. "I knew I should have erased it when I had the chance. It wouldn't be a good design for your annex."

"No. It's beautiful, but that's not what I meant. There's a place I used to go, before I got so busy with the sanctuary. It's a meadow in the Olympic National Park."

"And you want me to build a house in there? Not allowed, darling," Ken said, keeping her eyes on the road as she took the exit for Highway 104. "Although I'm sure it would be a peaceful place to live."

Bailey hesitated for a moment, caught in the fantasy of living alone with her birds in the middle of the national park. Not precisely alone, since she saw Ken there, too. She shook her head, as much to dispel the image as to deny Ken's assumption. "I thought you might be able to design my flight cages to resemble the meadow. If you're interested, I wanted Dani to be able to manage the sanctuary while we went on a day hike."

Interested? Right now, with her hand resting on Bailey's soft thigh, Ken was interested in anything she might offer. Did she think it was wise to go on a long hike with her, deep in the woods? Not at all. "Sounds like fun," she said. "Although our landscape designer might be a better choice."

"No. I want you. I loved how you interpreted the tree trunk and came up with the design for the house. I think you can do the same with my meadow. Capture its essence, I suppose."

Ken got snagged on *I want you* and slowly caught up to the rest of Bailey's words. "You have more faith in me than is warranted, based on one little design, but I'll do my best."

Bailey smiled in relief. She had been hesitant about bringing up the trip, but somehow the confined quarters inside the little sports car gave her a sense of intimacy. Maybe too much intimacy. She stopped stroking Ken's hand with her thumb and searched for a new topic.

"What made you choose architecture as a career?"

"Maybe because I never had a real home of my own, I liked the idea of designing them for other people. And other creatures and mythological beings, when I was young." Ken moved both hands to the steering wheel as she drove across the Hood Canal Bridge. Bailey felt the strong winds buffeting the little car. "My dad worked in construction, so we went where the jobs were and usually lived in worker's cottages and rentals. He spent his life building homes, but never owning one of his own."

Bailey watched a seagull hover on an updraft alongside the bridge. The gray water was choppy underneath the bird, but smooth and calm on the other side of the floating bridge. She liked the idea of Ken finally designing and owning her own house, after years of living in borrowed places.

"My parents tried to stay close to Seattle during the school years, so I could stay with my friends and not have to change schools all the time," Ken continued. "But during the summer we'd move wherever the better paying jobs were. One year, he worked out here on the Peninsula. My mom was working a temp job in Port Angeles, so I got to hang out on the construction site. I used cast-off supplies to design and build my own houses in the woods, and I fell in love with architecture."

They drove off the bridge and continued toward Poulsbo, but Ken kept both hands on the wheel even though the winds were no longer a factor. "I hated leaving those houses behind, but I imagined fairies and woodland nymphs moving into them. Most of the designs I made when I was young had some sort of fantasy element to them."

"I'll bet you drew some amazing creations," Bailey said. She wondered how someone with Ken's talent and uniqueness had ended up drawing squares for a living. "I'd love to see some of them."

Ken shrugged. The gesture might appear noncommittal, but she meant for it to end the discussion. Her first experiences with architecture had been solo attempts, but once she had returned to school in the fall, tanned and cocky after a summer with little supervision, she and Steve had turned her newfound hobby into a serious pursuit. But she'd keep those later years to herself. As far as anyone else was concerned, the story of her discovery of architecture was confined to that long-ago summer. "I don't have many left," she lied. She had them, but she had learned not to show them. Most of the time—barring her meeting with Joe—she remembered the lesson.

"What about you? What drew you to birds?" she asked as she followed Bailey's directions and exited the highway near the Scandinavian town of Poulsbo. "Were you a Hitchcock fan when you were a child?"

"No. Turn left at the light," Bailey said. "When I was a little kid, we had acres of woods behind our house in Bremerton. I used to play out there and pretend I lived in the trees."

Ken had seen how Bailey had blended into the forest at Dungeness as if she belonged there. She could picture a tiny, pale version of her, with twigs and leaves in her thick auburn hair, roaming barefoot along pine-needle covered paths like a sprite.

"And then right, at the next intersection. It's the paved driveway at the end of this road, winding through the trees." Bailey hesitated as Ken made the turn and drove slowly down the residential street. "You know how the birds get so quiet when loud people are walking by, like they did at Dungeness when we passed those families?"

Ken glanced over at Bailey and nodded, but she knew Bailey didn't notice her. She was lost in the past for the moment.

"They got still like that when I'd walk into the woods, but if I'd stay real quiet, they'd start to sing again. They let me know I belonged there, that they accepted me as part of their world. It was a good feeling."

"There it is." Bailey pointed needlessly at the huge wooden structure as they emerged from the woods and onto the Selberts' property.

"Jesus," Ken said softly. She hadn't meant to break the spell woven by Bailey's story, but the mammoth house demanded attention.

"It's something, isn't it? I think the poor eagle was so damned shocked by what he saw that he flew smack into the window."

Ken laughed. She had seen a picture of the house in Joe's office, but she had been too intent on Bailey's ass in the eagle photo to have noticed more than its general shape. The house was designed like an A-frame, but the front jutted out toward Poulsbo's Liberty Bay. It looked like a massive Viking ship about to head to sea. A huge blue-and-white Norwegian flag decorated its bow.

Ken got out of the car and shook hands with Joe, who had come out to greet them. Bailey was on the other side of the car being crushed in a hug by what appeared to be a Valkyrie, but must have been Vonda Selbert. Ken wanted to go to Bailey's rescue, but Vonda let her go and turned her attention to Ken.

"So this is your hotshot architect, Joe, the one who's going to design Bailey's new aerie. We expect something spectacular from you, Kendall Pearson." Vonda shook Ken's hand. "She's a looker, isn't she, Bailey? No wonder you're blushing."

"Come in, come in," Vonda continued, heading toward her house with her arm draped across Joe's shoulder. "We'll let this genius give you the grand tour of the house he designed, and then we'll have lunch and hear all about Kendall's plans for the rehab center."

Bailey trailed behind with Ken, a bit overwhelmed as she always was in Vonda's presence. "I wasn't blushing," she said. "I was trying to catch my breath after that hug."

"No kidding." Ken waved her right hand limply in the air. "I think all my fingers are broken. I'll never draw again."

Bailey laughed at the joke, but she saw the same closed expression she had seen on Ken's face the day they moved the osprey to his new cage. There was a wistful tone in Ken's voice, almost as if she wanted her words to be true. Bailey turned her attention back to the house. She must be wrong. Someone with Ken's talent must treasure it, not want it to be gone.

Joe gave them a tour of the house—aided by Vonda's frequent comments—and Bailey watched Ken withdraw further and further from the group. Bailey had seen the house several times already, but she enjoyed getting Joe's perspective as the person who had designed it. The spacious house was too huge for Bailey, and she'd never have felt comfortable living in it, but it suited the Selberts perfectly. Hearing how Joe had interpreted their dreams and made them real gave Bailey a glimpse into the type of work she knew Ken must be doing for his company. She had seen Ken reinterpret nature with her tree trunk design, and she had witnessed Ken's playful side as she drew a castle for Bailey. She would have thought the Selberts' home would fascinate Ken like it did her, but Ken offered little more than a polite but restrained comment every time she was addressed.

Bailey went down the spiral staircase to the patio door, sliding her hand along the rough-grained surface of the wide banister as she walked. The house was as grandly tactile as it was visually impressive. She ducked under a row of spiral-cut plastic sun catchers—just a few of the many and multicolored objects dangling across the plate-glass front of the house—and joined the others on the patio. Her curiosity about Ken's reticence disappeared as soon as she sat down and Vonda changed the topic from her own house to the proposed annex at Bailey's center.

"So, Kendall, tell us about your plans for the new rehab center," Vonda said as she handed out plates laden with food.

Ken took a bite of a boiled potato stuffed with goat cheese and herbs. She wanted to put off answering for a few moments, desperately hoping she'd come up with a brilliant idea before she had to swallow the mouthful, but Vonda saved her by answering her own question.

"I'm picturing a large surgical theater with mirrors where the students can watch Bailey as she works on the birds. And a great hall with display cages so public tours can come through and see various raptors. And maybe a large classroom where she can hold summer programs for local high school students…"

Ken forgot to eat while she listened to Vonda design Bird City. She had been growing more and more desolate as she walked through Joe's masterpiece. The house was as it should be—everything to do with Vonda Selbert and nothing like the unassuming and quiet architect who had designed it. Grand and livable and a celebration of Vonda's Nordic heritage. Ken's doubts about her suitability as an Impetus architect had grown in proportion with the huge house she had just toured.

She toyed with her stuffed cabbage while Vonda's plans grew in scope. What could she say after this monologue? *Well,*

I had an idea for a building with four equal sides and a few walls. She took a bite of the meat-filled cabbage and tried to chew while she looked for an escape route. She could run to her car and drive away before it was her turn to talk. Joe and Vonda were nice people. They'd give Bailey a ride home.

Ken glanced over at Bailey. She had been quiet during the tour, watching Ken with a curious expression most of the time, but now she was staring at Vonda with her mouth open like a baby bird waiting to be fed. Ken had been caught up in her own worries about her job and her ability to design anything worthwhile, and she hadn't been thinking how Bailey might be reacting to this discussion. Bailey, who treasured her privacy and the welfare of her birds, and whose house was now being turned into an avian three-ring circus by the woman controlling the finances. Ken flew to her rescue without stopping to think it through.

"Those are great ideas, Vonda," she said, interrupting Vonda's suggestion that Bailey travel to local nursing homes and schools with a crate full of falcons. "While education and PR will certainly be part of the new center's mission, the main function of the annex will be as a sanctuary for wild birds. Bailey and I are working together on a design that incorporates ergonomic elements with integrated raptor-friendly materials and eco-sustainable surfaces."

"Oh, my," Vonda said. She looked impressed by the fabricated description, but Ken thought she saw Joe laughing into his napkin.

"The sauce on these cabbage rolls is delicious, Vonda," Ken said, changing the subject before Vonda could ask for more details about the phantom annex. "Do I taste juniper berries?"

"Yes, you do. A remarkable palate and a brilliant architect. Quite a catch, isn't she Bailey? I'll print a copy of my recipe for you, Kendall."

"What are eco-sustainable surfaces?" Bailey asked once Vonda had disappeared inside the house.

"She means dirt floors," Joe said, laughing out loud this time.

Bailey joined in their laughter, as relieved as Ken looked to have gotten past Vonda's wild plans. She had been ready to start protesting, to engage in battle for her home, but Ken had handled the situation much more smoothly and tactfully. Bailey should have realized Vonda's ideas weren't going to happen just because she stated them—they were mostly too expensive and too ridiculous to be implemented at her small sanctuary. Ken had told Bailey she was on her side, that they'd work together to make Bailey's vision of the annex a reality. Until now, Bailey hadn't fully believed that Ken's words were true. She had felt alone and helpless, fighting against change yet convinced she didn't have any real control over her own home anymore. Now she had an ally. For the first time since they had sat down, she felt as if she might be able to at least try some of the food on her plate. Vonda came back outside with a stack of recipes for Ken, and Bailey took a bite of her cabbage roll while the other three started a discussion about cooking. Ken hadn't been lying about the sauce, either.

CHAPTER THIRTEEN

Ken paid for two loaves of bread and a half-dozen sticky buns in the small Poulsbo bakery before she waded through the crowd and emerged onto the sunlit street. She stood for a moment, letting her eyes adjust to the bright light after standing in line inside for over ten minutes, and then she walked away from the main street and toward the alley where she had left Bailey with her car.

As promised, she had removed the white convertible top for the drive home. They had decided to stop at the bakery—although both had proclaimed to be too full to ever eat again after Vonda's lunch—and Ken had been about to put the top up again while they were away from the car. Bailey had seemed happy to stay with it as guard, and Ken had left her parked in a quiet alley, away from the busy streets and looking tempting, with her head tilted back to catch the sun and her auburn hair draped over the back of the red leather seat.

Ken felt an unaccustomed lightness. Once the stress of talking about the annex had been removed, both she and Bailey had been able to relax. Ken had enjoyed talking about her hobby with two other accomplished cooks, and she had discovered that she liked Joe as a person when she wasn't worried about him as her boss. The food had been amazing, and Vonda's eagle had even made a brief appearance when he flew by them with majestic, shallow wingbeats before disappearing into the woods behind the house.

Ken climbed a steep hill leading away from Poulsbo's waterfront. Best of all, she and Bailey had been able to be around each other for a short time without the design plans for the new clinic hanging over them. Bailey didn't have to fight for her privacy, and Ken didn't have to fight to keep her job. A brief truce, but a welcome one. Bailey was technically a client and, Ken reminded herself, not her type, but she was intriguing company nonetheless. Smart and fascinating, she was quick to notice details and pull them together into jokes or astute observations. She'd never be boring.

Ken turned into the alley and came to an abrupt halt. Bailey was out of the car, frowning as she talked to a tall blond guy. Did everyone in this town look like a Nordic demigod? Ken shifted her bakery bag into her left hand. Her legs felt as if they'd turned to steel, with no ability to bend or move, but she forced them to propel her forward out of sheer will. She felt her heartbeat quicken and her eyes scanned the area for a weapon. She didn't see anything useful, but she couldn't stop moving. She had to get to Bailey.

As if hearing her name in Ken's thoughts, Bailey turned toward her and her face brightened into an easy smile. She didn't appear to be scared or in danger, but Ken wasn't taking any chances. She'd beat the guy to death with sticky buns if she had to—anything to protect Bailey.

"She's the owner, so she'd be able to answer you," Bailey said to the Thor lookalike. "Hey, Ken, he was asking about your car, but aside from knowing it's a Corvette, I couldn't answer any…are you okay?"

"I'm fine," Ken said, feeling her tension ease slightly once she was able to position herself between Bailey and the stranger.

"Hi, I'm Todd," the kid said with an easy smile. He reached out his hand and Ken shook it, keeping her stance low so he couldn't pull her off balance.

"I'm Ken," she answered, her own voice sounding far away because of the rushing sound in her ears.

"Your car's a beauty. What've you got in her?" Todd was wearing an open denim jacket and he held the bottom edges against his body as he leaned over to check out the dashboard.

Ken exhaled a little more easily. A car guy. She did the same thing out of habit whenever she was near someone else's vehicle, keeping any loose clothing from touching the car and possibly damaging a paint job. "A three twenty-seven with a six-pack," she said. She reached behind him to pop the hood, still keeping herself between Bailey and any possible threat.

"Nice," he said, drawing out the word for several beats. "What's that give you, three hundred ponies?"

"Very good," Ken said. "You know your engines."

"My dad has a fifty-eight, but he kept it stock with the original two eighty-three. If I could afford one, I'd modify it like you did."

Bailey stood back and listened to the two speak in what might as well have been a foreign language for all she understood of it. Ken was saying something about Rochester carbs, but Bailey didn't think she meant pasta. She was mostly relieved to see Ken's expression losing some of its vigilante edge. Ken had approached them with a lethal look in her eyes, probably thinking Todd was going to touch her car, but he seemed respectful of it and Ken was looking more at ease.

Once they had finished their tour of the car's engine, Ken waited until Bailey was in the car before she climbed in and started the engine.

"Nice!" Todd said again, giving Ken a thumbs-up sign before he walked away from them. Ken drove slowly in the opposite direction, occasionally checking her rearview mirror until they were out of the alley.

"He seemed like a good kid," Bailey said as Ken accelerated onto the highway. "This car must attract plenty of attention wherever you go."

"Yeah," Ken said. "I kept it in a garage when I lived in Seattle. Didn't need to drive it much."

Bailey still didn't recognize Ken's voice. She spoke as if her teeth were clenched so tightly she had a hard time opening her mouth. Bailey had wanted to touch Ken since they had stopped holding hands on the way to Poulsbo, but she hadn't been able to come up with a reason. Reasons be damned now. Ken looked like she needed touch, and that was all Bailey needed to know. She twisted in her seat and rubbed her thumb along Ken's tense jawline.

"He didn't touch your car, even when you weren't there. I wouldn't have let him."

"What?" Ken turned her head to stare incredulously at Bailey before she looked back at the road. "That's not what...I didn't care about that."

"Then what's wrong?"

Ken veered sharply off the highway and onto one of the small residential roads intersecting it. She pulled to the side of the road and stopped the car. Bailey was away from danger, for the moment. The adrenaline dump hit Ken hard, and she felt as if she had no choice but to lean over and kiss Bailey. To make sure she was alive and safe. Ken twisted her fingers in Bailey's thick hair, keeping the pressure from her lips steady until she felt Bailey's surprised response ease. The gentle touch of Bailey's tongue against her mouth changed the kiss from one of desperation and reassurance to something softer and even more frightening.

Even as Ken opened her mouth and welcomed the rough feel of Bailey's tongue, her mind still reeled from the brush with danger. Bailey was okay…this time. But she was too quick to trust, too naïve to understand how dangerous life was. Todd had seemed like a nice guy who was interested in cars, but the next person to come along might not be so friendly. And Ken might not be there to protect her.

Ken reached under Bailey's shirt and pressed her palm against Bailey's chest. Yes, she felt Bailey's nipple stiffen under her touch, and yes, she wanted her mouth and teeth on it, but mainly she needed the comfort of a strong heartbeat in her hand. She pulled away from Bailey's lips and trailed kisses along those exposed tan lines on Bailey's neck and arms.

Ken had been able to protect Bailey twice today. Once when Vonda was taking control of her annex, and again when she had been alone with Todd. Neither had been a true test of Ken's ability to rescue her. The change of subject with Vonda was only a stopgap—Ken didn't have any real design ideas to back up her nonsense words. And Todd had been a nice kid looking at a car, not a real threat. Bailey's skin felt fragile, precious under Ken's mouth. She didn't trust that she'd be able to protect Bailey when it counted.

Bailey felt Ken pull away before her lips had lost contact with skin. She was prepared for the feeling of loss when Ken sat up in her seat and looked at Bailey with the closed expression she had come to recognize. She wasn't sure what had brought on Ken's surge of passion, but she recognized when it was over.

"I'm sorry." Ken reached over and grasped Bailey's hand for a moment, giving her a squeeze before letting go.

"Heatstroke?" Bailey asked with a forced smile. "Drunk on juniper berries?"

"Maybe both," Ken said with a smile that looked as unnatural as Bailey's felt. "You're beautiful, Bailey, and I've wanted to kiss you for a long time. But I shouldn't have…we work together…"

"You'll still work with me?" Bailey asked. "We can still hike to the meadow?"

"You still want me to go with you?" Ken stared at her with something Bailey recognized as a deep weariness.

"Of course," she said. She had expected Ken to leave her eventually, once the osprey was healed and the annex designed. A kiss along the way had been a pleasant bonus. "We don't need to cancel plans just because of a small…lapse in judgment."

"Then we'll go hiking," Ken said. Her face relaxed into an easier smile. "For the birds."

"For the birds," Bailey repeated.

CHAPTER FOURTEEN

Bailey stood on the edge of the bluff and stared at the water below. Far below. A well-used trail of roots and rocks showed where Ken must make her way from here to and from the beach below. Sand, sky, strait. Blending together in shades of grays and blues, as if all forms of matter were linked by the common factor of dampness. Bailey ran her fingers through her hair, loosening the wet tangles. No rain, but the swirling mist saturated her hair and clothes. She shivered and wrapped her arms around her middle, hugging the quilted flannel shirt closer to her body.

She turned her back to the sea and surveyed the acre of land. She easily pictured Ken standing here, as windblown and romantic as Heathcliff on his moors. The property wasn't the prettiest or most tamable Bailey had ever seen. It was rough and beautiful and wild. Private. Perfect for Ken.

Bailey sighed and started back toward her car. She had felt restless after her kiss with Ken. Aroused and hurt. She recognized the inevitable path they would take. Ken obviously shared her attraction but was prepared to fight it, and everything in Bailey agreed it was the prudent course of action. Ignore the kiss, the heat between them. They were too different, too set on other goals than each other. Their relationship would end once the annex was designed. Still, the lingering effects of Ken's touch and tongue would take a long time to disappear. Bailey had come to this piece of land because she needed to clear her head, get a handle on her emotions. Ken had dropped her off at her house a few hours earlier, refusing to come in and check on the osprey because she wanted to get back to her apartment, so Bailey had known the property would be vacant, a place for her to get away in private and sort through her fantasies and confusion. But if she'd really wanted to exorcise Ken from her thoughts, she shouldn't have chosen a place that reminded her of Ken in every rock and blade of grass.

And in the car parking behind her own. Damn. Ken. Bailey pushed away the small part of her mind that had been hoping to see her and concentrated on the negative side of her presence here. She was trespassing on private property. And worse, she was revealing her feelings too much. Showing Ken she had been affected by the kiss, that she had been seeking her out. Her only way out was to lie until her pants started to smolder.

Ken took her time getting out of her car. She'd recognized Bailey's beat-up Honda immediately, but even if she hadn't had the car as a clue, she'd have known the shape and movements of Bailey where she stood near the cliff. Her olive drab shirt combined with the slate colors of water and sky, blending everything but Bailey's auburn hair into a wash of neutrals. And even at a distance, Bailey's face—pale and wide-eyed—was a splash of life on the rough, empty land.

Ken had needed time to decompress after her scare in Poulsbo. She'd had the experience before, the fear of danger, the need to protect, but it had never been as strong and intense as it had been with Bailey. Ken had to get out here, where the wind and salt air would wash her clean, but she hadn't been expecting to see anyone else, let alone Bailey. What the hell was she doing here? How could Ken get her to leave?

She got her small cooler off the passenger seat and walked toward Bailey. They met in the middle of the acre.

"What are you—" Ken started to speak once they were within earshot.

"I was just—" Bailey spoke at the same time.

Ken motioned for Bailey to continue. "I was doing some grocery shopping in town," Bailey continued. "I thought I'd stop by and see if I could spot signs of an osprey nest. To see if your osprey had been settling here."

Ken had been prepared to be angry with Bailey for being here, mainly because now she'd never be able to look at the bluff without seeing Bailey's slender and tousled form standing near it, but the mention of her osprey made her indignation drop away.

"Did you find a nest? That'd be great, to have ospreys here every year. They do return to the same place to mate and have babies, don't they?" Ken scanned the treetops around the edge of her property. She'd looked for a nest, of course, but maybe Bailey's trained eye saw something she couldn't.

Bailey looked around as well. "Well, no, I don't—didn't see anything. Still, it seems like a lovely place to release him, when he's ready to go. I'm sorry I bothered you, but I thought you were going to be in Sequim. I'd never have come if—"

Ken waved off her apology. She'd wanted to be left alone, but Bailey was already here. She attributed her relief at having company—at having *Bailey* for company—to a residual weakness from the afternoon. She was too tired to fight.

"I was going to have a quick dinner here before it gets dark. Want to join me?"

"I really should be going." Bailey backed toward her car. "I've left Dani alone long enough today."

"Stay." Ken put her hand on Bailey's forearm, feeling a hint of warmth under the damp fabric. *Let her go.* Ken ignored her common sense. She really *had* been weakened by today's experience in the alley. Maybe it would help her to stay with Bailey for a short time. Reassure herself that no harm had come to her. "I just brought a sandwich, but I'm still too full from lunch today to eat all of it."

"Well, okay. For a few minutes." Bailey stepped away from Ken's touch but stayed just within reach.

Ken walked toward an empty chair sitting in the center of the property. She sat on the ground next to it before Bailey could protest. The dampness of the grass seeped through her jeans, only adding to the wetness she knew was already there because of Bailey's closeness. She opened the cooler and brought out a plastic container. This would be a good test of her discipline. Stay close to Bailey without touching or kissing her. Resist any attraction she might feel because it was too dangerous to care about someone who seemed as much a part of nature as she was of humanity.

"I'm surprised you left Dani alone again, after being away this afternoon." Once Bailey had sat down with seeming reluctance, Ken handed her half the sandwich.

"Me, too. I'm trying to give her more responsibilities, and I've discovered it's easier to do if I'm not around. I try to take over if I'm there."

Ken laughed at Bailey's confession, delivered with a shake of her head as if she were scolding herself. Self-aware and charming. Ken turned her attention to her food, a mammoth sandwich with wedges of avocado, medallions of crab, and tiny round capers. She loved the combination of shapes and the colors of pink and green embedded in the creamy white of aioli.

"I'm not sure how to eat this," Bailey said. She turned the roll around in her hands. "I don't think my mouth is big enough."

"I'm sure you'll do just fine," Ken said, trying to look anywhere but at Bailey's mouth. "Just squish it together." She watched Bailey comply. "So…" Ken searched around for a topic of conversation that would distract her from Bailey's mumbled sounds of approval as she chewed. "Does having Dani there remind you of when you were an intern?"

"Yum. Not really." Bailey licked a dab of aioli off her lip and Ken squeezed her sandwich so hard, a wedge of avocado fell on her lap. She picked it up and ate it as if she'd meant to do so. "I didn't get into wild bird rehab until I was out of vet school a couple of years. My first internship was with a large animal hospital in Ellensburg. I had romantic ideas of being James Herriot and delivering cows out in the field. Cow fields don't smell very good, in case you're wondering."

Ken laughed. The thought of Bailey doing anything so rough-and-tumble seemed funny to her. She was born to the delicate healing of wings. "So you didn't find your calling in the muck?"

"No. I spent the summer wrestling livestock and trying to clean manure stains out of my clothes. The next year, I decided to try small animal work, so I interned at a cat rescue place. Turned out to be a crazy woman who lived with tons of cats in her house. She had to have everything just so, and she didn't let me do anything but clean litter boxes."

Bailey saw Ken roll her eyes before filling her mouth with crab sandwich. "Hey," she said, kicking Ken lightly with the toe of her tennis shoe. "Don't make that face. My situation is completely different from hers."

"Of course it is," Ken said with an exaggerated nod. "After all, cats don't have wings."

"Ha-ha. Anyway, I *am* trying." Bailey picked a chunk of fresh crab meat off her sandwich and ate it. "I guess my internships helped me clarify my goals. I learned what I didn't want to do, and I focused instead on what I *did* want. I always assumed I'd get a regular job, so I could pay off my student loans and feed myself while doing rescue work on the side. Going into rehab full-time is insane, a constant struggle to get grants and donations just to stay alive. But I came out of those summers with a vision for my clinic, and I started it as soon as I could, a few years after graduating. Even though I don't like what's happening with Wazzu, it's a godsend as far as funding and money problems go. What about you? How was your intern experience?"

"No actual manure, but plenty of metaphorical shit," Ken said. She popped the last bite of sandwich in her mouth and wiped her hands on a napkin. "My first boss had a healthy ego—and believe me, plenty of architects have them, but he had them all beat. He made me carry around a notebook, and every few minutes he'd say, 'Be sure to write this down,' as if he was about to reveal some inspiring trade secret. It was all nonsense, though, and I have notebooks full of sentences like *This guy's an idiot* and *Does he really expect me to write down this crap?*"

Ken grinned at the sound of Bailey's laughter. She hadn't heard it often, but she was getting addicted to the sound. "He designed small-scale developments. Nothing innovative, just plain and cheap houses, but I did learn a lot about the practical side of architecture."

"And now you're with such an exciting firm," Bailey said. She took the napkin from Ken's hands and wiped her own with it. "Joe is so talented, and he seems like a great boss. I'm sure when he tells you to write something down, it's worth doing. I guess we both learned what direction *not* to take when we interned."

Ken busied herself by packing up her container and their trash. Bailey wasn't right, but Ken didn't want to correct her. She'd interviewed for several internships and had been offered opportunities at firms more like Impetus where she'd have been expected to be creative, to give input, to learn and explore.

But she'd taken the less interesting job, where her duties and requirements were predictable and where any sign of originality was considered an insult to her boss. *She'd* made the choice to be there, and then to continue the unsurprising trajectory in her own career.

Ken stood up when Bailey did. "I'm sorry to trespass on your property, but I enjoyed dinner and our talk," Bailey said. She raised her arm and lowered it again, and Ken wasn't sure if she'd been about to shake hands or to move in for a hug. Any contact would have been welcome but dangerous, and Ken was relieved when Bailey kept her distance.

"It was nice," she said casually, wrapping her suede jacket closer to ward off the chill she felt. Even a hint of contact with Bailey brought her a sense of warmth. Having it taken away— no matter how prudent and wise it seemed to avoid it—made Ken feel cold in its absence.

Bailey stepped back again. The urge to touch Ken, to repeat their kiss here, in this place where they were relaxed and friendly and isolated, was overwhelming. She needed to get back to her birds, to her privacy.

"Maybe remembering my own internships will help me with Dani," she said. She realized she'd actually made it through ten minutes without fretting about the potential disasters taking place in the clinic. "She seems to care about this work, and I don't want to discourage her from it, like I was by those other jobs."

"You're making a good start," Ken said. "Good night, Bailey."

"'Night." Bailey walked back to her car, leaving Ken alone in the falling dusk. She wanted to stay, but she had no more excuses, no more energy to resist the need to go back home and check on her patients. At least she had proved she could be close to Ken, chat casually with her, without needing to kiss her again. Well, at least without giving in to the need. She'd keep her turmoil over their physical connection buried inside until they finally said good-bye.

Ken could barely make out the reddish color of Bailey's hair in the deepening twilight. She waited until Bailey's car disappeared down the road before she turned and walked carefully to the bluff. She had come here needing to be alone, but she had been resigned to entertaining Bailey for a few minutes as if she were a guest at Ken's home. Time to herself would have helped to ease the tension she felt after being prepared to fight in the alley, at least enough for her to be able to sleep tonight. But talking to Bailey, sitting beside her, had managed to relax Ken more than her acre of privacy would have done.

Dangerous. They were different people, glaringly so, even based only on the stories they had told tonight. Bailey decided what she wanted and threw everything into it. Ken held everything back. Bailey had made her feel better tonight, had given her a peace and calm she hadn't expected to find. But the gift was a temporary one, and Ken couldn't let herself forget it.

CHAPTER FIFTEEN

"The osprey is a picky eater, so make certain the fish is fresh. If you have to buy more at the market, smell it first," Bailey said. She added the fish warning to her growing list of instructions. "And when you change the dressing on the vulture's foot—"

"Be sure to wear a raincoat," Ken suggested. She pulled the pen out of Bailey's hand and tossed it on the table. "Come *on*. If you write any more, Dani will have to spend the whole day reading and won't have time to take care of the birds."

"We'll be fine," Dani said as she dropped her backpack on the kitchen table. "I've handled every patient this week, and I have your cell number and Ken's and the contact numbers for every rehab center from here to Portland."

"Portland, Maine?" Ken asked. She had been surprised when Bailey had suggested the day-long hiking trip. She'd be shocked if she actually got Bailey out the front door and into the car.

"Just about."

"Very funny," Bailey said. She flipped through several pages of notes. "I don't think I missed anything...Okay, I'm ready to go."

"Really?" Ken and Dani said in unison. Ken was still waiting for the last-minute emergency that would keep them from going.

She was ambivalent about the trip—and the extended time spent in Bailey's company after their shared kiss—and she was certain Bailey had the same misgivings. Part of her wanted to get out and see more of the Peninsula's recreational areas. Bailey was an ideal hiking companion because she saw nuances and details Ken missed when she took in her surroundings with a wider view. Her tendency to see generalities made her uncomfortable at times with Bailey, but they should be safe enough on a day hike in a secluded and sheltered part of the Olympic National Park. She'd be the guest in Bailey's world, and there'd be no need to play the part of protector or guard. Ken put her conflicted emotions aside. She'd walk some trails, learn some more bird names and facts. She'd have a nice day away from Impetus and her tiny Sequim apartment.

"Let's go before I change my mind," Bailey said.

Ken knew she wasn't kidding. "Bye, Dani," she called over her shoulder as she herded Bailey out the door.

"Have fun. And can I drive your car while you're gone? In case I need to make a trip to the fish market?"

"Not a chance," Ken said. She opened the screen door for Bailey and followed her to the car. "I'm taking my keys with me."

Dani waved from the porch as they got in Bailey's Civic and drove away. Ken watched Bailey tapping nervously on the steering wheel. She'd give her ten miles before Bailey made some excuse and turned around. Ken twisted in her seat and looked at the pile of gear Bailey had brought. Ken only had a small rucksack with some granola bars and a change of clothes sitting at her feet.

"How much did you pack?" she asked.

"You need to be prepared for emergencies," Bailey said. Ken saw Bailey's cheeks flush slightly.

She laughed. "Don't tell me. You have all the supplies you'd need to treat some injured bird we might find in the woods, but if I get a cut or a broken leg, I'm out of luck."

Bailey looked a little sheepish, but she joined in Ken's laughter. "I have splints in case you break a leg, but they're only a couple inches long."

"Great. I'm going to be trekking through the woods carrying a mobile raptor hospital on my aching back."

Bailey sighed and relaxed her hands on the wheel. She *had* raided the shelves of her surgery this morning when she packed. She never knew when she'd come across a wounded bird. She thought she'd packed a small human first-aid kit, too, but she didn't want to make any promises to Ken. It might still be sitting on her bed.

"How's work?" she asked. Most conversations she had were about her birds or her clinic, but she felt a loosening in her shoulders with every mile she drove. She had given Dani more responsibilities this week, and she had performed every task with an unruffled calm—even when the redtail grabbed hold of her thumb in her sharp beak and refused to let go. As long as Bailey was on vacation, she might as well make the most of it. Talking about Ken's job ought to distract her from the disasters she imagined befalling Dani and the birds.

"Not bad," Ken said. "We do these crazy team-building activities at every staff meeting. Waste of time, but they're amusing, at least."

"What'd you do this week? The one where you close your eyes and fall backward, expecting the person behind you to catch you?"

"Dougie—my project manager—knows better," Ken said with a wicked grin. "I'd definitely let him fall."

Bailey shook her head at Ken's joke. She guessed it was more likely Ken would be running around trying to catch every person in the room.

"So what *was* this week's exercise?" she asked. She took the ramp leading to Highway 101 and accelerated onto the road.

"Some brainstorming thing," Ken said, looking out the side window. "We started with a problem we've been having with the layout of the house, and then we had to toss a ball around the room. Whoever caught it had to give a solution, no matter how impractical or funny, before they could throw the ball to someone else. Some of the ideas we came up with were hilarious."

Bailey glanced at Ken and noticed her quick frown. One of her spontaneous and brief—but honest—expressions. "Did you eventually come up with an answer?"

Ken thought back to the game. She had been in her usual annoyed but indulgent mood during the first part of the game. Sitting back and staying aloof during the touchy-feely portion of the meeting, embarrassed because the focal problem was hers. She had turned in her initial design the day before, and it hadn't been up to the standards expected by Dougie, Impetus, or the client. She had come up with something more inspired than a square, but not by much. When the ball came her way, she had grabbed it and said the first stupid thing that came to her mind. She had thrown the ball to Dougie, who took her off-the-wall suggestion and pulled a thread of a brainstorm out of it. Angela developed it one step further. Then the ball-tossing game got more serious as the entire team built a fucking brilliant solution out of thin air.

"We did. Sort of a roundabout way to get there, but I guess it worked."

Ken changed the subject by asking about Bailey's early experience as a rehabber. She knew it was a gamble to get Bailey talking about some of her first mistakes because they might give her fuel for her worries about Dani, but Ken hoped for the opposite effect. Maybe Bailey would remember how she had managed to improvise and handle problems. What started as a way to give Bailey confidence in Dani while getting them off the sticky subject of Impetus turned into a damned entertaining conversation. She had to prod Bailey into telling her stories, but once she got going, Ken laughed until she was out of breath. Bailey's self-deprecation and dry delivery made the stories of clawed arms and undignified chases hilarious. She had expected the two-hour drive to seem more like five, but the ride was more companionable and entertaining than she had expected.

Bailey turned off Highway 101 and wound through the Olympic National Park. The forest soon gave way to temperate rain forest, and Bailey parked her car in a small, nearly empty lot near a trailhead, just beyond the more crowded Hoh Rain Forest Visitor Center.

Bailey got out of the car and stretched her lower back before shouldering her heavy pack and adjusting its straps. They had a four-hour hike ahead of them, but the terrain wasn't challenging. She looked over at Ken, who was shoving her small rucksack into the larger one Bailey had brought for her. Ken looked to be in great shape, so she shouldn't have trouble with the trek. Ken leaned over to adjust the laces on her hiking boots. Yes, great shape. Bailey admired the shape of Ken's legs, the shape of her ass, the shape of her breasts in the snug navy T-shirt.

Bailey turned away and fidgeted with the zipper of her lightweight jacket. She hadn't realized how badly she had been in need of a vacation. A few hours away from the clinic, and she was almost giddy with freedom. And almost tempted to make a move on Ken and try for a repeat of their kiss. It had been too long since she'd been at a conference or seminar where she felt free to have one of her tidy out-of-town flings. All she had to do was get through the rest of the day without making a fool of herself. She'd remain focused on the part of the future under her control—the beautiful new flight cages Ken would design after seeing Bailey's meadow. They were the goal for today's hike, not relaxation or the enjoyment of Ken's company.

"Ready to go?" Ken asked.

"Sure am," Bailey said. She started off at a brisk walk while the trail was nearly flat and even. She needed to burn off some of her excess energy. The path wasn't wide enough to walk abreast, so she led the way, turning now and again to point out a plant or a bird she'd spotted.

Ken easily matched Bailey's quick pace. She was accustomed to doing most of her exercising indoors, in the spare room of her Sequim apartment now that she no longer had access to the fancy gym in Seattle, but she had spent enough hours on the beach, jogging over rock-strewn sand, so the walk through the rain forest wasn't taxing. And instead of staring at a computer screen or television, she had plenty of nature to see. Big leaf maples and hemlocks with moss-covered trunks, spiky ferns, and more types of mushrooms than she had realized existed. The air was heavy with moisture and the smell of decaying logs. The occasional song of a wren or the hoarse, descending cry of a redtail filled the silences as they walked.

Ken didn't mind the view Bailey provided, either. The enormous pack covered most of her torso, but long, jean-clad legs were visible for Ken's admiration. Bailey walked with a definite spring in her step, clearly in her element deep in the forest with no other people around.

The moss seemed to dampen every sound, from the footfalls of their heavy hiking boots to their voices when they spoke. The hushed world and the feeling of being two tiny beings surrounded by huge, ancient trees made Ken realize how much her life had changed in just a few weeks. From downtown Seattle to Sequim to the site for her new home to the depths of the rain forest, Ken had been moving toward a quieter life. A different life. Bailey seemed more comfortable out here, where it was harder to fit in with the crowds because there were no crowds. Everyone stood out, everyone was an individual. Would she ever belong to this world as Bailey did?

Bailey skipped across the forest path whenever she saw a salmonberry bush, while Ken looked at her watch and tried to keep them on schedule. For some reason, the more dimensional and unrestrained Bailey got, the more Ken could feel herself closing in. Shrinking away from the brightness of Bailey, because anyone so unique and magnetic and fascinating was bound to draw attention. Even as Ken admired Bailey for being so free, even as she found herself more attracted and enthralled by this new Bailey, Ken realized how different they were. She cringed at the thought of being noticed. Bailey simply didn't care who noticed.

They crossed the Bogachiel River using a narrow wooden bridge, and then Bailey took a barely visible trail that branched off the one they'd been following. They started to climb, and the rapidly increasing elevation made even Ken feel her breath coming in shorter gasps. She stopped feeling so smug about the time she had spent on the treadmill and the beach because walking up a rough forest trail with a heavy pack was proving to be a more effective form of exercise. She was relieved when Bailey stopped to pick yet more salmonberries so she could lean against a mossy tree trunk and catch her breath.

"Almost there," Bailey said cheerily. She held up a big bag of salmonberries, their yellow and coral colors shining jewel-like through the plastic. "We can eat some of these for dessert after lunch."

The mention of food was enough to give Ken her second wind, and she pushed forward with more enthusiasm. Forty-five minutes later, Bailey led her off the trail and through some thick bushes. Ken was paying attention to swatting at bugs and pushing the scratchy branches away from her bare legs, and she didn't realize Bailey had stopped until she bumped into her.

"Oh," Ken said, looking around the small clearing and realizing at once why Bailey had wanted her to see this place. A stream meandered through one corner of the meadow and lacy purple, yellow, and white wildflowers dotted the grass. Several trees joined to make a lattice of branches overhead, and the brushy undergrowth was shelter for what sounded like hundreds of twittering birds.

Ken dropped her backpack to the ground and scrambled to get out her notepad and pencil. After weeks of worrying about her position at Impetus and her ability to design an annex Bailey would appreciate, she felt surprisingly confident about creating flight cages based on this spot. Ken might not trust her own talent or her desire, but she had no trouble agreeing to this task. All she had to do was copy nature. Adjust the dimensions, but keep the general proportions of plants and trees and light. It would be an easy exercise, and the area was stunning enough to inspire even the laziest of muses. "You're right," she said, already picturing an octagon-shaped structure in her mind. "This would make a perfect flight cage."

Bailey lugged the two packs over to the base of the trees. She watched Ken wander through the clearing, apparently looking for the right viewpoint before she started to draw. "Isn't it gorgeous? I wish I could have a stream in the cages. It's a more natural way for them to drink."

"I'll bet Randy could design some sort of self-filtering system. You'd need to have a way to keep the water fresh and clean."

Ken sat on a rock and started to draw, and Bailey left her to it. The hike had left her warm and sweaty, so she ducked behind some elderberry bushes and changed into shorts and a tank top. She heard the drone of a hummingbird and the raucous cry of a pileated woodpecker, but she couldn't see either one. She felt relieved that she hadn't chickened out at the last minute and refused to leave her clinic. The thought of having Ken recreate this lovely place in her own backyard—for her birds—made the effort of teaching and trusting Dani worthwhile. Bailey hummed quietly as she set up a makeshift kitchen and got a fire going in her small camp stove. By the time Ken finished sketching the area from several different angles, Bailey had their lunch almost ready.

"Hungry?" she asked when Ken sat down by the stove and set her notepad aside.

"Starving. It's been hours since breakfast."

"How about some Thai food?"

Ken sighed as she stretched out her feet. Bailey had switched from jeans to shorts at some point while Ken had been drawing. All her bird chasing had definitely paid off, if her slim but well-defined legs were any indication. Ken needed to concentrate on her own hungry stomach rather than the scanty parts of Bailey's anatomy still covered by clothing. "Yum. I love Thai food," she said, impressed by Bailey's camping skills. A fire and a gourmet meal. All in less than an hour. She watched Bailey pour a packet of ramen noodles into a saucepan of water. She might have to revise her definition of gourmet.

"Is that *ketchup*?" she asked when Bailey squeezed the contents of a small white packet into a bowl.

"No, of course not. It's hot sauce. And this one is peanut butter." She added the seasoning packet and the cooked ramen noodles, stirring the whole mess together before she handed it to Ken with a plastic fork.

"This is *not* Thai food," Ken said, sniffing the contents of her bowl before she took a hesitant bite.

"Noodles in spicy peanut sauce? Sounds Thai to me," Bailey said. She picked up a forkful of noodles and blew on it before putting it in her mouth.

"Sounds like dorm room food to me," Ken said. "But it's not bad."

They ate in silence, except for Bailey's random interjection of a bird species when one caught her attention. After they finished, Bailey got up to prepare dessert, and Ken noticed the jagged scar on her right shin. She reached out and grazed the whitish skin with her index finger when Bailey came close. Bailey didn't move away from her touch, so Ken rested her hand over the old wound. The scar was puckered and rough, but the surrounding skin was smooth under Ken's palm.

Bailey handed her a bowl filled with chunks of freeze-dried ice cream and salmonberries before she went back to her seat on the far side of the stove.

"What happened?" Ken asked.

"When I was five, I found a nestling hawk on the ground in the woods behind our house. I climbed the tree and put it back in its nest, but I fell and fractured my tibia."

The story wasn't unusual. What kid hadn't fallen out of a tree at some point during childhood? But despite the commonplace event and Bailey's dispassionate voice while recounting it, Ken felt something more powerful stirring behind the memory. Bailey and her birds. The relationship between Bailey and her obsession was a complex one.

"Must have been a serious break," Ken said. She decided to circle around the topic until she got Bailey to talk. Or maybe she should accept Bailey's abbreviated version and change the subject. Why dig into stories people didn't want to tell? She and Bailey didn't need more depth in their temporary relationship.

"Yeah," Bailey said. She picked up a cube of ice cream and ate it, licking her fingers. "I remember seeing the bone sticking out of my leg. I was horrified."

"Your parents must have been out of their minds with worry," Ken said. She was staring at Bailey's tongue as it slid over her fingers, and she almost missed seeing Bailey wince as if Ken's words were physically painful to hear.

"Yes. They were upset."

"Were you close to them?" Ken pushed harder. Bailey wasn't good at hiding her emotions on a normal day, and the intensity of her feelings was displayed clearly in the creases on her forehead and along the edges of her frowning mouth.

Bailey shook her head. "We...none of us were what I'd call *close*. Have you heard about those experiments where scientists stick a bunch of rats in a small cage, and the rats start to consume each other? My family was like that. They didn't need the crowds, though. Just put them in the same room, and the fights would start."

Bailey put down her dessert bowl and Ken saw it was still half-full of the salmonberries Bailey had been so excited about collecting on their way through the forest.

"When my parents finally split, the divorce was about as messy as one can get. They fought for custody, each accusing the other of abuse. I was in foster care on and off for a few months, and my parents had supervised visits with me that were little more than ranting sessions about whatever parent wasn't there."

Ken felt her back stiffen with anger. If she'd been a dog, the hair along her spine would be standing on end. How dare any parent treat a child that way, let alone a sensitive and unshielded one like Bailey. "Had they ever...were the allegations true?"

Bailey held her hand out in a calming gesture. "No. They never paid much attention to me unless they were using me as a weapon against the other. They never hurt me."

Physically. Ken knew precisely how much damage emotional abuse and bullying could do. She wanted to get revenge, to lash out, but instead she got up and walked over to Bailey. She sat close, not touching, and waited for the rest of the story.

"They were divorced with joint custody when I fell out of the tree. I remember lying on the couch, crying because no one would let me go back to the woods so I could check on the baby bird. My parents were in the next room arguing over which one had to take care of me. Mom had a new boyfriend and Dad was busy with work. I didn't help by being nearly hysterical because of the nestling."

Ken laced the fingers of her shaking hand with Bailey's. "Don't even consider blaming yourself for any part of what happened. You acted out of compassion. You were just a child."

Bailey curled against Ken, resting her head on Ken's shoulder. Her right hand settled below Ken's collarbone and she felt the strong, angry beat of Ken's heart. A grounding friend, the expanse of sky above her. She fought her way back to the present and out of the hurtful and confusing past.

She felt Ken's fingers twisting in her ponytail. "Is that the reason you've devoted your life to rescuing birds?"

Bailey shrugged. She had often wondered the same thing. "It's part of the reason, at least. I think I was born to do what I do. It's hard sometimes because I rarely know what happens after a release, just like I never found out about the baby bird. You just let go and hope."

Bailey pulled out of Ken's arms and sat up, refastening her mussed ponytail. She cast about for a new subject when all she wanted to do was drape herself against Ken's side again. Her hand still pulsed with the memory of Ken's heartbeat, and she wished she hadn't had the barrier of Ken's shirt between her hand and Ken's skin.

"Will you show me your tattoos?" she asked, bending her knees and hugging them to her chest.

"How did you know I had any?" Ken asked. She looked vulnerable, as if she had been experiencing the rejection and pain Bailey described.

"When we were working on the osprey, I could see down your shirt," she said.

"You were staring down my shirt," Ken repeated.

"Not staring. Only the briefest of glances. Will you show me?"

Ken hesitated. No wonder Bailey approached strangers with wariness. Her parents, the people she should have trusted without question, had rejected her. Ken couldn't do the same now, but she wished Bailey had asked for something, anything else. A hug. Sex. Something far less personal than the tattoos.

She grasped the hem of her T-shirt and pulled it off so she was wearing only a sports bra. No one got this close to her, not even girlfriends. She either kept the room in total darkness or wore a tank top during sex, and Ginny and her predecessors had accepted her insistence on those rules. But the image of Bailey with her leg in a cast, crying over the fate of some bird while her parents fought, broke Ken's resolve to never share her body in this way.

Bailey rose onto her knees and traced the outline of the dragon arching from Ken's rib cage and over her left breast. Bailey's fingers shifted her bra out of the way, and Ken was shocked to feel desire stirring at Bailey's touch. She had been aroused by Bailey before, every time there had been physical contact between them and during their kiss—hell, every time she had looked at Bailey, or thought of her—but she hadn't expected her body to react when her emotions felt so completely bare. She dragged her fingers through the dirt at her side, making deep gouges in the earth and erasing them with her palm, as Bailey's attention turned to the half eagle, half lion on her belly.

"What kind of creature is this?" Bailey asked as she circled Ken's navel with her fingernail, following the curve of the beast's talons.

"A griffin." She shifted on the ground so she had her back to Bailey. "And this one's a chimera."

Even though she couldn't see it, Ken had every line of the tattoo etched in her mind, and she was able to track Bailey's tactile but feather-light examination of the mythological creature. When Bailey had reached the end of the serpent's tail, Ken pulled her T-shirt over her head and turned around again.

"You have a beautiful body," Bailey said with a slight catch in her voice. She cleared her throat and looked away. "The artwork is stunning. Is it yours?"

Ken stared at her hand. It was caked with dirt from digging in the earth, and she rubbed at the marks. "No. Steve, a friend from school, drew them. We both loved mythology, and we created cities together. I'd design the buildings, and he'd draw the gods and creatures that lived in them."

"Oh," Bailey said, her voice barely audible. "He's very talented."

The memory of Steve's drawings as they wafted through the air to lie scattered on the pavement remained frozen in her mind, like a still photo of a shaken snow globe. "He was."

Ken got up and started to shove her drawing materials into the large backpack. Bailey watched her in silence for a moment before she stood.

"I guess we should start back," Bailey said as she dismantled the camp stove. "We'll have plenty of daylight for the hike back to the car."

Ken hoisted the heavy pack and buckled the straps around her waist and chest. Bailey had been respectful, not asking more questions about Steve when Ken made it clear she had difficulty talking about him. But as they walked along the path, away from the private sanctuary Bailey had shared with her, Ken felt the burden of her memories more acutely than the weight of her pack. Bailey had seen Steve's creations. She should know his story, as well.

She started talking in a quiet voice, unsure if Bailey could even hear her since she didn't turn around or say a word. Ken kept her gaze on the path directly in front of her feet.

"I met Dougie and Steve in grade school. I was new, and they were nice to me from the start. I had more in common with them than with most of the girls. We liked science, math, robots, rockets. Dougie was into sci-fi and astronomy, and Steve and I were almost as obsessed with mythology as you are with birds. We were inseparable all through grade school and into junior high. That's when everything changed."

Ken followed her around a large boulder blocking most of the path. Bailey shifted her pack and Ken could see her profile and her downcast eyes. Ken reached out to straighten Bailey's heavy backpack while Bailey tightened her straps. Once they were on the move again, Ken resumed her story.

"Hanging out with boys wasn't a big deal until kids started separating by sex. All of a sudden, I was something strange because of my interests. One year it was fine for me to be interested in dragons and rockets, the next I was treated like an alien because I wasn't into girly things. Dougie and Steve were targets, too. They were teased because they were friends with the weird girl."

Teased. Such a harmless-sounding word. Inadequate. She paused, and Bailey spoke for the first time since they had left the meadow.

"I get that the other kids changed their minds about what was socially acceptable," Bailey said. "But what made *you* change?"

Ken cringed inside. Bailey had captured her childhood hell in one question. She had scoffed at the other kids at first. Laughed with her friends about the girls who'd troll the malls for clothes and shoes and guys. And the boys who strutted around in their half-man states. Both so weak compared to the strength

Ken felt in her mind and in her heart when she was in her own make-believe world.

"Steve was an amazing artist. I could make outlines of the creatures I saw in my imagination, but he gave them expressions. He made them real." Ken rubbed a hand over her chest, feeling the prick of the tattoo gun instead of her fingers. "One day, a group of popular kids caught Steve with a notebook full of his pictures. I remember standing there, frozen while they ripped them out, one by one, and threw them around the schoolyard. Steve tried to stop them…"

Bailey wanted to stop when she heard the tremor in Ken's voice, to turn around and hold Ken while she talked, but she kept walking, step after step, as the story unfolded. Bailey felt as frozen as Ken had been as she listened to the pain in Ken's voice and was helpless to ease it.

"They beat him up pretty bad," Ken continued. She seemed to have control of her voice again. "He was lying on the ground, bleeding and trying to fight back but just too weak to stop them. And I stood there the whole damned time. I couldn't move. That's when I realized how stupid our games were. We thought we were so brave and strong, but we were nothing. When it really mattered, I did *nothing*."

She was silent for a long time. Bailey waited for a few minutes before she interrupted the stillness with another question.

"What happened to him?"

"They made his life a living hell after that. Waited for him after school, jumped him every chance they got. He made it through a few months, but everything was different. He had always been quiet, but he withdrew completely. He was silent. With me and Dougie, in class, everywhere. He stopped talking, and then…"

"What?" Bailey asked, her voice barely above a whisper. She couldn't resist the flicker of hope. Maybe she was wrong about the end of the story…

"He shot himself. With his uncle's gun. He must have been planning it for weeks because he left notes for all of us, apologizing for what he'd done. *He* apologized."

Bailey heard the rage and disbelief in Ken's last statement, and she knew Ken's anger was directed at herself.

"What happened to you after he was gone?" Bailey asked the question, but she knew the answer. She might not have all the details, but she knew what Ken had done after the incident. She had closed down, protected herself. Tried to live up to her ideal and protect everyone around her. Bailey wondered if Ken had really been concerned about her car in Poulsbo, like she had originally thought, or if Ken had been trying to protect *her* from danger.

"Those kids started doing daily inspections of my book bag and locker. The first time they did, they found drawings of castles Steve and I had designed. After that, I got rid of everything they might use against me. I stopped hanging out with Dougie and the others and started working out instead." Her voice was dispassionate, as if giving up all her interests and friends meant nothing. "I got strong enough to take care of myself. To stop even the biggest of the bullies the next time he tried to hurt someone who was weak and different."

Bailey's hands gripped the straps of her backpack. Ken had erased any sign of her own individuality, but she fought for the rights of others to be unique and original. Poor Ken would have had a full-time job protecting Bailey if they'd been in the same school.

"And Dougie?"

Ken hadn't been powerless the day the same bully tried to hurt Dougie. She had stepped in, finally able to take action and fight back. And then she'd walked away from Dougie and everything he represented from her past. Walked away from his invitations to come back into their circle and to rejoin their games.

"We work together now, temporarily. He got me the job at Impetus, and I had no choice but to take it. But as soon as I can, I'll get out. I don't want anything in my life to remind me of my past."

Except the tattoos cutting across her chest and stomach. Bailey turned her full attention to the trail when Ken stopped talking. She and her raptor center would always be linked to Impetus in Ken's mind. And Impetus was inextricably linked to Dougie. Bailey would be one of the ties Ken cut. Bailey hadn't expected anything different, hadn't thought her relationship with Ken meant anything beyond a mere work project, so why did Ken's vehement pronouncement leave her as gaping and raw as if the severing of ties had already begun?

❖

Bailey eased the pack off her back and pulled back the strap of her tank top. She already saw dark bruises where the unbalanced weight of the backpack had dug into her flesh. She hadn't wanted to stop and adjust the contents while Ken had been talking, and after the conversation had ended, Bailey had wanted to get out of the forest without delay. She had hoped the long hike would wear away some of the emotional residue from her and Ken's confessions, but instead she had grown more upset with every step.

She threw her backpack into the car. Physical exertion was no match for the impotent anger seething through her. It was aimed in too many directions for her to feel any control. Her parents, Ken's bullies, Dougie, Ken. Every kid who had teased and ridiculed Bailey, every bird she had lost. Even Steve, for throwing away a talent she could barely comprehend and for the scars he'd left on Ken's psyche. Bailey clenched her fists. She was heading toward a meltdown, and she had no way to stop it.

"Oh no. Your shoulder is bruised," Ken said. She shoved her pack onto the backseat next to Bailey's and came close, massaging the area with gentle pressure. "You should have told me. I'd have carried some of your supplies for you."

"Stop trying to rescue everyone," Bailey snapped at her. She rubbed her temple. She had a headache.

Ken frowned at the sharp edge in Bailey's voice. "I would have lightened your pack a little. Hardly worthy of knighthood."

"Well, I can take care of myself. I don't need your help."

Ken looked behind her at the trailhead. She seemed to have missed part of the conversation with Bailey. They were fighting, but Ken had no idea when it had started. After talking about Steve, they had been silent except for the occasional comment about the footing or low-hanging tree branches.

"Suit yourself," Ken said. Bailey's intensity was contagious, and she felt her own anger stirring. "You're the one with the bruises. We could have fixed your pack, but apparently you wanted to be a martyr."

"Me?" Bailey asked, with disbelief evident in her tone. "You're the one wearing a shrine on your body. Those tattoos of yours are gorgeous, and they could be an amazing way to honor your friend and the sense of wonder you shared. But instead, you've turned yourself into a monument to *his* talent. You stopped living your own life the moment he stopped living his."

Ken stood perfectly still. She processed Bailey's words and waited, with a sense of detachment, for her body's reaction. Would she slap Bailey? Walk away? Cry? Nothing. Not even a cold rage.

"I'm living my life," Ken said. "You're the one stuck in a cage, afraid to take a chance on anyone or anything besides your birds." Ken held her hand out for the keys. "You look like you have a headache," she said calmly. "I'll drive us home."

Bailey seemed deflated after her outburst. She tried to apologize, but Ken shrugged it off and started the car. Bailey was silent for a long time, and when Ken finally glanced over at her, she saw Bailey was asleep, her cheeks marked with trail dust and tearstains.

Ken was relieved to have peace while she drove back to Sequim. She was amazed by her self-control and her lack of anger, but she waited for the numbness to wear off and fury to take its place.

It wasn't until Ken, sore from the hike and bruised deep inside, had driven over halfway home that she finally realized why she had reacted with indifference to Bailey's harsh words. She knew they were true.

CHAPTER SIXTEEN

Bailey woke the next morning with the lingering effects of a migraine blurring her vision and pounding behind her right eye. She eased out of bed, as woozy as if she'd had a fifth of vodka the night before, and squinted in the sunlight seeping around her bedroom curtains. The drive home from the rain forest was a hazy memory, and she had no recollection of getting undressed and under the covers. What she *did* recall, with almost obscene clarity, were the words she had hurled at Ken after their hike. She had crossed a line as deep as the geologic faults buried under her state. What she said had been true, but she had had no right to criticize the way Ken chose to honor her friend.

She stumbled down the hall on autopilot. Her birds needed to be fed even if she felt nauseated at the thought of making any kind of food, human or avian. Maybe she'd repay the vulture by vomiting on *him* this time.

Bailey saw a pile of blankets on her couch, and when she went into the kitchen she found Dani at the counter fileting a fish and humming along with whatever was playing on her iPod. Bailey stood in the doorway, at once repelled by the briny smell and grateful Dani had stayed. She stepped into the kitchen and tapped Dani on the shoulder.

"Good morning, Dr. Chase," Dani said in a hushed voice. "How's the headache?"

"Long way from the heart. I'll survive," Bailey answered with Sue's favorite saying. "Did you spend the night?"

"Yes. I hope you don't mind. Ken was worried about leaving you alone. She would have stayed, but I did instead so I could feed this morning."

"Of course I don't mind," Bailey said, somewhat surprised to realize it was true. For once, she was relieved to have help, and she sat at the table while Dani finished preparing the tray of breakfasts. She had figured Ken would be far too angry to care whether or not Bailey made it through the night, but she appreciated her token offer to stay, anyway.

Bailey trailed after Dani and watched her feed. The sight of all her patients tucked safely in their cages and eager to eat went a long way toward easing the remnants of yesterday's headache, but once the physical symptoms had vanished, she was left with guilt and sorrow over her behavior. She knew only one way to rid herself of the unpleasant emotions—to take the focus off herself and turn it on her birds.

"I want to catch up the redtail again today," she told Dani while they washed dishes together. "Her wing seems a bit stiff, and I want to check it. She might need a few sessions of physical therapy."

"Great," Dani said with an exaggerated moan. "I'm barely healed from the last time we caught her."

"I'll have the first-aid kit handy, just in case," Bailey said. She went into her surgery to gather the supplies she'd need. Dani leaned in the doorway with a frown on her face.

"Something on your mind?" Bailey asked as she sorted through a tray full of hoods. She found the right size for the hawk and added it to the pile on the examination table.

"Well, yes. I don't want to overstep, but I've been thinking of the nets we use for catching the birds, and it seems it'd be safer to use wider ones. Less chance of snagging a wing or foot with the rim of the net."

Bailey pulled a pair of gloves out of a drawer. "True, but the wider the net, the more unwieldy it is."

"Not if you use a shorter pole."

"True, again," Bailey said. "But then you have to get closer before you can use the net, and that's more stressful for the bird."

"I've come up with an idea I think might work," Dani said as they walked across the yard to the flight cages. The redtail flew up to the far corner of the cage, as if reading their intent. Dani went into the supply shed and came out with two poles. One was short, with a wide net on the end. The other was longer, with a wedge-shaped padded sheet of plastic.

"See, we can use this longer pole to corner the bird against the mesh wall of the cage, and then step forward and catch it in the net. I added a lever to the long pole, so the plastic can move any direction we need." She clicked a lever on the handle, and the plastic sheet moved between a vertical and horizontal position.

"Interesting." Bailey heard the hesitation in her own voice. Change. She was still so determined to resist it. "Have you tried it?"

"No, of course not. Not without your permission."

Bailey exhaled a sigh of relief. Dani wasn't trying to take over or push Bailey aside. She was trying to add something to Bailey's program, not take anything away from Bailey herself. Bailey let go of her need to dismiss Dani's idea, or to take over and try it herself. "Thank you. So, do you want to try it now?"

She stood between the cage's double doors and watched as Dani angled the plastic sheet and gently moved the redtail toward an open space in the cage, where she wouldn't be able to duck under branches and avoid capture. The light plastic sheet seemed easy to maneuver, and once Dani had the hawk in a clear spot, she stepped toward her and easily contained her with the large net. Bailey was inside and securing the hawk's wings the moment the net dropped.

"Well done, Dani," she said. "I'd like to try it myself sometime, but I believe you've come up with a more efficient method than I was using. Great work."

Bailey kept her voice positive and casual, but she felt shaken by what she had seen. She'd been consumed by the pain of her headache and the memory of the hurtful words she'd flung at Ken. Now some of Ken's words to *her* were floating through her mind. She went through some wing manipulations with the captured hawk, letting Dani try them after she demonstrated each one, but her mind was stuck on the catch up. The modification to Bailey's usual method was slight, but Dani's system was safer and less distressing for the birds. Bailey didn't care whose idea it was, but she was disturbed by how close she had come to missing out on it. If she had gotten her way and Dani had been fired, if she'd remained as unwilling to take a chance on anything new as Ken had accused her of being, she'd never have learned a new way of helping the raptors. How many more advancements would come in the future as new interns and students spent time here, watching her ways and improving on them?

Bailey had been one pair of eyes, looking at her patients and slowly figuring out how to manage them. She had fought the university's presence because it interfered with her solitude, always trying to convince herself she was doing what was best for her raptors. But she had been doing what she thought best for *her*. Now, as she and Dani practiced in the yard with the two-pole system, laughing and taking turns pretending to be the bird, Bailey started to realize Ken was right. She had built a cage around herself, heavily guarded and unyielding. She had thought it was what she wanted, to keep people from intruding on her life because she didn't need companionship. But instead she had only been protecting herself against people who would come into her life, make her care about them, and leave her again.

Bailey's defenses hadn't been strong enough to protect her from Ken. She had broken into Bailey's life and changed her. Made her want something deeper and more lasting. Bailey had chased Ken away, and it was too late to keep her heart from breaking. But she had learned her lesson in time to help her birds. She'd let the university students, with their fresh perspectives and new ideas, into her center, into the new annex Ken was designing for her. She had kept her sanctuary closed and private, concealed like Ken's tattoos, almost at the expense of her birds. And she'd done the same thing with her heart, pulling back and pushing Ken away when she got too close. Was she too late to open the cage around her heart so Ken could enter? Would she even want to, after Bailey had defensively pushed her away?

Bailey locked the shed door and walked back to the house with Dani. For the first time in months, she felt hopeful about the direction in which she and her center were heading. But her personal life seemed far less promising. Because as much as Bailey had been determined to keep her distance and independence, Ken seemed even more inclined to be alone, not needing—or needed by—anyone.

CHAPTER SEVENTEEN

K en sat in a khaki-colored folding chair with her feet propped on a boulder and an open sketch pad on her lap. An occasional breeze off the strait rustled the heavyweight paper, and Ken used her palm to keep her place. She had a stick of black chalk in her other hand, but nothing in her head to draw.

She'd already designed the flight cages. She'd come home after the hike to the meadow, worried about Bailey's painful expression and chilled by the harsh words hanging between them, and she'd finished the sketches in one sitting. She'd sat up for hours after, sweating and exhausted following the cathartic effort, and fought to keep from returning to Bailey's house. If she'd had a clear reason to do so, she might have gone. To finish their fight? To finish what they'd started in the meadow, when Bailey's hands had stirred her arousal and her memories? She hadn't known why she wanted to go, so she'd stayed home.

The flight cages would be worth the pain of the hike. Even in her emotionally chaotic state, Ken could see their beauty and practicality. They mimicked Bailey's meadow, but they were suited to birds in transition. A taste of freedom, within the safe confines of soft mesh. Ken could picture Bailey in them. Watching her birds, tending to their healing wounds, catching them one last time before their release into the wild. She wanted to actually *see* Bailey in them, or at least to see her face when she studied the designs for the first time, but Ken needed to keep her distance. She'd handed them over to Randy, and he'd added his own landscaping elements before delivering them to Bailey. Now all Ken had to do was design the new annex, and she'd be finished with what had become so much more than a simple work assignment.

The annex. She needed to finish her design and move forward. Get out of Bailey's life and go back to living her own. She drew a square on the page and smiled at the memory of Bailey's expression of disgust when Ken had shown her the first design attempt. She looked at the four-sided shape. A cage. Thinking inside the box. Neither interpretation fit Bailey or her center.

She was still reeling from Bailey's words after their hike last week. She had called Bailey a martyr, and Bailey had thrown the word back at her. Ken had no argument against the accusation. She covered her tattoos and her memories—both of Steve and of the open and creative spirit she used to have—keeping them caged and static like a grounded bird. The possibilities of life had seemed endless when she was young, both in the world of the senses and of the imagination. Limitless thoughts, needing no basis in reality, were brought to life with paper and pen. Somewhere along the way, Ken had stopped seeing with her mind and had focused on what was visible on the surface. Clothes, job, apartment, girlfriend, all designed to make her fit in.

No, not to fit in. To *appear* as if she did. But the land where she sat and the car she drove had been her small ways of rebelling against the expectations she set for herself. She had put her Muse houses in her portfolio for the same reason. To whisper her individuality even as she shouted her bland conformity. She turned to a clean sheet of paper, but she was still unsure what to draw. She had lived by the rules for a long time. But now Dougie had forced her to reconnect with her past by bringing her to Impetus and back into contact with him. This land had given her a safe place to breathe and move without any concern about how she'd be perceived.

And Bailey? Bailey had given her a chance to see what life would be like if she lived unfettered by concern about image and reputation. A life without fear, aligned with values and compassion rather than a desperate attempt to find security through conformity. Ken had convinced herself the only way to survive with her individuality intact was to shield it with a visible barrier of convention. But she had been wrong. She had buried herself far too deep.

She had to reconnect with the Ken who had been ready to believe a chimera or a griffin might be lurking behind the rhododendron bush in her backyard. She'd recapture her old self eventually because Bailey had healed her. Bailey's life-giving hands had reached beyond the layers of skin and ink shielding Ken's soul, and Ken would always be grateful, every time she was able to sketch or create something authentic. Bailey needed healing as well, but Ken wouldn't be the one to provide it. Even if she wanted to, even if the thought didn't terrify her, she couldn't be what Bailey needed. She'd failed before, when Steve had needed her protection. Bailey was like him—unique and special, caring so deeply for her birds, like he'd cared about art and imagination. Ken would look for someone else, someone to drive Bailey from her mind and from her body's memory. After she took care of her obligation to Bailey.

What did home mean to Bailey? Because, no matter how far the annex was removed from her house, Bailey's home would be where her raptors were. The new building couldn't be designed with only its intended purpose in mind. More important than function, it had to be a fit for Bailey's personality. Ken let her mind wander, free-associating her impressions of Bailey. She thought of Bailey's hands as they had wrapped the osprey's wing and as they had gently traced the contours of Ken's body. Healing and letting go.

Ken drew an arced building, hinting at the shape of a wing. The inner curve would be paned glass, so the internal workings were visible from Bailey's house or from any point within the building. Rooms for seminars and examinations branched off the central hallway like primary feathers, separated not by walls but by panels made of the same mesh as the flight cages. A safe place for any escaping birds, and easy to reconfigure as needed. A small, traditionally enclosed section at the far end could be used for darkened recovery areas and private rooms for the interns.

Ken pushed her windblown hair out of her eyes and held her sketch at arm's length. She took an imaginary tour of the halls and rooms. Pretty and practical at the same time, with comfortable visibility for Bailey, direct light from the glass front and diffused light through the mesh. Bailey would love it. Even more important, the birds would love it.

Better than a box. Ken used the black chalk to draw markings similar to those on her osprey's wing on the roof of the building. A touch of whimsy no one but the birds would see. When she had finished, she closed the sketchpad and rested back in her chair. She'd let the idea simmer overnight and work on the structural details tomorrow.

A gull swooped upward from the sea, borne on a wind current Ken only saw in its effects—in the ruffled feathers and in the otherwise stillness of the bird's wings as it hovered near the bluff. She closed her eyes, blocking out the sun but still feeling its warmth. She'd show the sketch to both Bailey and Joe next week, and then she'd be done with her part in the project. Construction crews would step in to finish the work, and soon her concept would be given mass and dimension. From an image of a wing spread in flight to a building full of students and raptors. Birds would be healed within the mesh walls, moving toward freedom.

And after so many years in stasis, Ken would move forward, too. Responsible only for herself, not for anyone else.

❖

Bailey parked behind Ken's Corvette and got out of her car. She stood on the side of the road, strangely reluctant to cross onto Ken's property. She didn't know if she'd be welcome or not, and Ken had every right to be furious with her. Finally Bailey moved, drawn forward by the song of a house finch, and followed the little red bird until he disappeared behind a spiny clump of Oregon grape. Once Bailey was on the property, she could see Ken, stretched and motionless in the sun. Her feet were crossed at the ankles, and a sketch pad dangled from her hand, only inches from the grass.

Bailey stayed where she was for a few still moments, content to observe Ken in this place where she had chosen to make her home. Bailey heard the rhythmic beat of the rugged and active strait, just below the bluff, but the ring of trees around the property gave it an atmosphere of privacy and quiet. The acre was level where it fronted the road, but the lower portion of the land sloped down from east to west. Bailey saw stakes and bright yellow string in the grass, and she recognized the shape of the tree trunk house immediately. She envisioned Ken's tiered house being built, stick by stick, in her mind. Imagining it here, rather than on the back of her car's registration, she realized she had been wrong when she had called it a showcase. Instead, it would be a haven. Simple and beautiful as it hugged close to the ground but looked out toward the sea.

"Bailey."

Ken's voice made her jump. She had been focused on Ken's future home, hoping to have a place within it, and she had momentarily forgotten the present.

"Hi, Ken," she said.

"What are you doing here?"

Bailey took a deep breath before she spoke. She felt the same tension in her body as she did when stalking an injured bird. Keep steady, don't make sudden movements. Carefully sidle toward the wild creature until she was able to control its movements. "Randy came by today with the plans for the flight cages," she said. The message had been clear. Ken had sent Randy in her place because she didn't want to see Bailey. Bailey had ignored the message. "I wanted to thank you. They're going to be even better than I dreamed. I wanted you to copy what you saw in my meadow, but you captured the spirit of the place instead."

"I'm glad you like them," Ken said. Her expression was as closed as it had been when they had first met. Bailey wanted to see her laugh or even frown. To show some sign of emotion, rather than none at all. But Ken wasn't trying to run from her or to push her away. She had disappeared behind a wall as impenetrable as the one she'd drawn for Bailey's castle. Bailey felt a sense of panic. She had been trying to sneak up on Ken, to slowly reveal the love that had been building inside her without giving too much away until she could gauge whether her feelings might be reciprocated. But Ken wasn't giving any indication of what she was feeling. Love, anger, disgust—Bailey had no clue. Either she tipped her own hand and risked rejection, maybe even ridicule, or she kept silent and under control.

"I had been hoping you would bring the plans yourself," she said. She felt an ache inside as she struggled to keep her feelings contained. It had always been so easy to do, but the emotions she felt now were as unwieldy and uncooperative as a flailing raptor. "So I could apologize."

Ken looked away, toward the water. "Randy will be better at choosing native plants, and he has some ideas already about the stream you wanted."

Bailey wanted to stay in the safety of the meadow, too, but she pushed past it to the argument they had on the way out of the woods. "Ken, I'm sorry for what I said after our hike. I shouldn't have—"

"Yes," Ken said. "You should have. I needed to hear it."

Bailey felt her heart thud against her rib cage. She felt bruised from battering against the sanctuary she had built inside. Maybe she had a chance to fix their relationship, to have Ken in her life again, but only if she could summon the courage to set her love free. "I needed to hear what you told me, too. All of it. I fought having an intern for the same reason I was pushing you away. I *was* living in a cage. One I built myself because I was afraid of rejection, of being left alone rather than making the choice to live alone. I'm making changes and letting Dani and the university in my life. But even more, I want you in my life. Ken, I love you."

Ken wanted to move forward, to take Bailey in her arms, but she couldn't. She understood the depth of Bailey's courage, and she was in awe of her strength. Embracing change, opening her life and heart not only to the students, but—even more intimately—to Ken. Willing to be weak and strong at the same time. Ken didn't deserve Bailey's love. She could never be worthy of it. "I'm glad you're accepting what the university has to offer. Your birds will be better off, but so will you. You won't have to do everything alone anymore."

"What about us?" Bailey asked, although her eyes were red and she seemed to know Ken's answer before it was spoken.

"Bailey, you were right about me. I spent so many years being careful about what I said and how I acted. I fell into the habit, I guess, of being someone I wasn't. I need time to relearn who I am." Focus on the externals. The need to dress or act the right way, her ability to create and design. The inside work—being able to risk caring for someone else, being responsible for them—seemed an impossible task. Bailey deserved more.

Bailey wiped a tear off her cheek with the back of her hand. "Do you need to do it alone?"

"I do." Ken felt made of stone, but she lifted a heavy hand and cradled Bailey's cheek, rubbing her thumb over a falling tear before sliding her hand through Bailey's hair. Deep and soft, it anchored Ken to Bailey for a brief moment. "I was the strong one. I took care of myself and defended other people, but I never did enough. I always knew I had failed, because of Steve. When we first met, I assumed you were the kind of woman I'd need to protect, but I was wrong. You are the strong one, Bailey. You are confident and unwavering. You've found your calling and you follow it wholeheartedly. I gave up my calling because I always felt guilty getting credit for my sketches or plans when Steve was the real talent. He's the one who should be alive now, and getting the recognition I avoided."

Ken pulled her hand away from Bailey's warmth and rubbed under her collarbone. "It's time to stop living in his shadow, trying to avoid success because he'll never have it." She ripped the wing-shaped design out of her sketch pad and handed it to Bailey.

"This building will be a new start. For both of us," she said. Bailey would find life in her annex. People who would protect her and care for her. A university full of students and professors to give her support. Even now, after declaring her misguided love for Ken, she had a lightness about her. A sad but bittersweet expression, as if saying the words, attempting the connection, had been enough to set her free. Ken was relieved that Bailey would be okay, better than okay, without Ken in her life. She walked back to her chair, leaving Bailey in the center of the clearing.

CHAPTER EIGHTEEN

K en sat on her usual bench outside the office building. No crossword puzzle, no lunch. Nothing except the black and gold watch she checked every thirty seconds. She was waiting for her client presentation, and every passing second brought her closer to failure.

Her black veneer desk upstairs was still bare and impersonal, even after she had been sitting at it for almost two months. Today it had some remnants of her on it. A 3-D model of a large and decidedly mediocre house, and a series of neatly laminated specs and sketches. Randy's landscaping and Angela's interiors were brilliant and inspired, but Ken's house—the centerpiece of it all—was unimaginative. She had filled it with all the goodies money could buy, but it was nothing more than a pricier version of her mass-produced boxes.

At least she had tried her best. Ken sighed as she watched a flock of pigeons erupt into the sky as a young girl ran past them. No, not her best. Far from it. She had been so intent on losing this job, but now that she was on the verge of accomplishing such a mind-numbing feat, she was having second thoughts. And third thoughts.

Joe had loved the annex she had designed for Bailey. Ken had known from the moment her pencil hit paper that Bailey would adore it. The big surprise was how much Ken herself had enjoyed the process, so long neglected, of bringing something truly unique out of her mind and into the world. Combining form and function to create a building that would be beautiful to see, beautiful to use. A thing of grace. Yes, her boss loved the annex, but she knew she was expected to produce such results consistently. She had managed one good attempt but had failed with today's paying client.

She looked up from checking her watch yet again and saw Dougie walking toward her. He sat next to her and rested his elbows on his knees. His bangs dropped in his eyes as he stared down at the cement, but he didn't bother to push them away.

"Do you have a backup plan?" Ken asked. She hid her shame behind dry humor. He had put his faith in her, had staked his reputation on her, and she had failed not just him, but herself as well. Just as she had expected.

"Yes," he said. "Once we saw the direction you were going, Joe had me draw up another set of plans. I'll present them if Vince doesn't like yours."

"If?" Ken repeated with a snort of humorless laughter. "You might as well do the full presentation. Even *I* wouldn't want to live in the house I designed."

"There's nothing wrong with it," Dougie said. Still coming to her defense, no matter how hard she tried to push him away. "But there's nothing right with it, either."

"So why put anyone through the embarrassment?" Ken asked. The high of designing the annex, of connecting with Bailey's deepest desires and needs, had evaporated. She felt empty again, unable to create. Her talent, and Bailey herself, seemed so far away right now. Ken would be alone in front of the client—naked and vulnerable—and she couldn't face the humiliation, made worse by her too-recent realization of what this job really meant to her. She'd wanted to fail but somehow deep inside had hoped she wouldn't. "Go ahead and present your ideas. I'm sure the client will love them, and you'll—"

"No!" Dougie sat up and pushed his bangs aside with a brusque swipe. "You produced crap, so you stand up in front of everyone and present it. I can't try to save you, Ken. I've been trying since Steve died, but I can't do it anymore."

"Don't bring him into this," Ken said, her voice sounding like a dangerous growl. She had broken her rule, going against her better judgment and sharing Steve's story with Bailey. Ken had revealed her secret shame, her inability to protect the ones she loved most, but Bailey had misunderstood. She had loved Ken anyway, in spite of her weakness. "I won't talk about him."

"But I will. You lost a best friend when Steve killed himself, and I'm sorry for you. But I lost *two* best friends that day. How do you think I feel?"

Ken looked away, unable to bear the pain she saw in Dougie's tear-filled eyes. She brushed angrily at the wetness on her own cheek. "I'm still here," she said. *But I don't deserve it.* She didn't speak those words out loud, but they hovered in the air between them.

"Ken," Dougie said more softly. He took one of her hands and cradled it in both of his. She pulled against his touch, but he didn't let go. "What happened back then was horrible, but it wasn't your fault. What Steve did to himself, that was horrible, too. A shame and a loss. But it wasn't your fault. You couldn't save him back then, just like I can't save you now. You aren't the one who died, but you buried the part of you that you and Steve shared."

Ken used her free hand to wipe the tears away. She agreed with Dougie about one thing. She had buried her creativity, the part of herself so connected to Steve, deep inside. Where she could finally and forever keep it safe. It emerged now and again, in random designs or sketches, but most of it remained underground. She had managed to access it for Bailey, but only because Bailey somehow managed to drive her far inside herself, where her most basic needs and emotions were hidden. Ken couldn't get there on her own.

"How do you manage to go on?" she finally asked. "To keep remembering him and thinking about him?"

"Because I think of the work I do as a way of honoring his memory. Every drawing I make or idea I create has a little of him in it, because he'll always be part of me. How much more would that be true for you? The two of you were so close, and the worlds you created together shaped the artists both of you would have become. Every time you draw a line, a room, a house, there'll be a part of him living in it. That's a better way to preserve his memory than by shutting it away from the world."

Dougie stood up. "There's Vince. I'll walk him upstairs and stall for a few minutes. I really hope you'll do your presentation, Ken. Sell the house you designed, and maybe Joe will give you another chance."

Ken trailed behind Dougie and Vince before ducking into the bathroom on the first floor of the building. She splashed cold water on her face and stared in the mirror. Except for her puffy red eyes, she looked the part of conservative professional. Her white dress shirt was buttoned nearly to her throat and covered with a pin-striped blazer. A carefully chosen wrapping to hide the failure inside. She had known all along that she wasn't talented or daring enough for the challenging job at Impetus. And that she wasn't brave enough or strong enough to love and protect a wacky, sensitive, unique woman like Bailey. She was destined for a bland and boring career, a passionless and predictable love life.

Dougie's words today had echoed the harsh ones Bailey had spoken after their hike. They had both tried to give her a chance to live again. Dougie, with this creative and challenging job—and Bailey, with her love. Ken had turned them both away because she had been too afraid to stand out, to live as bold a life as they wanted for her. They'd seen potential for something more in her, but they'd been wrong. She had tried to protect herself and had ended up hurting all three of them. They'd tried to protect *her*, to love and support her, and she'd failed them.

Ken took a step back from the mirror. She hadn't failed them, she'd failed herself. They had stood by her, waiting for her to decide whether to step up to the challenge or to step away. Like Steve. Ken raised a hand to her mouth, almost afraid to admit the truth. As if it was a betrayal of Steve and how much she had cared about him. She had tried to help him back then, but her efforts had been doomed because he hadn't taken part in the healing. Bailey and Dougie could only do so much for her. *She* had to take the step toward healing, toward proving she wasn't the failure she was trying so hard to be. Toward love.

Ken took off her navy blazer and unbuttoned the top two buttons of her dress shirt. The head of a dragon with a ruby eye was just visible along her lowered neckline, and the rest of her ink showed indistinctly through the thin fabric of her shirt. She left the bathroom and went upstairs, tossing her blazer on her desk.

So she'd try to be more daring, more herself. To prove to Dougie and Bailey that their faith in her was justified. To keep Steve's memory alive instead of hiding it. But her new resolve couldn't change the bland house she had designed into something spectacular.

Ken sat at her desk and tapped her fingers on the stack of laminated posters as she searched for inspiration. She had nothing. She had been able to come up with a plan for Bailey for one reason. She loved her. She knew Bailey and saw the heart of her, so designing a place for her to work was simple.

She didn't love Vince Larue. She wasn't even overly fond of his Seattle Mariners. She flipped through her notes from previous meetings, searching for some way to sell the house to him. He liked to watch movies, he was on the road a lot, his favorite color was blue. Ken thought about Bailey and her flight cages. She planned them with the bird in mind, not designing the cage she thought they'd want, but observing them in nature and replicating what she could.

Ken remembered a comment Steve had made when she was drawing one of her first fantasy houses. *If you're building a house for a dragon, you gotta make it wide enough for its wings.* Ken had designed the right annex for Bailey because she knew Bailey. Knowing Bailey meant understanding the importance of her raptors, of transparency and visibility, of light and natural beauty. With Vince, she had been designing a house for one guy, but she wasn't taking into account the way he lived, what defined him. Vince had never said *he* liked watching movies. He had said *we.* Everything had been about his team, his teammates. Ken had been trying to design some version of a standard house for him, but the guy wanted a damned locker room.

Ken left the model and specs on her desk and grabbed a pad and a pen instead. She burst into the conference room just as Randy was finishing his landscape presentation.

"Are you ready, Ken?" Joe asked, seemingly unfazed by her altered dress and her lack of models and sketches.

"I am, thanks. Vince, good to see you again." She shook hands with him and sat down, opening her pad to a fresh sheet of paper. "I believe I've designed the perfect house where you and your teammates will be able to relax and enjoy each other's company."

Ken rapidly sketched out a building with four connected wings. A hint of a baseball diamond. She tapped the section corresponding to home plate. "This central part will be your main entertaining space. A sunken living room, movie screen, plenty of seating. I'm picturing a pizza oven as the central focus of the kitchen, because let's face it, even a frozen pizza tastes better when it's made in a pizza oven."

Vince laughed and leaned over for a closer look at her sketch. "What's along this wall?"

"Cubbies for all your friends," Ken said, darkening the cross-hatching along the wall. "A playful version of your team's locker room, so everyone has a place to store personal items like beer mugs."

Ken turned to a new page and sketched the wings of the house. She felt Joe and the others clustered behind her, watching her draw, but her hand didn't falter as she worked. She described the apartment suites where out-of-town guests would have privacy and comfort, a weight room large enough to accommodate an entire team, and a game viewing room with an entire wall covered with a whiteboard for writing notes and plays. Dougie had been right. She was designing a house just for Vince, but there were memories of Steve in some of her lines and curves. And hints of Bailey in some of her shapes.

Ken finished her impromptu presentation and sat back in her chair. Vince flipped through the pages one more time, pausing on a detailed sketch of the main kitchen.

"You'll show me how to use the pizza oven?" he asked.

"I'd be delighted," Ken said. "I'll make my top-secret version of Hawaiian pizza for your housewarming party."

"I'll count on it," Vince said, shaking her hand again. "I love your ideas. You designed the exact house I didn't know I wanted."

Joe patted her shoulder. "Excellent job, Ken. As I expected, of course."

Ken smiled. She hadn't expected it herself, but she had pulled it off. With some help from Dougie and, in a way, Steve. And Bailey. Always Bailey.

Dougie stopped her as they were leaving the conference room. "You're back?" he asked.

Ken gave him a quick hug. "Getting there. It's a start," she said. A good start.

CHAPTER NINETEEN

K en got out of her car and stared at the mammoth skeleton. Her design had been a series of lines and curves on a piece of paper only weeks earlier, but now it was taking shape right in front of her. She walked over to the wing-shaped structure and stood inside, looking down the long, arced hallway just as she had imagined doing when she had first drawn the sketch. She had seen hundreds of her box-shaped houses brought to life, but she had never felt such a sense of possessiveness, as if this building contained a part of her.

It did, in a way. It represented her imagination and her ability to take a vague concept and turn it into a functional and tangible building. She had already created several more designs for Impetus, each feeling as personal and authentically hers as this one and the one she'd designed for Vince, and she didn't plan to stop. She could no more go back to rehashing old floor plans than she could go back to living in the city and not close to her land.

Ken ran her hand over the smooth side of a two-by-four before she left the building through the space where a door would eventually be. She was heading toward Bailey's house when she heard laughter and voices coming from the backyard. She changed course and came around the corner of the house to find Bailey standing near her new flight cages. The steady music of an artificial stream was a pleasant backdrop to the sound of

Bailey's voice as she talked to a group of students sitting cross-legged in front of her.

Ken edged nearer, out of Bailey's direct line of sight, and listened to her lecturing about restraining raptors during treatment. Bailey told a story about her first attempt to put a hood on a falcon, and Ken laughed along with the students when she recognized the story as one Bailey had told her on the way to their hiking trip. As if recognizing the sound of her laughter, Bailey turned toward her. Ken had been rehearsing this moment for weeks, but all of her careful notes and phrasing flew away on the light breeze. She'd have to follow her heart, not her planned script, and hope Bailey understood.

Ken ran a shaky hand through her hair while she watched Bailey signal for Dani to take over her class before walking across the lawn toward Ken. She had no idea what kind of reception she'd receive, and Bailey's wary expression didn't give her any reassurance. Ken realized her entire life was approaching her. Bailey could so easily walk away, leaving Ken empty and bereft.

"Did you bring me another bird?" Bailey asked. She stood a few feet away and only needed to cross her arms over her chest to give the full *don't touch me* effect.

"Not this time," Ken said. "Well, unless you count the eagle half of a griffin."

"It depends," Bailey said, with a hint of a smile. "I hear they can tear your heart out with their talons."

Ken clenched her fists at her sides. "I'm sorry, Bailey. I should never have let you go. I just…What you said on our hike cut deep, but it made an opening for the part of me I'd buried inside to get out. I've been designing again. Dreaming again. But you're the only dream I really care about coming true."

Bailey avoided eye contact and looked toward the shell of her annex. "Good, Ken. You deserve to be recognized for your talent, but more important, you deserve to be happy doing the work you love."

"I don't only mean architecture, Bailey. That's one part of me you brought back to life. But more than my job, you gave me something else." Ken wrapped her fingers around Bailey's upper arm and tugged her toward the annex. Maybe the beams and shapes would help her say what Bailey needed to hear. What she so desperately needed to say. "I accused you of keeping people out, but I was the same way. I was terrified to let anyone trust me again, scared I'd let them down like I did with Steve."

Ken stopped once they were standing on the plywood floor of the annex. Bailey opened her mouth as if to protest against the comment about Steve, but Ken pressed her index finger against Bailey's lips. She fought to concentrate on words instead of the feel of Bailey's soft mouth. "I know what happened to him wasn't my failure. I could only do so much to help him, and I tried my best. I'm working to come to terms with that. But I let that event shut me down, pull me away from everything and everyone I used to love. I almost let it pull me away from you."

Bailey felt her universe pause for a long moment. The words *love* and *you* placed so close together made her inhale with hope. So close. She moved Ken's hand away from her lips, wrapping her fingers tightly around it while she gestured behind her with her other hand, toward the students who were scattered around her lawn. "I understand. I was afraid of rejection, of getting close and being hurt, and when you turned me away, I thought I'd learn my lesson and not trust anyone again. But I didn't. I've let people in, Ken, and it's because of you. The birds and I are getting accustomed to having more activity in our home, and it wouldn't have happened if you hadn't shown up with the osprey."

"Home," Ken repeated the word. She took a step closer and raised her hands to cup Bailey's chin, turning her head so Bailey looked directly at her. "A couple months ago, Dougie asked me what home meant to me. I've had different answers come to mind, but yesterday when I watched them break ground on my property, I knew the truth. I had thought that acre was my home, but I was wrong. Bailey, *you* are home to me. Wherever you are, however many birds you bring with you. Even if there are bags of mealworms thawing on our table. If you're there with me, then I'm home."

Bailey raised her hands to cover Ken's and, for an agonizing second, didn't know if she was going to push Ken's hands away, or if she was strong enough to hold them close.

"We can keep the mealworms in the intern's fridge," Bailey said, and then she reached up and kissed Ken quickly on the mouth, feeling Ken's smile forming against her own lips. She moved away and looked over at her class, but Dani waved her off with a grin. She had plenty of stories already, in her short time as Bailey's intern, to entertain the students for the last few minutes of their orientation.

"Speaking of the intern's living quarters…" She walked quickly through the annex toward the walled-off section at the far end. She'd wanted Ken for so long, had been resigned to losing her. She couldn't bear to go another second without touch, without crawling out of her own skin and under Ken's. "Maybe you'd like a tour?"

"I'd love one." Ken followed Bailey through the unfinished wood door leading to the enclosed portion of the annex. She stopped suddenly once they were inside the empty room, pulling Bailey off balance and into her arms. She burrowed her nose in Bailey's hair, inhaling the scent of apples and woods and meadow breezes. "And in case I haven't been clear, I love you."

Bailey turned to face Ken, hooking her arms behind Ken's neck and leaning their foreheads together. "I love you, too," she said, before finally allowing herself the kiss she'd been wanting to share with Ken for so long.

Ken sighed as Bailey's tongue slipped into her mouth. The kiss was everything she'd expected from Bailey. Agile and expressive and sensitive. Matching her in desire and strength. No desperation or fear, as there had been after the trip to Poulsbo. A familiarity in their touch, as there had been in the meadow. Ken pulled Bailey's pale yellow T-shirt out of the way of her mouth, and finally—careful not to rip the soft fabric—slid it over her head and threw it onto the floor. She dragged her tongue over the sharply defined tan lines on Bailey's chest and neck, and the increased pressure from her mouth was directly rewarded by the tightening grip of Bailey's hands in her hair.

Ken pressed Bailey gently against the particleboard wall and dropped gentle kisses around her mouth, watching her eyes change from a deer-like reddish brown to the deeper shade of a forest floor after a rain as Ken unhooked her bra. She tentatively circled Bailey's breasts, teasing her nipples with only her fingertips as she kept vigilant for any sign she was moving too fast.

Bailey sighed, arching toward Ken's elusive hands. She had expected Ken to be on her like a bird of prey mating, taking her with all the passion and intensity she knew Ken possessed. Bailey wasn't opposed to leisurely lovemaking sessions, and she could definitely imagine spending entire days in bed with Ken, but she sensed something else. A holding back. A hint of fear. Giving her too much time to think and not enough to feel.

"Ouch!" Ken moved her head a few inches away, an expression of surprise mixed with laughter on her face. "You bite like a falcon."

Bailey shook her head. "If I did, you'd be bleeding." She grabbed the belt loops on Ken's jeans and jerked Ken's hips firmly against her own. "Ken, I won't break. I can be scatterbrained and oblivious at times. And I think I cry more than most people. But I'm not fragile. I'm strong, and I love you, and I want you. You can love me without worrying about hurting me."

A series of emotions seemed to cross Ken's face. Bailey thought she could identify some of them. Hesitation, relief, gratitude. Feelings as complex and varied as Ken herself. Bailey didn't have long to sort them out, though, as Ken descended on her once more, with no doubt or caution. A thrusting kiss, naked breasts pressed against slippery silk, Ken's thigh between her legs. Bailey's thoughts and concerns were shoved out of her mind, replaced by a wild and shared longing, a jumble of sensations. Her legs were pushed apart, and she drove her crotch against Ken's leg. Before she could form the words *I'm coming*, she'd collapsed into the support of Ken's embrace. Her mind raced frantically to catch up with her body.

Ken laughed, feeling Bailey's hair tickle her face when she did. "Was that what you needed?" she asked. She braced one hand against the wall and cradled Bailey in the other.

"Why, yes, it was." Bailey's voice stammered slightly, and Ken felt an absurdly proud *I did that to her* awareness rush over her. "How'd you know?"

"I guess I figured it out when"—Ken's own voice hitched when Bailey unbuttoned her shirt, using her fingers and tongue to trace the ornate tattoos—"when I stopped worrying about what I might be doing wrong and concentrated on you."

"Very good," Bailey murmured against her skin. She unzipped Ken's slacks and pressed her palm against Ken's stomach, sliding lower as she grazed her teeth gently over Ken's nipple. "Because I want you to love me without restraint or fear. And I'll return the favor."

Ken moved her other hand to the wall, struggling to hold herself upright while Bailey's hands explored her. The smell of arousal and the woodsy scent of the construction site enveloped her. The slight sucking sounds of Bailey's mouth and Ken's own wetness brought her to the edge of a climax faster than she'd expected. Bailey's fingers stroked inside her, but she'd already gone far deeper into Ken. Into her past, her fears, her dreams and longings. Ken came hard, releasing more than pent-up energy as she gave herself over to the healing power of Bailey's hands.

CHAPTER TWENTY

K en stood at her drafting table, a beam of spring sunlight falling over the blank paper in front of her. She was trying to work, but she was too busy listening for Bailey's car to concentrate. She gave up the pretense and stared out the heavily paned window at the Strait of Juan de Fuca. The water was choppy today, but brightly lit by the May sun. A beautiful place to live, and soon it would be a real home for her and Bailey.

The tree trunk house Ken had planned and designed had been finished for over six months. She and Bailey had decorated it together, but they wouldn't officially move in until June when Dani graduated from WSU and moved into Bailey's house as her full-time assistant, joining Luke, Bailey's latest intern. Ken would finally be home after so many years of roaming and searching. She had found everything she wanted.

The sound of tires on gravel brought her hurrying out the front door and over to the car. Bailey jumped out, smiling even though her eyes were red with tears. Ken was very familiar with Bailey's release-day emotions. The sadness of letting go, the joy of a healed bird being set free. She slid her fingers through Bailey's hair and leaned over for a kiss. She pulled away all too soon, not wanting to keep Bailey's cargo waiting.

"How'd the capture go?" she asked as she and Bailey each took a side of the heavy wooden carrier and lowered it to the ground.

"He led us on quite a chase, but Luke finally got him cornered. I tried to explain where he was going, but he didn't want to leave the flight cage."

"Who could blame him? You've made the clinic into a wonderful sanctuary."

Bailey kissed her on the cheek. "We did that together," she said. "But no matter how nice it is, it's no match for freedom."

"No, it's not. So let's give this guy a chance to fly free again."

Ken lifted her side of the carrier and they slowly carried it behind the house and down to the edge of the bluff. Ken was surprised by the feel of her breath constricting in her chest. She had watched Bailey release birds before and she always felt a thrill of excitement as they flew away, but this was different. This was her osprey. It had been a long winter, but now he was ready to move on.

They set the carrier on the edge of the lawn. Bailey stepped back in silence, giving Ken the honor of unlatching the lid. The bird stood on the wooden platform for a long moment. He hopped to the edge of the carrier and tilted his head, looking up at her with golden eyes before turning his attention to the trees and sky above him. In a sudden burst of movement, he spread his wings and launched into the air.

Bailey came up behind her and wrapped her arms tightly around Ken's waist. Ken covered Bailey's hands with her own, grateful for the touch as she thought about the day when she had first stumbled upon the injured bird. Almost a full year ago. She had taken the osprey to Bailey's for healing, never expecting to be healed herself. By Bailey's love, her touch, her spirit.

Ken watched the osprey until he disappeared from sight. She turned in Bailey's arms and let her lover wipe the tears out of her eyes, let her kiss away the sorrow of saying good-bye.

"They change lives, these birds of yours," Ken said. She led Bailey to one of the chairs by the bluff and sat down. Bailey curled in her lap, her long legs crossed and draped over the arm of the chair and her head resting on Ken's shoulder.

"If you hadn't found the osprey…"

"And if Vonda hadn't found the eagle…"

Their voices trailed off. Bailey knew neither one of them wanted to finish their sentences. A year ago, she had been dreaming of a life of solitude, just her and her birds. Then one small osprey had wedged his way into her life, bringing with him Ken and her past and her visions for the annex, forcing Bailey to open her heart to the others who were trying to share her life.

She pressed her lips against Ken's neck, unable to express her gratitude for all the changes she had been so determined to resist. The students who brought excitement and fresh perspectives, the faculty of WSU who had become an indispensable resource, the birds who benefitted from the expansion. The greatest expansion had taken place in Bailey's own life. She had wanted to fight her attraction to Ken, but how much would she have lost if she'd been successful? Everything that mattered.

Ken's legs were falling asleep, but she didn't want to move. She kept her arms wrapped around Bailey as they sat on the bluff. She'd never get tired of this place or this woman. The sound of the surf, the misty fog, the screech of gulls. The connection to Bailey as they searched for a glimpse of the osprey and talked in hushed voices. The simultaneous inhale when a comfortable embrace shifted naturally to one of awareness and arousal.

Ken's fingers twisted gently in Bailey's hair as Bailey turned for a kiss before sliding to a kneeling position between Ken's legs. Communication became more basic—but more meaningful—as whispered sighs and soft touches replaced words. Ken lifted her hips and Bailey slid her jeans down her legs, drawing away for a brief moment to toss them aside, but returning with demanding lips and tongue.

Ken's world condensed until there was only her and Bailey. The hard swipe of a tongue and the teasing brush of teeth. The remembered taste of Bailey in Ken's mouth—soon to be a reality once more. The sense of utter safety and love that Ken had never known before. Ken let go, completely giving herself over to Bailey, her heart unfurling and soaring, as if on wings.

About the Author

Karis Walsh is a horseback riding instructor who lives on a small farm in the Pacific Northwest. When she isn't teaching or writing, she enjoys spending time outside with her animals, reading, playing the viola, and riding with friends.

Karis can be contacted at kariswalsh@gmail.com

Website: http://www.kariswalsh.com/

Books Available from Bold Strokes Books

Wingspan by Karis Walsh. Wildlife biologist Bailey Chase is content to live at the wild bird sanctuary she has created on Washington's Olympic Peninsula until she is lured beyond the safety of isolation by architect Kendall Pearson. (978-1-60282-983-1)

Night Bound by Winter Pennington. Kass struggles to keep her head, her heart, and her relationships in order. She's still having a difficult time accepting being an Alpha female. But her wolf is certain of what she wants and she's intent on securing her power. (978-1-60282-984-8)

Slash and Burn by Valerie Bronwyn. The murder of a roundly despised author at a LGBT writer's conference in New Orleans turns Winter Lovelace's relaxing weekend hobnobbing with her peers into a nightmare of suspense—especially when her ex turns up. (978-1-60282-986-2)

The Blush Factor by Gun Brooke. Ice-cold business tycoon Eleanor Ashcroft only cares about the three P's—Power, Profit, and Prosperity—until young Addison Garr makes her doubt both that and the state of her frostbitten heart. (978-1-60282-985-5)

The Quickening: A Sisters of Spirits Novel by Yvonne Heidt. Ghosts, visions, and demons are all in a day's work for Tiffany. But when Kat asks for help on a serial killer case, life takes on another dimension altogether. (978-1-60282-975-6)

Windigo Thrall by Cate Culpepper. Six women trapped in a mountain cabin by a blizzard, stalked by an ancient cannibal demon bent on stealing their sanity—and their lives. (978-1-60282-950-3)

Smoke and Fire by Julie Cannon. Oil and water, passion and desire, a combustible combination. Can two women fight the fire that draws them together and threatens to keep them apart? (978-1-60282-977-0)

Asher's Fault by Elizabeth Wheeler. Fourteen-year-old Asher Price sees the world in black and white, much like the photos he takes, but when his little brother drowns at the same moment Asher experiences his first same-sex kiss, he can no longer hide behind the lens of his camera and eventually discovers he isn't the only one with a secret. (978-1-60282-982-4)

Love and Devotion by Jove Belle. KC Hall trips her way through life, stumbling into an affair with a married bombshell twice her age. Thankfully, her best friend, Emma Reynolds, is there to show her the true meaning of Love and Devotion. (978-1-60282-965-7)

Rush by Carsen Taite. Murder, secrets, and romance combine to create the ultimate rush. (978-1-60282-966-4)

The Shoal of Time by J.M. Redmann. It sounded too easy. Micky Knight is reluctant to take the case because the easy ones often turn into the hard ones, and the hard ones turn into the dangerous ones. In this one, easy turns hard without warning. (978-1-60282-967-1)

In Between by Jane Hoppen. At the age of 14, Sophie Schmidt discovers that she was born an intersexual baby and sets off on a journey to find her place in a world that denies her true existence. (978-1-60282-968-8)

Secret Lies by Amy Dunne. While fleeing from her abuser, Nicola Jackson bumps into Jenny O'Connor, and their unlikely friendship quickly develops into a blossoming romance—but when it comes down to a matter of life or death, are they both willing to face their fears? (978-1-60282-970-1)

Under Her Spell by Maggie Morton. The magic of love brought Terra and Athene together, but now a magical quest stands between them—a quest for Athene's hand in marriage. Will their passion keep them together, or will stronger magic tear them apart? (978-1-60282-973-2)

Homestead by Radclyffe. R. Clayton Sutter figures getting NorthAm Fuel's newest refinery operational on a rolling tract of land in Upstate New York should take a month or two, but then, she hadn't counted on local resistance in the form of vandalism, petitions, and one furious farmer named Tess Rogers. (978-1-60282-956-5)

Battle of Forces: Sera Toujours by Ali Vali. Kendal and Piper return to New Orleans to start the rest of eternity together, but the return of an old enemy makes their peaceful reunion short-lived, especially when they join forces with the new queen of the vampires. (978-1-60282-957-2)

How Sweet It Is by Melissa Brayden. Some things are better than chocolate. Molly O'Brien enjoys her quiet life running the bakeshop in a small town. When the beautiful Jordan Tuscana returns home, Molly can't deny the attraction—or the stirrings of something more. (978-1-60282-958-9)

The Missing Juliet: A Fisher Key Adventure by Sam Cameron. A teenage detective and her friends search for a kidnapped Hollywood star in the Florida Keys. (978-1-60282-959-6)

Amor and More: Love Everafter edited by Radclyffe and Stacia Seaman. Rediscover favorite couples as Bold Strokes Books authors reveal glimpses of life and love beyond the honeymoon in short stories featuring main characters from favorite BSB novels. (978-1-60282-963-3)

First Love by CJ Harte. Finding true love is hard enough, but for Jordan Thompson, daughter of a conservative president, it's challenging, especially when that love is a female rodeo cowgirl. (978-1-60282-949-7)

Pale Wings Protecting by Lesley Davis. Posing as a couple to investigate the abduction of infants, Special Agent Blythe Kent and Detective Daryl Chandler find themselves drawn into a battle over the innocents, with demons on one side and the unlikeliest of protectors on the other. (978-1-60282-964-0)

Mounting Danger by Karis Walsh. Sergeant Rachel Bryce, an outcast on the police force, is put in charge of the department's newly formed mounted division. Can she and polo champion Callan Lanford resist their growing attraction as they struggle to safeguard the disaster-prone unit? (978-1-60282-951-0)

Meeting Chance by Jennifer Lavoie. When man's best friend turns on Aaron Cassidy, the teen keeps his distance until fate puts Chance in his hands. (978-1-60282-952-7)

At Her Feet by Rebekah Weatherspoon. Digital marketing producer Suzanne Kim knows she has found the perfect love in her new mistress Pilar, but before they can make the ultimate commitment, Suzanne's professional life threatens to disrupt their perfectly balanced bliss. (978-1-60282-948-0)

Show of Force by AJ Quinn. A chance meeting between navy pilot Evan Kane and correspondent Tate McKenna takes them on a roller-coaster ride where the stakes are high, but the reward is higher: a chance at love. (978-1-60282-942-8)

Clean Slate by Andrea Bramhall. Can Erin and Morgan work through their individual demons to rediscover their love for each other, or are the unexplainable wounds too deep to heal? (978-1-60282-943-5)

Hold Me Forever by D. Jackson Leigh. An investigation into illegal cloning in the quarter horse racing industry threatens to destroy the growing attraction between Georgia debutante Mae St. John and Louisiana horse trainer Whit Casey. (978-1-60282-944-2)

Trusting Tomorrow by PJ Trebelhorn. Funeral director Logan Swift thinks she's perfectly happy with her solitary life devoted to helping others cope with loss until Brooke Collier moves in next door to care for her elderly grandparents. (978-1-60282-891-9)

Forsaking All Others by Kathleen Knowles. What if what you think you want is the opposite of what makes you happy? (978-1-60282-892-6)

Exit Wounds by VK Powell. When Officer Loane Landry falls in love with ATF informant Abigail Mancuso, she realizes that nothing is as it seems—not the case, not her lover, not even the dead. (978-1-60282-893-3)

Dirty Power by Ashley Bartlett. Cooper's been through hell and back, and she's still broke and on the run. But at least she found the twins. They'll keep her alive. Right? (978-1-60282-896-4)

The Rarest Rose by I. Beacham. After a decade of living in her beloved house, Ele disturbs its past and finds her life being haunted by the presence of a ghost who will show her that true love never dies. (978-1-60282-884-1)

Code of Honor by Radclyffe. The face of terror is hard to recognize—especially when it's homegrown. The next book in the Honor series. (978-1-60282-885-8)

Does She Love You? by Rachel Spangler. When Annabelle and Davis find out they are both in a relationship with the same woman, it leaves them facing life-altering questions about trust, redemption, and the possibility of finding love in the wake of betrayal. (978-1-60282-886-5)

The Road to Her by KE Payne. Sparks fly when actress Holly Croft, star of UK soap Portobello Road, meets her new on-screen love interest, the enigmatic and sexy Elise Manford. (978-1-60282-887-2)

Shadows of Something Real by Sophia Kell Hagin. Trying to escape flashbacks and nightmares, ex-POW Jamie Gwynmorgan stumbles into the heart of former Red Cross worker Adele Sabellius and uncovers a deadly conspiracy against everything and everyone she loves. (978-1-60282-889-6)

Date with Destiny by Mason Dixon. When sophisticated bank executive Rashida Ivey meets unemployed blue collar worker Destiny Jackson, will her life ever be the same? (978-1-60282-878-0)

The Devil's Orchard by Ali Vali. Cain and Emma plan a wedding before the birth of their third child while Juan Luis is still lurking, and as Cain plans for his death, an unexpected visitor arrives and challenges her belief in her father, Dalton Casey. (978-1-60282-879-7)